CU00869616

Fragments

Punam Farmah

Copyright © 2017 Punam Farmah

All rights reserved. No part of this publication may be reproduced, distributed, or transmitted in any form or by any means, including photocopying, recording, or other electronic or mechanical methods, without the prior written permission of the publisher, except in the case of brief quotations embodied in critical reviews and certain other noncommercial uses permitted by copyright law

Cover art 'Fabric of the universe' Punam Farmah Copyright © 2017

All rights reserved.

ISBN-13: 978-1542854405

Printed by Createspace

www.horticulturalhobbit.com

www.twitter.com/horticulturalh

Also on Facebook.com Search for Horticultural 'Obbit

Also by Punam Farmah:

Playing with Plant Pots: Tales from the allotment

Sow, Grow and Eat: From plot to kitchen

DEDICATION

<u>Law of conservation of energy:</u>

Energy cannot be created or destroyed.
It can only be transferred.

Ram Lok and Lajwanti

Hussen Lal and Amro

Indra Devi

Contents

Contents 1

1 The Anands

    Early days 4

2 Matthew

    Grandmother's Sponge cake 17

3 Michael

    The mourning afterwards and again 45

4 Maya

    A mother's loss 62

5 Daniel

    When all the colour has gone 78

6 Christopher

    A boys best friend 89

7 Aldo

    My baby too..102

8 Michael

    Pieces...115

9 Caliope

Growing pains 125

10 Matthew

In your shoes 136

11 Christopher

Words on a page 148

12 Daniel

A shared grief 157

13 Joyce

Lend an ear 173

14 Lydia

In the mood for swing 184

15 Nandini

Soul food 203

16 Death

Destroyer of worlds 216

17 Saying Goodbye

Journey's End 258

18 Marcy

Someone to walk with 295

19 Lydia

Ask 324

20 Aldo

Bunting...339

21 Michael

Bundle 347

22 Christopher

Paw print 356

23 The Anands

Parting Gifts 365

24 Daniel

Adventuring..374

ABOUT THE AUTHOR 387

1 The Anands

Early days

Caliope was bored. Tapping her pencil against the desk, she watched the clock on the wall and willed the hands to move towards ten to the hour. That was when this double lesson of Psychology would end. She was looking past the whiteboard on the wall and just a little off centre. The curly penmanship of Mrs. Hardcastle seemed to merge together. Making it even more difficult to understand the concepts relating to Behaviourist theory and its application to how attachment was formed between a small human child and their primary care giver. Rolling her eyes Caliope turned her gaze towards the door. In her mind, she was running out, crossing the threshold of the classroom with a spring in her step and making a sharp exit out into the corridor.

"You will see from your handouts, a series of key words," Joyce spoke as she moved down the central aisle that bisected the classroom into halves. "The same key words that are written on the board," she said shining a laser at the board. The red dot danced on the plastic. "And attached to the modelled example. Using the key words and the sentence starters on the slide, I would like you to create a paragraph containing your own example of how attachment is formed between a child and their primary care giver."

Turning on her heel, Joyce clutched her pointer into the middle of her left palm and surveyed the panorama of eighteen teenagers. A sea of largely dark haired students, though the single, solitary red headed individual and four or five newly blonde bouffants did offer some variation. She had been about to retreat to the teachers desk in the corner where the classroom desktop PC displayed the lesson slides. Instead she moved two paces and towards the seat of a very distracted Caliope Anand.

Caliope was largely out of the classroom. That was how far the day dream had progressed. In her head, she had already exited and was taking a walk down the admin corridor. Her imaginary self was meters from the doors that exited the building and out onto the front entrance. Her dark eyebrows were arched, and betrayed her imaginary perambulation. There had been a rain shower this morning when her father had dropped her and her little brother at school. Caliope was wondering if the rain had dried up. A walk down to the rec ground would be a welcome break from school if the weather was better.

Placing her pointer softy next to Caliope's pencil case, Joyce stood at the edge of the desk. It was not entirely lost on her as to how distracted and distant Caliope was. Nor was it a surprise. There had been a quiet trickle of information from both the pastoral team and the senior management. A family bereavement was always hard. However, to lose a parent and a parent who was still relatively young with a young family did pain Joyce somewhat. She had not really expected Caliope to be in school or to even be in her class.

Feeling the shadow of Mrs. Hardcastle loom large over her, Caliope felt her day dream snap to an end. Even the motion of the pencil being tapped came to an abrupt halt. So much so that the red and black pencil, slipped from Caliope's fingers. It rolled to the edge of the desk at which Caliope was sat and started to descend to the floor.

It took Joyce a second to register the movement of the pencil. Yet she was quick enough to catch it as it travelled half way to the floor. A practiced manoeuvre for Joyce. She knew that time spent in the classroom was now officially eighteen years too long. The students sat here before her, had been but puking, mewling babes when she had first qualified. Joyce delicately placed Caliope's pencil in the dip of the

6

open, but unused this lesson, textbook. There was no need to reprimand her. The breaking of her reverie had been just enough.

***

Raj couldn't remember how he had done it. How he had managed to drop off Caliope and Koby at the school gate and then drive back home. Sat frozen in his seat, his hands were clamped around the steering wheel. Raj had been holding on that long and his fingers were exerting that much pressure; that the steering wheel was now hot, clammy and uncomfortable to hold. When he had left home with the kids, the dark clouds overhead had parted to let forth a deluge that been forecast for days. He had yet to switch off the windscreen wipers. The rain had fallen in near horizontal drops given the wind direction and force. The wiper blades squeaked their disdain abrasively across the windscreen at still being operational. The one blade actually needed replacing and the noise was an unwelcome reminder.

The whole process this morning had occurred as though they were all on autopilot. Raj had come down the stairs to see Caliope sat at the breakfast table, eating her way through the soggy bowl of cereal that she ate most mornings. The only difference being her puffy eyes rimmed in pink. Even Koby was still momentarily on course, arguing with the dog as to where his rugby boots were. This particular interaction between boy and dog also happened every Wednesday.

Wednesday morning. It had only been two days.

Gingerly, Raj uncurled his fingers from the now very warm and clammy curves of the steering wheel. The engine of their family car had been idling whilst parked. Eight minutes had passed on the clock that sat next to the speedometer. Realising how long that he had been sat there, Raj fumbled at the clutch of keys that were suspended from the ignition.

Turning the car keys, he silenced the rather robust but reliable family car. With the keys sat in his hand, Raj realised just how slowly he was going. He never went this slow. He might have ambled and taken his time. But never this slow. Time seemed to be like treacle, and he was wading through it. Ordinarily, he wouldn't have been able to get out of this car quick enough. Wednesday's were his day off; he and his wife would have a coffee before finding some adventure to fill the day with. The one day, where being a parent and a professional was suspended in favour of quality time and being together. He really couldn't move.

Nandini watched her son from the window. A finger from a hand that was crepe-like in texture was hooked around a heavy drawn curtain, as she peered around it and through the glass of the window. She had been standing there just under ten minutes. The time spent standing at the window, hiding behind the curtain was starting to take its toll on her knees. The damp weather was already playing havoc with the arthritic inflammation. Skulking with stealth and sadness really wasn't helping.

Stepping back, Nandini shuffled around the fabric of the curtains. She was convinced that if Raj hadn't already spotted her, then the already twitchy neighbours certainly would have. The one's either side had yet to come around to offer the condolences. Perhaps they shared the family shock at the sudden bereavement, rather than avoiding a polite social nicety. Rubbing her hands together. Nandini felt the damp softness of a sodden tissue. It was in fact a piece of kitchen towel that was starting to crumble and disintegrate. A facial tissue really wouldn't have been up to the job demanded of it.

Slowly, she turned away from the window. Her slippers shuffled across the deep pile of the carpet, that further slowed down her age wearied gait. Nandini liked the carpet, and had whole heartedly agreed with the choice that her daughter-in-law had made in buying it. In her mind, the quality of the carpet was astounding. What she had disagreed with had been the price and she had told Raj quite pointedly her views. Especially as the children still had the tendency to trample in mud with the school shoes. Her daughter-in-law had still made a good choice. Her other choice had been to marry Raj. Nandini had been relieved to hear that Raj's days of being restless and a wholly feckless bachelor had come to an end when he had asked Rachel to meet her and her late husband. That had been a nice time. The memories were still vivid, and offered a warmth even now. Especially now, given the circumstances but were tinged with a bittersweet sadness.

Nandini trudged slowly from the lounge into the hall way. The plush pile of the carpet gave way to the smooth surface of ash coloured laminate. She paused a moment and with her slipper clad foot nudged, together a pair of Koby's well-loved trainers. The boy was growing fast, and shoes didn't seem to last him very long. With the shoes paired neatly, Nandini continued her slow walk towards the door. She had heard the car door open. The robotic beep of the car alarm signaled that Raj was ready to come into the house.

Tucking the crumbling piece of kitchen towel into the pocket of her cardigan, Nandini needed both of her hands to open the door. One to depress the handle, and the other to unclick the mortice lock. With the gap between the door and the step, she could see the shadows formed by her son's feet fall on the laminate and meet her slippers. She then heard the metallic clunk of keys as they fell from Raj's hands and onto the step below the door. Nandini pursed her lips, as she heard her son let loose an expletive. A rather loud expletive, that Nandini shuddered at. It had been her belief that her son had been raised well enough not to be so crass on his doorstep and within earshot of the neighbours. That was spur enough for her to open the door, and let Raj step in.

***

His mum would always remind him about his kit. Every time and without fail, mum would remind him that he would need it for that day. After school, it was his job to empty his kit bag and put the contents into the washer. He wasn't to leave his muddy kit in the laundry hamper; it was categorically imperative that the jersey, shorts and socks were washed as soon as he got home. This morning, Koby had fumbled around on autopilot looking for his boots. Looking for his boots had become a habit. A conditioned response given how his mum had reminded him so frequently. The praise when he actually followed her instructions also helped. Her words reinforced the fact that he was mature enough to do something for himself and didn't rely on his mum to do it for him. Koby had looked for his boots as though everything was normal. As though his Mum was still here; as though there had been no death. Carrying on as normal actually made him feel angry. There was some small comfort it in, he liked the routine. He was angry as it felt disrespectful and as though everything was being glossed over.

Sat in Maths, he was supposed to be trying to get his head around area and volume. At least he looked like he was trying to do that. He was satwith his shoulders hunched over his book to feign the look of being on task. In reality he was doodling on the squared pages of his Maths book. The exercises that had been set were nothing more than a jumble on the page. Numbers and words danced and swirled around the page, making no sense to him whatsoever. He had favoured doodling instead and had abandoned the questions that the rest of class were attending to rather conscientiously. His fist was curled and pressed against his cheek, his gaze cast downwards; Koby appeared to be concentrating. That was what the teacher sat at the front of the class would see, him with his eyes down, and focused on the task at hand.

He was okay with Maths; it was English that he struggled with. Koby found comfort in numbers. They were fixed and changed only when used in equations and formulae. Words changed all the time, with different meanings and descriptions. Words could change everything and using a verb or adjective could make a whole world of difference to what you felt, thought or did. He didn't like the ambiguity or double meanings that could occur when words changed. Change unsettled him. Change caused his world to start blurring at the edges, and the ground to become less firm beneath his feet. Change made him feel lost and as though he was being tossed around in the sea, without the hope of ever reaching land. At this moment, change was intense and overwhelming; Koby couldn't understand how he might cope with everything that change might bring with it into his world.

So far in this lesson, Koby had spent twenty or so minutes looking at the exercises and attempting to do some of the questions. He had then started to doodle as the numbers had begun to move around on the page and dancing to a tune that only they could hear. No matter how much he had tried to skewer the numbers to the page with his pencil, he just couldn't get a handle on the task set.

This was all so immensely frustrating, uncomfortable and made his brain feel as though it was being pressed with a spoon through a fine sieve. Trying to do the questions had been painful and awkward. In comparison, the doodle was comforting and allowed him to escape. Doodling allowed him to stop thinking about all of the questions that swirled around on his head. Questions such as why did his mum have to die, why had the doctors not been able to keep her alive. Why did everything that had happened, happen so quickly. These questions were whizzing around his head; each question feeling as though it was hitting the walls of his brain as he thought about it. Each time a question clunked against the inside of his head it made his heart throb, his eyes hurt and for them to prick with tears.

These tears were now dropping from his eyes and falling freely across the page in front of him. Each one plopped gently across the doodle that he was creating, a blue ball point pen rendering of his mother's face. A face that was rather different from the one that he had seen only a few days ago. As Koby filled in irises with cross hatching, he remembered when his mum's eyes had sparkled. Hers were eyes that sparkled when she laughed; eyes that would become dark when she was angry. A few days ago, her eyes had become duller, darker and no longer sparkled. His mum had told him that she was tired. So tired of fighting, and all that she wanted do, was to sleep.

There had been such absolute fear. He had found the experience frightening. That much Koby was sure of as the thought bounced into his head. The singular and intensely frightening thought of his mum being so tired; that she wanted to go to sleep so badly and then not waking up. Koby had told Caliope, he had said the words out aloud as they had stood in the corridor outside their mum's room. He had just said it, blurted the words out and that was when Caliope-his big sister-had wrapped her arms around him. She had wrapped her arounds him and let her limbs envelope him in the biggest hug that he had known her to give him. They didn't hug often. He could count the number of times on his one hand; and this hug was so different to all of those.

It was at that point that Koby had realised. He had realised that what he thought might actually happen. Up to that point, no one had told him. No one had tried to drop the possibility casually into conversation or awkwardly hover around him, to then sit down next to him and placing a hand to his shoulder actually demolish the universe as he knew it. His mind had been keeping safe before Caliope had wrapped him up in her arms. He had been telling himself that it would all be okay, his mum would get better and that she would go home as soon as possible. With Caliope's arms around him, he had felt the impact of the bombshell, and the walls of his universe shuddered and juddered. As she squeezed the hug around him, Koby realised that this was not going to end well for them or for his mum.

Right now, nothing felt real. Everything felt as though it was a part of a dream. A dream that would end at some point. He would go home, and his mum would still be there. She would check the washing machine for his kit; she would switch it on as he would have forgotten to do so having put in the detergent and fabric softener. He had to get through the school day first though. Koby looked up from the blur of tears that covered his eyelashes and looked at the clock on the wall. The movement of the hands told him that there was still another fifteen minutes left of this particular lesson. Lunch would follow, and then there was History and finally PE at the end of the day.

Returning to his doodle, he found that he had sketched out of much of his mum, and was now concentrating on his smile. That was how he wanted to remember her, smiling and laughing. He hoped that if he remembered like this, then perhaps this wouldn't hurt so much or make him feel so angry. The hurt and anger, it was all too much and was starting to crawl around inside like an army of ants. A horribly intense sensation and all he wanted to do was to make it stop.

2 Matthew

Grandmother's Sponge cake

He had gone to take the cover of the cake stand. To lift of the mesh cover and have a look at the layered sponge cake that he anticipated being there on the orange and white ceramic cake His hand sat on the cover gently, with the peak of the dome hitting the fleshy centre of his palm. The way in which he had planted his hands onto the cover caused his fingers to curve across the surface of the meshed fabric.

More often than not, the cake that he anticipated would have been left to cool and he would have been able to feel the warmth of the freshly baked cake radiate towards his fingers. He had a high level of expectancy and as per his usual routine he had gone into his Grandma's kitchen to make her and Grandad a pot of tea. Their tea was routinely a little wet and therefore required whatever cake Grandma may have baked during the course of the week. Matthew did this every time that he would visit his grandparents. That would mean every weekend and without fail. With his hand sat on the cover, Matthew registered the fact that he couldn't feel any heat whatsoever. His internal mental schema was suddenly paused and he actively looked at the cover having largely been on a sort of auto-pilot.

Very slowly, he peeled away his fingers and moved his hands from the mesh cover. Sat in the centre of the stand was indeed a cake. It was however, much smaller than the twenty five centimetre diameter of the cake stand. Rather than there being a dual layered sponge that might have been approximately fifteen centimetres high from its crumbly base to its domed risen surface, an entirely different cake was sat there. No more than fifteen centimetres in diameter and eight centimetres high, the cake that Matthew saw was most certainly not homemade.

Two layers of really synthetic looking sponge were sandwiched together with a glossy looking jam and cream that peaked out between them. Matthew recoiled in disgust, his lips pulled into a sneer before turning downward at the corners. His grandparents very rarely bought a shop made cake and generally dismissed them as being soulless and entirely unpalatable.

Shoving his hands into his pockets Matthew stood by the worktop and stared at the covered cake stand. His eyebrows rose as he mentally questioned how a shop bought cake had managed to make into his grandmothers kitchen. Matthew could feel his jaw tighten and his hands start to curl into fists at his sides. Inhaling sharply, there was that horrible sensation of anger starting to flame up inside and a warm flush creeping across his cheeks. As innocuous as it looked, the cake beneath the cover infuriated him beyond a reasonable level of contempt.

Raising his arms as though he was an eagle about to take flight, Matthew moved swiftly towards the cake stand. A fit of fury descended upon him and he pulled off the cover and dropped it onto the worktop where it bounced on its peak and fell aside. His other hand landed heavily on cake, fingers splayed across the icing sugar covered surface. The pressure of his digits caused the cake to squelch; the filling exited from between the two thin layers and seeped down the sides.

Sticky red gloop that shone trickled down the sides in something of a grotesque fashion. Beneath his fingers, the texture of the cake was smooth and almost rubbery. So unlike the grainy and textured surface of the cakes that he was used to, the feel of the sponge made Matthew grimace still. Exerting further pressure with his fingers, he broke through the crust in the same way you put your fingers through the holes of a bowling ball. With the cake firmly in his grip, he employed some of the skills that he had acquired as teenager learning to play basketball. One foot was planted firmly onto the floor, with the other moving swiftly to the pedal of the waste bin close by. Rising swiftly the lid snapped open and Matthew flicked his wrist to send the cake flying in. In moving his foot, the pedal bin closed as quickly as it had opened. Matthew rubbed hands together to remove the powdery residue of icing sugar and sticky sweetness that that the cake had left behind on his palms and digits.

There was even a smell. It was sickly, sweet and syrupy; a scent that couldn't compete with the warming fragrance of a homemade cake that was infused with love and tender care. Matthew's anger had started to ebb away as the cake had clipped the rim of the waste bin and taken a tumble into the plastic bag of household waste. The offending article was gone and he didn't feel quite so annoyed.

Matthew did however still want cake and he could not tolerate the thought of his Grandad having his afternoon pot of tea without the pre-requisite cake. Especially when at this moment in time, they could both do with a slice of cake that that had something to do with Grandma. It just had to be Grandma's cake. She would have wanted them to have had proper cake and to remember. Having cake would go toward remembering the good times. Remembering her; Lilly, wife, mother and grandmother. The last two weeks had been really very difficult for them all as a family and there was still a level of heaviness in the atmosphere that had yet to lift even though a funeral had taken place. This somberness made Matthew feel as though his head was fuzzy. As he looked around the well-kept kitchen, he realised exactly what he had to do. He would need to find his Grandma's recipe collection to help realise his plan. A cake was required, but not a shop bought cake such as one that he had just thrown away. There would have to be a homemade cake and as close to the ones that his Grandma used to make

His Grandma Lilly's kitchen was square in shape. Cabinets hung on the opposing walls, one side had a worktop with additional cupboards beneath. On the other side was an imposing aga style stove. Behind him stood a rectangular dining table with matching chairs. This was where his grandparents always ate their Sunday dinners. Sliding his hands to his hips, he turned to face the stove and to think. Her books were definitely somewhere in this kitchen, and most likely near the stove for easy access.

He would probably have to rummage through a few drawers. This was not really an issue; he didn't think for one moment that Lilly would mind if he rifled through to look for her recipes. Biting his lips, he felt his brows knit together. Matthew's face had now become more reflective and somewhat pensive as he tried to remember Lilly moving around the kitchen in her apron. The question that arose in his mind, was how difficult could this really be? 'How difficult', he thought to himself, 'would it be to make Grandma's sponge cake?' Matthew's hazel eyes darted around the kitchen, desperately trying to visualise Lilly's path around the kitchen.

His gaze travelled from the 'fridge that always hummed, to the deep and wonderfully archaic kitchen sink. Finally his eyes tracked towards the oven with its shiny almost yellow handle over which she would drape tea towels. As he remembered, Matthew's hands slipped from his hips to hang loosely at his sides. In his mind the images of were wonderfully vivid and his Grandma Lilly was full of life.

He remembered being sat at the end of the table and being no more than six years of age. He must have been that age as Matthew had the distinct memory of his legs dangling over the edge of the chair and he is feet not touching the floor. Lilly had placed a bowl in front of him, part filled with flour, butter and sugar. She had then asked him to rub the mixture together until it looked like fluffy breadcrumbs. After a while, the softened yellow butter and fluffy flour had combined with the granulated sugar so that they could make a crumble for after dinner.

Mentally fast forwarding to a few years later and he

started secondary school. On one particular occasion Lilly directed him to cream together mixture for fairy cakes. Matthew had asked for her help, and for a very specific reason. At school, as part of his food technology class he was being taught how to make fairy cakes. Knowing that his Grandma like to bake, he had banked on her giving him some guidance. In reality, Matthew had wanted to impress his classmates; some of whom thought that baking and making cakes in particular was best left to girls. He had held her beige mixing bowl under his arm and stirred with some difficulty. No longer a child and not quite an adult; his adolescent strength only just did the job.

At the time Matthew had lacked the physical strength in his arms to cream the mixture to his Grandma's exacting standards. He had desperately pleaded with her to allow him the use of an electric whisk; she was however having none of it. Lilly had told him an in no uncertain terms that creaming was best done manually and using the whisk was just plain lazy. In addition she had never had such gadgets when she was younger and learning to bake. His arm had been sore, but the cakes that he subsequently made at school were beautifully fluffy and made up for the aching limbs that training had inflicted upon him.

Matthew had watched Lilly throughout his entire childhood and his teenage years. When he had left home to go to university, Lilly would proudly tell her friends he had gone away to read food science and all because of how he had helped her in the kitchen as a child. He would call her from time to time during his course, and she would ask him if had learned to make proper food rather than doing experiments in his classroom. That was the general theme in all of the conversations that they would have. Conversation that he enjoyed immensely though he would feel a sharp pang of homesickness on hanging up the 'phone.

It was different now; he would never hear her voice or the rasping laugh that Lilly had sounded when he had explained about his rice pudding experiment going completely and utterly wrong. Matthew would never hear his Grandma Lilly again and that was very difficult for him to process. As his chin dropped to his chest, he felt his throat catch slightly. Grandma Lilly really disliked rice pudding.

There would definitely be no rice pudding made today. A rice pudding wouldn't have the same impact or offer the same solace as a sponge. The memory of Lilly's dislike had poked a wound that was still fresh and had not yet started to heal. He could feel the sensation of so keenly that he wrapped his arms around his torso to give himself a hug. This was part to give him comfort, part to contain the pain that he felt. Matthew remembered the whole event with such clarity and immediacy. Summoned by his father to the house, he and Lydia were in this very kitchen when Lilly had decided to leave. Sat at the table, they had been drinking yet another cup of tea and had been waiting. They had both been waiting to hear that Lilly was no more, and that her fight was at an end. In the run up, Matthew had retained his habit of popping in to see his grandparents. He had used the visits to steel himself for when his Grandma was no longer in her room and eyeing the door as she waited for him to arrive.

With Lydia, he had gone home to get some rest. To also have something of a break from the overwhelming atmosphere that had started to gradually descend upon the house. When they had left, the nurses looking after Lilly were still on duty. His mum and dad largely had everything under control and looked as though they were on top of things.

There was just that something that Matthew had observed in his dad that did somewhat undermine that conclusion. Usually, when his dad smiled you could see a bright glimmer. Now almost absent, the smile that Matthew knew so well had become less bright and on the odd occasion looked very forced. Having just surfaced and got themselves together, they were about to leave for breakfast at nearby café. His dad had called Lydia. Matthew's his own 'phone had not been charged and sat on the coffee table where he had left it on their return home. Lydia had thrown on her coat and pulled him through the front door in something of a frenzied hurry.

They were to come back to Grandad's and as quickly as they physically could for what Grandad was describing as Lilly's last round. When they had arrived back at the house, the atmosphere had changed entirely. Voices had become quieter, the television had been switched off. Everything appeared to be in the shadow of darkness. The colour and spirit of the house felt as though it was slowly ebbing away. Even the movement of the nurse on duty had slowed down to a more reverent and solemn rhythm. It was almost as though he was anticipating the end coming sooner rather than later.

Seeing Matthew and Lydia at the door to Lilly's room the nurse had departed. Lydia had stopped before the door as they had both gone to enter. Giving his hand a gentle squeeze, she couldn't find the strength to go in with him. Holding his hand in hers, she kissed his fingers and then turned to leave back down the stairs. She would wait for him in the kitchen and put the kettle on for them both. With his hands still wrapped firmly around his torso, he could feel the depth of every breath that he took. Each and every breath was drawn in edged with sharp hurt. Matthew could not yet bring himself to think about his goodbye. How he had held Lilly's hand and spoken to her in a low whisper. The very thought made his eyes prick with hot tears. He had said his goodbye and then joined Lydia in the kitchen. All so fresh, the memory was still too immediate and intense.

Unfolding his limbs, Matthew moved towards the large Aga style stove that occupied the far side of the kitchen. To the right of the stove were drawers and he remembered that in one of them was a tin box. In that in box was a collection of recipes that Lilly would refer to when she was baking. There was also a set of note books where she would write things down when trying something or paste into them recipes that she would clip from magazines.

One by one, Matthew pulled out the drawers. Each one was heavy and deep. The kitchen had been built in a time when quality and durability had been paramount. First, was the cutlery draw and he chided himself for not having remembered that fact.

Pushing the drawer closed, it was possible to hear the sound of the runners slide in a weary fashion. A creaky abrasive groan betrayed the age of the fittings. In the second drawer he found tea towel, and moving a few aside he couldn't find what he was looking. Shoving it closed with his fist there was an increasing level of frustration. Kneeling on the floor he hoped that he would find the tin and books in the third and final drawer. Sliding this drawer out slowly, the first thing that he saw was a pile of neatly folded up carrier bags that had been hoarded away.

Sliding these aside Matthew found his quarry. Kneeling was uncomfortable, so he shifted his legs to sit upon the floor cross legged. His immediate reaction was that the floor was actually cold. Then as he had his hands pressed against the front of the drawer, Matthew felt a strange sense of deja vue. He had probably done this as a small child and had not been expecting to be sat here as an adult and looking for his grandma's recipes. Sat in the box was a rather battered looking tin, and to the right of it was a pile of paperback notebooks. Each and every one of the books was dog eared. This was a testament to how much they had been used over the years.

Putting his hand to the tin, Matthew lifted it out of the drawer and cradled it in his hands. The box felt rather cold as he passed a thumb across the curved lid and the tired looking logo that had been punched into it. No bigger than an egg carton, he remembered how the container had looked so much bigger when he had been a boy.

As an adult he could hold onto the box quite comfortably in his hands. As a small boy he had struggled to keep a hold of it and had even dropped it on to the floor. He slid a finger into the dent that had been made and was still there now. Even now Matthew could hear in his ears the ringing echo of the box landing on the hard kitchen floor. He had been so scared at the time, and Grandma Lilly had scolded him into a sulk that his parents couldn't understand.

Holding the box in his fingers, he used his thumbs to push open the lid. Some force was required as the box had been closed quite firmly. It was most likely that it had not been used in a while. As the lid rose, the recipe cards that his grandmother used came into view. Each card was approximately five by four inches and as he pinched one by the corner between his thumb and forefinger he could see his grandmother's cursive handwriting. Words written in black curled with rhythm across the pale blue lines. The ink that Lilly had used to write them was starting to fade and become less clear.

This particular card was for Dundee cake, and the thought of making one caused Matthew to grimace. He was grimacing because of the effort required to making one, and didn't particularly fancy soaking currants in whiskey. In addition, Dundee cake didn't feel right for what he wanted to do. A Dundee cake would further require a trip to the supermarket and that would demand additional effort. Tucking the recipe card back into place, he flicked through the others.

There was uniformity to the cards. On one side there was the name of the recipe and the title was neatly double underlined with a ruler. This was then followed by a list of ingredients and the quantities required. All of these quantities were given in imperial rather than metric. Matthew remembered getting confused about this when helping and having to do the appropriate maths to keep up. Flicking the card over, he saw the step by step method that was painstakingly and neatly written out. His own penmanship was something of a disgrace compared to his grandma's. He couldn't help but admire the handwriting that curled beautifully with the lettering leaning to the right. Not all of the cards were written in the same hand; and as he flicked through the cards there were a few that weren't so neat or beautifully scribed. These were the cards that most likely written by his grandad Albie as Lilly had become frailer and started to deteriorate.

"Oh, Matt, what did you do with the cake?" Unbeknown to Matthew, Lydia had come into the kitchen and was standing by the now vacant cake stand. "Your Dad bought for tea time. Don't tell me that you…." Seeing that he was in fact sat on the floor with a drawer open, she realised that something wasn't right. "What exactly are you doing down here?" she asked moving towards him and kneeling beside.

Turning to face her, Michael pursed his lips to speak. Only the words wouldn't come out. He turned back to the card that he had been looking at, held between his finger and thumb poised to be taken out. "It didn't look particularly nice," said Matthew, taking card out and snapping the tin closed. He let the tin rest in his lap, with the card flat against his palm. "Probably wouldn't have tasted that good either," added Matthew, studying the list of ingredients on the card.

Uncomfortable in having to kneel upon the floor, Lydia leant across Matthew and gently took the card from his hand. "A home-made cake might taste better, I suppose," Lydia held onto the card as she spoke and rose up to her feet. She read through the ingredients, using her finger to work down the list and then turned it over to scan through the method. "You know, Matt," continued Lydia, "I've never actually made one. Lilly would always say that I should try to make one; even if I end up burning it."

Matthew pushed the drawer closed by pressing the front with his palms. Splaying his fingers on the floor either side of him, he used his hands to springboard himself up to his feet having unfurled his long legs. Dusting off his hands he waited for Lydia to finish reading the recipe card.

She promptly held the recipe card out towards him, knowing that she didn't even need to ask. "If you make a mess though," she said pulling out the second drawer, "You clear it up," added Lydia, rifling through the drawer to find an apron that she knew was stashed in there. "You follow the instructions," she spoke whilst unfolding a cornflower blue apron and pulled the neck strap overhead. Luckily for her, on her wrist was a black elasticated band. Sliding it over her wrist and off her hand, Lydia gathered up her wiry brown hair and tugged the locks into a pony tail. "I can be your glamourous assistant, and well, assist." Lydia arched her brows having stated the obvious and took the two short strings that snaked towards the floor either side of her hips to tie them tightly at the base of her spine.

Matthew momentarily looked up from the card, said "You look very pretty," and then returned back to the recipe. The itemised list of ingredients was fairly simple. The list was straightforward in that he wouldn't have to make a trip the supermarket. All of the goods listed would have been in this kitchen anyway.

Whilst he was occupied, Lydia had wandered and was starting to empty the oven of the assorted trays and baking sheets that were stored within. In doing so, she had found two circular sponge tins and a wire cooling rack. Setting these upon the worktop, she moved the trays into a corner of the kitchen where they wouldn't interfere with the baking process. She then leant against the worktop and watched Matthew weave a path across the kitchen.

The path that he moved along was familiar in that she

seen Lilly take the same path when she had been baking. Lydia could see that Matthew was staying true to it; she could see no deviations or variations to it. He too had watched Lilly and carefully at that. With his movement he knew exactly which cupboards had to be open, which jars he would need and even located the same mixing bowl and utensils that his grandmother would have used.

"There should be a set of scales behind you," Said Matthew as he aligned two jars together, "Could you find them, we need to weigh sugar and flour."

With her thoughts derailed, Lydia set about finding the scales. She had to open a few of the cupboards to find them having forgotten their exact location. When she did find the scales, they comprised of a colourless bowl that sat on a square platform with gradations that were marked in black and white. As she placed the scales next to the jars that Matthew had aligned, it struck Lydia just how dated the scales looked. A lot like the rest of the kitchen, the scales were showing their age and were probably older than both her and Matthew.

"Spoon," Matthew wiped flour from his hands onto his jeans and progressed across the kitchen and to the cutlery drawer.

Not looking as he moved, Lydia had to bite her lip and not reply with 'no thank you'. All things considered, such a reply would have been in poor taste. "Wooden?" she asked instead, pointing to a pot that stood by the aga and held not one but three wooden spoons.

"Yes," replied Matthew taking one from the pot and clunking it flat onto the worktop. "And one of those," he said raising aloft a metal spoon that had been fished out of the drawer. "And we still need to weigh things," he added shifting himself towards the 'fridge.

Taking the hint Lydia unstoppered the jars of dried goods. This was no easy process as she was so used to unscrewing lids of things.She was however, in this instance, confronted by cork bungs and therefore removing them was hardly second nature. Gripping the first jar into the crook of her arm, Lydia had to tug out the bung with some effort. Initially non-compliant, she had to tease the bung along the neck of the jar with her finger before grasping her fingers around the circumference and yanking it out in one fluid motion. She lurched backwards with the motion. Had she not clamped the jar with her elbow, she might have dropped it to the floor in losing her grip and smashed the ceramic jar. Looking at Matthew with a view of frustration she opened the second having learned how not to do it.

Lilly's mixing bowl was biscuit beige on the outside and white on the inside. It was one of the very first things that Matthew had located in opening and closing cupboards. A fairly traditional mixing bowl, it was probably used by grandma's like Lilly up and down the country. Lydia was about to ask how much of the flour and sugar needed to be weighed out. As she turned, Matthew arrived next to her with Lilly's recipe card and a butter dish. To be helpful, he had already diced up the butter into cubes.

"Equal quantities," said Matthew slapping the recipe card onto the worktop. "The same amount of both sugar and flour. This stuff is probably soft enough and needs to be creamed with the sugar." Picking up a wooden spoon he dropped it into mixing bowl where it thudded against the ceramic. The way that Matthew stood pivoting on one foot suggested that he was on the move again and quickly at that. "When you are creaming, this means to mix up the butter and sugar into a paste." He said, as he did something that he did very rarely and to emphasis a point. Holding up his finger, he waggled it repeatedly. "Creaming takes elbow grease," he added as he disappeared off to the 'fridge.

Biting the inside of her cheek, Lydia refrained from making a barbed comment. All things considered, this was not the time to start a fight. She was supposed to be helping, with the cake and helping Matthew process this all in whatever way he needed to. At any other point she might have entered into a war of words, just not today. The sugar had been weighed, and combining it with the sugar in the bowl, Lydia did her best to mix the two together. What Matthew had said about the butter being soft enough was far from the truth, and it did take some effort to combine the smooth butter with the gritty granulated sugar. The bit about elbow grease was certainly true, and it really did take time to do.

As Lydia struggled with the creaming process, Matthew was looking for some more butter and the four eggs that the recipe demanded. He had expected to find the eggs in the 'fridge; that was where he would look for them at home and that was his conditioned response. What he eventually remembered was that in this kitchen, the eggs were kept beneath a dark brown ceramic chicken. He felt as though could have kicked himself, a look evident from the look of despondence that had flashed across his face.

Finding the chicken, he moved the heavy ceramic bird and liberated the eggs that he needed. These were scooted over to Lydia, and his instructions were clear as he adopted the pivot foot stance again. "Could you beat these in one by one? The flour we fold in after." Said Matthew as he turned away and headed to the 'fridge. Whilst the décor of the kitchen was rather dated and betrayed the age of the house and its occupants; some of the appliances were actually quite modern and somewhat anachronistic. Opening the 'fridge demanded a hefty tug; the doors were rather broad and weighty. Matthew wondered just how easily his grandparents were able to use it. There had been a few grumbles when it first installed, so using it on a daily basis no doubt bothered them. Even the 'fridge in his own kitchen wasn't so stout or so robustly built.

He needed another pack of butter from the fridge and fortunately there were a few to choose from. Wrapped in a golden metallic cover, any notion of butter being bad for you was burnished away by the shiny packaging that made it look rather attractive. Matthew tore away a once inch strip from all the way around the block to allow him to grease the cake tins. These had been washed and dried whilst Lydia was still creaming the cake mix and now sat next to the drainer with a tea towel draped across them.

"Now what would you like me to do?" Lydia enquired, the wooden spoon that she had been using was raised high as though she was about to beat a drum with it. "Eggs are done," she said waving the spoon around. She had caught Matthew in transit along his flight path in the kitchen, and waited till she had his attention. He had stopped as though he was gliding across the floor in a similar way to a ballerina might have in acting out a scene from 'Swan Lake'. Seeing him made her fixed expression of concentration give way to a smile that became an irrepressible burst of laughter.

"Fold in the flour with a metal spoon," said Matthew, before he heard her laughter. "And what's so funny?" he asked heading towards the waiting cake tins.

Shaking her head, Lydia picked up a metal spoon to start folding in flour. "You were gliding across, like a ballerina." She was still laughing, but managed to fold in the flour carefully. "You just don't do that in our kitchen," she added. "It doesn't matter. Was just a bit funny, that's all."

Embarrassed, Matthew could feel his cheeks become warm. He had been somewhat lost in his own world, focused on what Lilly would have done. "Just fold in the flour," he said rather sheepishly. "Should pre-heat that thing," he muttered clutching at a tea-towel still and trying to realign himself with the process that he was supposed to be following. Draping the tea-towel over his arm, he pressed the ignition on the oven and turned the oven knob to the required gas mark. Hearing the click of the ignition and the subsequent thud, Matthew peered through the oven doors with his knees bent.

The muffled thud chimed with the appearance of blue flames that he could now see dancing at the back of the oven. Leaving the oven he returned to the tins to try and grease them. Matthew remembered Lilly using so much butter on the tins that there would be a thick coating all the way around the circumference. In his determination to follow her footsteps he had forgotten that these tins had a non-stick coating. These tins were another relatively modern development in the kitchen. This jarred with his previous experiences; so much so that Matthew felt a little flummoxed and unsure of how to proceed.

To grease or not to grease; that was the question as he held onto the packet of butter. He could feel his thumb press into the metallic cover and start to move into the softening butter. Lilly would always grease the tins and that was all he remembered. These still looked very new, suggesting that she hadn't even used them. His mum had brought them and put them into the kitchen, with the hope that Lilly would be well enough to use them. He would take risk, and there was very little that he had to lose.

Matthew could hear Lilly's voice in his head, telling him to grease the tins properly. There would no doubt be an eye roll and some loud tutting. Lily wouldn't have been disdainful or disparaging, just annoyed that Matthew was doing something that wasn't her way of doing things. Pressing the butter against the metal of the tin, he then dragged the packet across the surface and all the way around the circumference of the tin. He had to repeat this action again to ensure even coverage across the whole tin and then there was the sprung base as well with its textured surface. Matthew really didn't fancy chipping away baked on cake mix that might weld itself to any ungreased spots.

"Now what?" Lydia had appeared at his shoulder, having become a little bored. "I've folded in the flour for you. Are we ready to bake yet?" In her arms was the mixing bowl containing the now ready cake mix.

A trend was developing as Matthew squeaked. His concentration had been broken again, and this time he rocked a little on his heels with the motion of being startled. He had been entirely engaged within his own world; immersed in wanting to be exact and on task. Being at home, he and Lydia were able to use a kitchen and without getting in one another's way. Being here and under these circumstances; this was altogether different and not particularly pleasant. Usually, Matthew could tolerate her help in the kitchen; her assistance was within reason. Right now however, it was unsettling and upsetting his cake making momentum. "Now we pour, and almost," replied Matthew as he put down the second tin and held out his hands for the bowl.

Lydia complied and handed the bowl over; glad to be rid of it as really was quite heavy. Not before removing the wooden spoon and tapping it against the side to remove excess mix that clung to it. Passing a finger through the mixture that coated the back of the spoon, Lydia did the done thing and pressed her finger to lips before licking away mixture. All perfectly innocent and in her head, made the situation a little lighter.

Peeved that she had licked the spoon, Matthew pulled his lips together in disdain. With the bowl in his hands, he started to pour the mixture into the greased tins. There was the initial plop sound as the mixture landed into the tin and then it silently descended and pooled. In tin was filled in turn, and with the bowl empty he passed a finger across the rim to then lick it away. From the corner of his eye, he could see Lydia's eyes narrow at him as she walked towards the sink. It was a slightly different matter when he decided to lick the bowl. With all the mixture scrapped into the bowl, Matthew pressed his wooden across the surface to smooth it out.

Observing Matthew closely as she washed her hands beneath the tap; she saw him drag a finger across the concave surface and once more take a small mouthful of mixture. All she could see was a little boy lost. Matthew looked like a lost little boy who had spent hours in this kitchen learning how to bake from his grandmother. Lilly had truly meant the world to him. He had yet to speak openly about her death, how he might have felt having to say goodbye. Lydia knew better than to rush. If he needed her, she was definitely going to be there to support him.

Looking at the curved surface of the spoon, Matthew was convinced that he had got all of the mixture off and away. Setting the spoon onto the worktop, he picked up one of the tins, and asked, "Could you bring the other?" as headed towards the oven. Balancing the tin on his left palm, he used his free hand to open the oven. As the door lowered he could feel the intense heat across his face and was trying not to be blinded by the light coming from the side. Sliding the tin onto the middle shelf he then stood aside to let Lydia slide the second tin into the oven. As she moved away, he took the oven door in both hands and closed it.

They would now have to wait for twenty minutes for the two sponges to cook through. Twenty minutes during which they both took turns to peer through the door and will the sponges to rise and puff up at the surface. Lydia hovered and even made a cup of tea. It was only when Matthew jumped from his seat that she realised that their wait was over. Handing him a pair of oven gloves she then watched Michael make sure that the sponges were done. For each sponge, he pressed an index finger into the centre where the golden brown surface had domed and cracked with the heat of the oven. The sponge was springy to the touch and that told Matthew that it was most likely done. However he wanted to be entirely sure and his face became pensive.

Lydia watched silently still, as he moved towards the cutlery drawer once again and this time removed a metal skewer. Jabbing the skewer into each of the sponges, Matthew checked for any mixture that might have clung in its uncooked state to the skewer. With there being nothing left on the skewer, Matthew was going to rest assured. Looking at Lydia, he needed her help for the next phase.

She took the hint easily enough and stood alongside him. Side by side they both unclasped the hinges that held the tins closed and released the sponges. Two domed and golden brown sponges were removed from the tins still resting on a base. There were a few burned bits on the edges, but nothing to spoil the sponges. Both of the layers looked a great deal more palatable compared to the cake that Michael had dropped into the kitchen bin. Sat onto the wire cooling rack, they looked fairly edible.

Sliding a little closer to Matthew, Lydia moved her had from her side and curled it around his, to give his hand a gentle squeeze. She wasn't going to pretend that she knew exactly what he was going through, or that she felt the loss as keenly as he did. What she did know, was that if he wanted to make another cake, or a hundred more; she would be there to help him through it. There were worse things that she might have to do compared to eating slightly crispy cakes. The cakes would have to cool down, and from what she remembered from the recipe; they would require filling with raspberry jam and be dusted with icing sugar. The cake may not have been all singing and dancing, It was Grandma Lilly's sponge cake and that was all that mattered.

3 Michael

The mourning afterwards and again

Blue. Beautiful, baby blue. An entire layette sat on top of the changing table, and its colour was in pronounced difference to the table's utilitarian plainness. The clothes had been sat there for some time waiting to be worn. Ever since they had found out, that firstly there would be a boy, and secondly that they should have hope. This time, they could cross their fingers for a definite result.

Sat there now, the clothes were positioned as though someone had forgotten to tell them. Forgotten to communicate that whilst the plan had been for the garments to be worn there had been a distinct change of plan. The layette would have to be disappointed; its fate was to remain unworn. Brushed cotton would be not be pressed delicately against the skin of a newborn right now or anytime soon. Sat next to the layette were a stack of romper suits, still packaged in crisp and colourless cellophane. Something of an impulse buy when the new arrival had been first discovered. At that point there had been no discovery of the gender; with this the colours selected had been deliberately neutral. The romper suits and other gathered bits and pieces fell into the categories of yellow, white and purple. They had not needed much encouragement to go shopping. With this pregnancy supposed to end on positive, there had been a whole gamut of emotions and sensations. A feeling of uncertainty-in light of some previous disappointment-with a parallel flutter of excitement that this time there was going to be a baby at the end of such an arduous journey.

Pressed against his chest was a stuffed animal. The creature was an elephant to be exact. Made from a plush fabric, the cuddly elephant was warm against his fingers and a very deep shade of grey. They had decided that the entire nursery would be elephant themed.

His eyes travelled from the stack of cellophane romper suits and towards the images painted onto the wall above the changing table. These were images of an elephant and its child that had been painstakingly created over different weekends. Coloured and crafted using a number of different colours to create a patchwork effect. Vibrant colours had been selected from a range of small pots of paint that would otherwise be used as testers for decorating. They had amassed something of a collection in experimenting with different combinations. A stencil still hung in place, taped to the otherwise very magnolia wall; waiting much like the romper suits, for a grand unveil. Each and every little square was complete and a colour burst waiting to happen. Perhaps the stencil was a little fed up of waiting. The top left and bottom right corners were starting to dog ear and pull in resistance to the tape that currently anchored the entire thing to the wall.

He had been standing here in one place for a while, and in the middle of the nursery. To his left was the cot, for when their baby was bigger. Above which was suspended a mobile, brightly coloured and more elephants in an assortment of colours. They might not have used the cot for a while, and for the early days there was a Moses basket left on the floor in the height of anticipation.

The shrill cry of a 'phone from downstairs momentarily broke his thoughts. Turning his head a little to the right he heard the call be taken by his father. His father's voice was deep at the best of times, but now took on something of a more sonorous sound in trying to be discreet and gentle in the current circumstances. The grandparents had arrived in haste having received the call. Labour was underway and they were to assemble here at the house as soon as physically possible. What they had not been expecting was the sad news that their grandchild-a grandson-had been born asleep. It had taken them-him and her- a while to make the telephone call. They had made it together, holding each other's hands. The previously jubilant grandparents had arrived a little later at the hospital and there had been a family gathering of a sort. A very quiet and sombre gathering, brief as the immediacy and intensity of an eternally sleeping baby was just too much.

Michael and his parents had eventually left to return home. Allowing his wife to rest a while and alone. He had not wanted to leave her, but they could not look at one another without curling their fists and starting to cry. Still able to hear the muffled sound of the call being taken, he couldn't make out the exact words; but the tones was clear from the rise and fall of his father's tone. The tone was a genteel response that acknowledged condolences and sympathies.

Hugging the grey plushy elephant closer, he heard his father draw the call to a close and the clunk of the telephone handset being placed back into its base. There was more discussion that could be heard but only just. Once he was home, he had retreated immediately to the nursery. The three other had adults had occupied themselves with things to do such as tea making and examining the cupboards for food. Actions carried out in an attempt to cover up the feeling of walking on eggshells. An overwhelming feeling of loss, that was at complete odds to the expected jubilation and a rosy future cloaked the whole house.

He had to move, he could feel his knees tremble and about to buckle from beneath him. He made an attempt to move towards the armchair that had been brought up to the nursery from the lounge, in anticipation of nursing. His legs wobbled with intensity, and before he knew it, his knees had met with the floor. Still he held the stuffed elephant tightly and closely towards his chest. His fingers curled around the toy trying to get comfort, the smallest solace as all he felt was pain.

There was absolute agony as he tried to breathe. It was so hard to breathe, as his chest pulled and felt as though it was aflame with every laboured breath that he tried to take. From his navel to his sternum; the physical sensation was that of a white hot blade searing through flesh. This then combined with the further sensation of feeling as though someone had smacked you straight in the stomach. Not just the once either, but repeatedly as though you were a speedball in a gym. Striking you time and time again; beating you into pained submission. It was safe to say that the butterflies of excitement that had been present with their fevered fluttering had been well and truly squashed. The butterflies of expectancy were altogether annihilated. Letting go of the elephant, his hands landed before him onto carpet. His fingers splayed out into the pile to support his weight. This prevented him from falling further and flat face down onto the floor. Michael let out a gasp. A deep breath that he had been holding in for what felt like a lifetime; it had been forced down deep into his gullet. Only now, which the feeling of having been punched in the gut; did the breath exit between his lips. With this breath came tears and the deepest of sobs.

At first he tried to stop; he tried to stop crying, making pained noises. No matter how much he tried, Michael could not get himself to stop. The tears and sobs would not abate, and the sensation of being caught in the tugging currents of a flood did not subside. In his head there had been so many dreams. So many hopes of what the future might hold. For the child that was expected so keenly, for the three of them as a finally complete family. They had both hoped and dreamt about what might happen.

Yet for now, he had no words, no thoughts to say to her and help make this be less painful. At the time, when they had been expecting the first cry; there had been nothing. They had heard nothing but a heavy and foreboding silence. Then there was a flurry of noises from the medical team as they sprang into action. They had looked at one another; no words spoken but their faces had stretched with anxiety. Kneeling here, a physical mess; Michael felt paralysed by the grief that he and his wife shared. His limbs felt so heavy right now.

Only hours ago, at that moment when it came became apparent that there was happy ending; he had been unable to put his hand into hers. Michael had been fixed to the spot with fright. He was fixed again now, prostrate on the carpet and wanting to curl up. Curl up and shut out the whole world. Pressing his eyelids down, he momentarily cleared the tears that had welled up. Forcing them to tumble down his cheeks and leaving behind what felt like a greasy film clinging to his skin.

What was he to do now? He could not think, his head was already hurting in trying to process what had happened. At his temples he could feel a constricting pressure that was starting to travel and move across his forehead. Lifting a hand, Michael swept his fingers across his face to clear away tears and mucus.

It hurt less to breathe now, as the tightness across his chest had started to loosen and allowed him to breathe more freely and deeply. Taking in air, he could hear the swooshing sound as it travelled through his nose and filled his chest. Watching his chest swell, the movement triggered him to move his limbs. Pulling his legs and feet from behind him, Michael then drew his knees toward his chest to rest his chin upon them. Once again he closed his eyes, squeezed out the residue of tears and focused upon the elephant stencil. His dark eyelashes glistened with the trapped tears that had not travelled down his face. By batting his lashes a few times, Michael was able to dislodge them. The tears took flight away and into the air. He caught sight of one shiny tear flying away. The shiny globule of moisture moved through the air quickly and silently landing onto the carpet where it was quickly absorbed into the deep pile. Even though he had his arms wrapped around his knees in what felt like a safe cocoon, Michael could feel himself trembling still.

A sort of delayed shock was starting to kick in and he felt distinctly quite cold. Looking at his forearms he could see his skin rise in goose bumps and feel rough to the touch as he passed a hand over his arm to warm himself up. He was definitely cold, and he registered that fact in sudden awareness of the physical sensation. Being dressed in only a thin t-shirt and jeans and with the central heating yet to kick in certainly didn't help matters.

Despite the feeling of having been punched in the stomach, Michael remembered that it had been some hours since he had eaten. Grumbling and gurgling sounds from his now empty stomach alerted him to do something about the lack of sustenance.

He could hear voices in conversation downstairs.

Only now there was the additional sound of the television being on. This was a little staccato, and not the same voice. Suggesting that whoever was watching it was channel flicking. The family had most likely got bored or felt increasingly more uncomfortable with the atmosphere that shrouded the house and clung to all of the walls. Michael was definitely hungry; a small spikey ball of pain was discernible as forming beside the other deep throbbing pain. The pain of hunger rolled around inside, a spikey ball wanting to get out and be remedied. It would keep moving around and causing him discomfort, the sensation would abate only if he actually ate something.

He wanted to move, but he felt grounded and anchored to the spot. His limbs were heavy still, as though the weight was keeping Michael together and preventing him from fracturing into millions of tiny pieces. Whilst it was scientifically impossible, he was convinced that the force of gravity acting upon him had changed. The weight of the world pressed upon him in a far greater way than he had ever experienced. Gravity had become denser, more concentrated than with all the previous disappointments. There had been miscarriages, quite a few. Some had happened very early on, if they hadn't been so invested, they might have blinked and missed the events to occur in the first few weeks. A couple of the sad endings were a month or two into the pregnancies. With those, gravity had swirled around him; it had swirled around them both. The force was acting as though it was trying to keep them both standing and standing together. With this sad ending; this time the sensation of gravity was different. They had been so close to a positive and guaranteed outcome that the effect of gravity was no longer supporting. Gravity was no longer acting as a scaffold to help support them both.

This time the gravity that Michael himself was experiencing was a heavy and damaging force that had knocked him down squarely onto his backside. With the effect on him being so harsh, how might she be feeling to have been at the centre of not just this storm but all of them combined? He would have to stand again, uncurl from his cocoon and find out. As to how he might do that; that would come to him. Hopefully.

Downstairs three adults milled around somewhat tentatively. All three of them had experienced something similar involving their children before. A sad and difficult telephone call or a face to face chat where they had been told that at this time, things were not meant to be. There was to be no grandchild, that they could put away their knitting needles until there was. May be next time, they had been told, if the universe was to allow it. One of the adults was stood in the kitchen by the kettle making tea once again. This was the role that she had elected to take up when there had previously been sad endings. The second was making a ham and salad sandwiches with soft white bread. She was the feeder of the triad; they all had to eat after all.

Adult number three had retreated to the lounge and was watching the television. He was sat at the side of a three seater sofa. A sofa that was new and the upholstery still had the stiffness of being factory fresh. Unsure of what he was to do and how to do it; this was his role. To retreat and wait in the wings until he was required in some shape or form. He would definitely be available, for whatever purpose; he had always stressed that to his son. All being well, the boy in question would no doubt show or tell him how his father might help. The voices and faces on the screen were different. They were not family or the doctors and nurses who had been part of the last twenty four hours.

The sounds and images were all a jumble of movements and garbled noise. This was a distraction from the knot that had form in his stomach as well as the catching of emotion in his throat. A single slip in attention would unravel that knot and unlock that catch to bring forth a torrent that was being suppressed. A moment of emotion that was supposed to be joyful was once more replaced by devastation and profound sadness for his son and daughter-in-law.

Adult number one heard the sound first. It was the sound of her son walking down the stairs. She looked at the second adult and nodded that should hasten the preparation of the sandwich that were being. She herself continued to make hot drinks for them all. Four mugs sat on a tray next to the kettle. Two teas were required as well as two coffees. One of the coffees was to be black and with two sugars. She was aware of the specific stipulation and had been for a number of years. To alter that combination of coffee and sugar or event to forget it, was to invite episodes of insufferable childish tantrums. For now, she could do without those.

The kettle had just boiled and a plume of hot steam floated from its dark spout. Adult number two sliced the sandwich that she had prepared down the middle, pressing her palms flat onto the slices to keep it all together.

Michael's footfall down the stairs wasn't particularly heavy or noisy. The sound of his movement broke the rather sedentary sense of status quo and alerted the gathered family of his presence. He looked into the lounge first. Only briefly but he saw his father looking sombre and reflective whilst flicking through channels. The digital package that they had was rather extensive, and the range would no doubt keep his father occupied for some time. At the end of the short carpeted hallway was the kitchen where he found his mother and his mother-in-law. Michael's first thought was how much they looked like two soldiers at their posts ready for duty. The thought brought the smallest and briefest of smiles to his mouth.

He pulled out a chair from beneath the square kitchen table and sat himself down. Placing his palms onto the surface of the faux pine table, Michael felt cocooned again. The chair back was keeping him from slouching and forced him to sit upright. His feet were planted firmly onto the cold tiled floor. He could feel the pressure of the chair seat pressing into the back of his knees. Otherwise he might have flopped forwards, his head onto his arms as though he were a marionette that had been cast aside from a much merrier time.

The two women moved from the sentry posts. Adult number one placed a green mug before her son. A mug of medium brewed tea with the tea bag left in and a spoon. The spoon would be needed to stir in the two teaspoons of sugar that for now sat in the bottom in want of dissipating.

Adult number two then discharged her duty by placing next to the mug a matching plate. On top of which lay the sandwich that she had prepared. Moving back to their posts as quickly as they had left them, the two women kept their distance and hoped that the food and drink would be taken and their concerns about an empty stomach alleviated. Adult number two busied herself with making the three remaining beverages. She watched from the corner of her eyes to see if her son was eating and drinking. She knew that he hadn't for some time and her maternal instincts would not allow her to bear the thought of him being hungry. Dipti had become strangely accustomed to this situation; it had happened in a similar way so many times before. The only difference between those occasions and now being that the definite and positive outcome had been within reach.

This situation was supposed to be resolved with a success, a new born baby that they would all cuddle and coo over. A happy and healthy, much anticipated child that would have been loved and spoiled rotten. Making a cup of tea for herself and then the two coffees; in her head she imagined all that might have been. From the other side of the kitchen, adult number two saw to making more sandwiches. Perhaps now they could all eat. She would make enough for them all and perhaps some spares. After which, she would say her goodbyes to return to the hospital and be with her daughter.

They had barely spoken whilst they had been there. The disappointment and shock had been painfully palpable and intensely immediate. It wouldn't be any less now, but a small amount of time had passed to allow going back and seeing how she might be.

Hopefully, her daughter would have had some rest, a little sleep. Even if she wasn't awake or they didn't speak, they would at least be in the same space and together.

Michael could feel their gaze flit upon him from time to time. He loved them both and knew that this was the way in which they would show their affection. The two mothers made for an effective and efficient tag team. Over the years they had honed their mothering to complement each other and in doing so avoided there being any conflict to sour things. He had picked up half of the sandwich and holding it between his hands took bites from the corner. Small bites at first, there was still some resistance in having to eat. Three small bites then gave way to mouthfuls, and short work was made of half the sandwich. He really was hungry, the sustenance essential and he would not be loath to eat the rest of the meal.

"Any news on that coffee?" asked Adult number three having now joined the fray. He had left the television on in the lounge to join his wife, her opposite number and his son. He moved towards Michael and placed his right hand gently on his shoulder. The touch was meant for reassurance, and was indicative of a close father and son bond that had never shied away from displays of affection and signs of support. "Or do we have to go all the way to Columbia and pick the beans ourselves," he added after a pause. It was all he could think of saying to make the situation a little lighter and more bearable.

His wife, Dipti, adult number one, frowned at him and shook her head. She had just finished making the coffee in question. Instant granules had been doused hot water, and stirred up with two teaspoons of sugar. The granules were most likely not up to her husband's usual standards, he was something of a coffee connoisseur; sadly this was unavoidable for the moment. "Here," she said softly, handing over the drink that was also in a green mug. "It's hot, so mind you don't gulp it down."

"Thank you," her husband acknowledged, taking the mug delicately into his hands and blowing across the surface of the liquid. He could tell from the smell that wafted towards him that the quality wasn't the best, not to mention the way in which the dark liquid had frothed around the edges on stirring. "Hot is good," he said, yet to take mouthful. "Hot warms you up."

"Hot has you fuming," returned his wife, as she moved away and gave a second coffee to her opposite number. "When you take a gulp," she continued as she moved back to her post. "As you are impatient, burn your mouth and then turn the air blue."

Michael watched and he listened as he ate the rest of his sandwich. The exchange made him feel even more ill at ease. It all sounded so normal. It all sounded so mundane.

4 Maya

A mother's loss

Intense, vigorous, and all-consuming waves of agony. She could feel were waves and waves of sheer pain crashing over and over across her heart. Every time that she felt as though she composed herself, the sensation would start again with the tiniest of niggles. The feeling of abject grief would manifest itself in an almost human form, similar to a small child peering round a wall and chortling with juvenile glee as her eyes met with his.

Caught in the crosshairs of the gaze, she would feel immobilised and fixed to the spot. Having gained her attention, eyeballs boring through her, the grief demon would then scream. Shriek like a banshee and as the sounds in her mind tried to pierce through her ear drums, she would clamp her hands over her ears. The creatures shrieking would rise to a crescendo that would become a swirling mass of waves with her in the middle of a vortex. Only when the harsh, discordant sound had subsided did she realise. Realise that the screaming was her own sound and that she had screamed so hard and so much that her throat throbbed. Then the need arose to clear it as phlegm had accumulated and was about to trigger a gag reflex. All the phlegm and mucus that gathered in a dense ball had to be moved; that was what would happen when you cried. Cried and for long periods of time when you thought that no one could hear you or see you. Her eyes were slick with tears that streamed and cascaded down her cheeks in fat, greasy, globular drops. Their paths ended at her jawline and from there the tears dripped away onto her clothes. Pressing two fingers into the hollows of her eyes she swept away an accumulation of moisture. Deciding that this wasn't enough, her hand followed flat across her cheek and swept away a combination of tears and make up.

Make up. She felt as though she was wearing a mask. A mask that was thick, heavy and applied to cover up the greyness. The greyness was an overwhelming shroud that would otherwise indicate a distinct lack of joy, warmth and life. Without the façade, her appearance was that of a washed up and wrung out individual who could have done with a few extra hours of sleep.

Last night, she had lain in bed unable to settle and to fall asleep. She had whiled away the hours by tossing and turning, her mind was whizzing through all of her questions. The 'what ifs', the' why nots' and 'how comes' that had plagued her every moment and every day since the tragedy had happened. There were hundreds of questions that whizzed around and filled her brain, all begging to be answered.

Where she found herself now, sat upon a cold closed down toilet seat with her knees drawn up tightly towards her chest was far better than being sat at home. At home she had established a routine of waking, washing, breakfasting, A routine with the feeling of being enveloped inside a world where nothing had happened and nothing was different. She could sit in front of the television, flick through the channels and consume a monotonous diet of daytime dramas that numbed her brain rather than stimulated it.

To be cocooned and safe, with the world beyond the television set buffered away had been acceptable and comfortable. She was however now at a point that being inside what she could only describe as a bubble, was suffocating. The sheer monotony and onerous gentleness was overwhelming to such an extent that it had fostered a fierce drive to escape. Here she was, having taken the bus in the teeming rain and arriving at the office to try and work. Officially, she was supposed to be on leave. The hushed whispers and questioning eyes of her colleagues had made her bristle somewhat when she had gone into the kitchen to make a cup of tea. Strewn around the base of the toilet were squares of toilet tissue. Some of the squares had been scrunched up into damp balls that had been used to stem a flood of tears that had preceded the almost rather primal and unrestrained episode of screaming. Had she been in a better frame of mind, the offending litter would have been picked up and flushed down the toilet. At this precise moment in time, such an activity seemed a rather herculean effort from where she was seated. Beneath the mass of tissue was a pair of black court shoes that were splattered and water marked. The rain had not been kind to them during her commute. The shoes looked rather forlorn and not really fit for purpose.

She had started this whole situation so well. Getting up this morning, the covers had been kicked off in defeat. She had been defeated in not being able to sleep, defeated by the mental barrage of questions, defeated by this entire experience. There was the still the sense of being on auto-pilot and going through the motions, as well as trying to retain a sense of normality.

Lifting herself from the bed that she shared with her husband, her movement had caused him to exclaim and curse at there being a draught. She had showered, changed and applied her makeup to start her day in the same what way that she had before everything had happened. Standing in the bathroom, her hair had been dried, combed and pulled tightly back into a neat and tidy ponytail. Her age was somewhat betrayed by the shimmer of a few silver strands that had been tucked behind her ears. These were a reminder to book in for a cut and colour at the next available opportunity. Usually, the process of making herself look somewhat presentable was carried out quickly and with as little fuss as possible. Make up and its application was always something of an inconvenience but prevented questions being asked of health and whether it was serious. No doubt women all over the world despised being in such a position; allowing the makeup industry to reap reaped the benefits of this self-flagellation and boom because of it.

She would take time today. Looking at her reflection in the bathroom mirror, the harsh light emanating from the spherical fitting accentuated every part of her features. Every pore, every crease that was half way to becoming a fully-fledged wrinkle was defined by the hue from the lighting. Blinking her eyes, she focused upon the almost deep purple skin beneath her eyes.

The colour was a deep bruise-like purple, and was horribly pronounced without the heavy coverage of concealer. The pigmentation was a stark contrast with the rest of her skin. Even olive and somewhat Mediterranean looking skin could pale against such a dense shade of puce. Such a dense shade that her eyelashes were struggling to cast a shadow and break up the colouration. A pigmentation probably caused by a multitude of different factors. Genetics for one, rather than just recent events that caused her to toss, turn and be bereft of a good night's sleep.

Reaching for the door of the mirrored cabinet, she delicately pulled the panel towards her with her fingertip on the bottom right corner. A small red rectangular pouch was lifted from the shelf inside and removed from the cabinet. A bottle of moisturiser that was almost three quarters full was also taken out and held precariously between her fingers by the pump top. Closing the door she placed the makeup case and the bottle on the side of the sink.

Depressing the pump top of the bottle, she held two fingers beneath the spout. More than one pump was required to release some of the cream, and eventually the liquid that exited the pump was wonderfully thick and luxurious. A testament to the price, it was an expensive lotion and therefore used sparingly. The time that it had taken to for the bottle to remain at three quarters full extended into years. Ordinarily a less pricey moisturizer product tended to be used on a daily basis. This was done purely because this particular lotion was perceived as being something of a decadent luxury.

Even the smell of the full bodied lotion permeating to her nostrils had an exorbitant accent to it. An accent that was somewhat comforting with the offer of her worries being eased away as she proceeded to rub the dollops onto the apples of her cheek in a circular motion. Being a parent, her sense of smell had become educated to an extent and was becoming increasingly more refined with the exposure to the vast array of smells that her child had presented to her over the years. Base notes of vanilla and top notes of spiced chocolate were an entire world away from the earthy damp mud and stale socks that had once been found to be festering and forgotten in a dark corner of a gym bag.

Continuing to smooth in the scented cream across her skin, Maya passed her fingers over years of love, joy, sadness and anger. Her skin was a tapestry; experiences and emotions that caused the corners of her eyes to crinkle into crow's feet when she smiled. Agonies and ecstasies that pulled her jowls back when she was irate or anxious. A whole life time was etched across her face. Maya would not have had things any other way, and any thoughts of cosmetic surgery that might have been fueled by the fantasy of one day winning the lottery were filed away into a mental box.

A mental box that would only be opened and the fantasy revisited when suitably drunk and further emotionally further compromised. Her skin certainly felt refreshed; the cold tautness from having washed her face had been softened and soothed away. There were few opportunities to do this and to look at her features so closely in the mirror. Ordinarily this process was done so quickly, quietly and without much reflection as to what might improve her skin tone, whether she ought to use a better brand of foundation or did that shade of eyeliner have to be such a harsh shade of black.

Opening the red make up bag required sliding a golden zip across matching metal teeth. The bag was velveteen and quilted, soft to the touch beneath her fingers. Maya let her lips twitch into the faintest of smiles as she remembered that the bag had been a gift from Millie for her birthday. The bag had been gifted to her filled with several small bottles of nail varnish and a manicure kit. With the bag unzipped, the toothy edges were apart like the mouth of a very hungry crocodile.

Agape, the mouth of the bag looked rather intimidating and likely to snap shut with her fingers sandwiched between the teeth of the zip. Maya's fingers entered the bag and took from it a tube of foundation, a small circular pot of concealer and a rather blunt and not altogether serviceable eye pencil. Once upon a time, Maya would have had a much larger bag and it would have been filled with an array of different cosmetics. That was however many years and an entire misspent youth ago. Here she was, right now; older, wiser, less fanciful and definitely more frugal. Make up was simpler now and not the prestigious brands that she had used in her younger years. Carefully Maya unscrewed the lid of the pot of concealer and tore away the silver foil that formed a second barrier. She dipped two fingers of her left hand into the pot and scooped out the small amount that was required. Two peaks formed in the mousse like substance, making it look like dollops of Angel Delight that had been whipped up and were full of air.

Returning her gaze to her reflection, Maya dabbed the concealer into the hollows of her eyes. Patting it across the deep shades of puce that tinged the sockets and made her look as though her eyes were deep set. She did the same across her eye lids, one eye open at a time to allow the concealer to be smoothed into the creases and the corners. This was easier to do with fingers in comparison to using a sponge. That was a waste; her fingers could blend and glide across her skin so easily without a sponge absorbing the concealer into its synthetic fleshiness. Her fingers dabbed into the pot a second time and this time her fingers moved along the curves and creases around her nose and few spots of high colour around her jawline. There was precision and process in the position of each delicate dab.

Her next task was to apply foundation from a tube. This would need a brush rather than using her fingers.

Stepping back from the sink Maya open a door beneath it to locate a black and blue roll of make brushes that had been sat on a shelf next an assortment of bath and shower products. The roll was securely tied with shiny faux satin ribbon, and too securely for her liking as she had to fiddle to untie a rather tight knot. With the knot undone the roll softly fell open and was the size of piece of A4 paper. With small elasticated hoops the roll held about a dozen different brushes. Each and every one had a very specific job; there was blusher brush, a concealer brush and an eyeshadow brush to name a few.

Once upon a time this assortment would have been used with gusto and with a vast collection of cosmetics. Today however, the number of brushes and the varied functions was overwhelming. Maya's hand hovered over the roll, and then her fingers dropped gently and glided across the cold handles. Settling on the foundation brush with its flat bristles with rounded edges, Maya slid it free from the loop that anchored it down.

Tucking the brush between the two fingers of her left hand, Maya unscrewed the top of the foundation tube. This was then placed between the hot and cold taps, as she would otherwise forget where she had put it and risk being late to work in trying to locate it. Squeezing the tube from the bottom, Maya watched blobs form on the foundation brush. She was not yet finished with her reflection and paying close attention set the brush to her skin. Carefully the brush moved across her skin, around the curves and contours. She was able cover half of her face before returning once more to the tube and covering the other side. The liquid was smoothly dragged by the brush across her cheeks, her forehead, and the bridge of her nose. Foundation created an evened out canvas with blemishes and high colour all now blended away. Her eye sockets were now less purple and Maya looked a little more alive.

The signs of being sleep deprived had been painted away and she didn't look so drained anymore. Satisfied that a suitable foundation had been laid, she returned the top to the tube and placed it back into the bag. The eye pencil needed sharpening and she set to giving the pencil a sharp point with a double barrelled black plastic sharpener. Cream and black ribbons descended from the sharpener and onto the sink. Scooping them into her palm, Maya dropped them into a peddle bin that sat next between the sink and the toilet. Using the sharpened pencil, she carefully lined both her upper and lower lids.

She didn't get as far as mascara or lipstick. Instead she had left the bathroom and gone down to the kitchen. There she had breakfasted on black tea and bowl of supermarket own brand flaked corn. Fed and watered, Maya had picked up her handbag and taken her coat from the cloakroom. Closing the front door behind her, she had walked to the bus stop and caught the next bus that would stop a five minute walk away from school. Maya had tried. Tried to keep herself together as school had started, students and staff were starting to mill around in anticipation of the shrill bell that heralded a new working day. Seeing the students amass had not been as easy as she had expected. From the tender looking year seven all the way up to the non-uniformed sixth former who was coming to the end of their school career. Each student that she saw was a reminder of the different trials and tribulations that a child might experience at different ages. So much so, she was unable to focus whilst sat at her desk and she had beaten a retreat to the ladies staff toilets. And here she was.

***

The noise. Joyce had been washing her hands and having a cursory glance at her reflection in the mirror to the left of the hand dryer. She was somewhat startled to hear the sharp and almost animal like wail coming from one of the locked toilet cubicles behind her. Shaking off her hands Joyce moved closer towards hand dryer. She listened, not yet drying her hand. What she heard were sobs, sniffles, the squelch of a nose and rustling of tissue paper. Joyce placed her palms beneath the hand dryer but watched the cubicle doors. Following the frame of the door down towards the floor, she focused on the gap between the door and the floor. The gap was about fifteen centimetres high and she could make out toilet tissue debris and also a pair of dark shoes. Being the staff ladies toilet, there was only a specific group of people she might expect to be in here. From the sobs and sniffles she could also take a guess as to who might be behind the door. There had been announcements made in the recent staff briefings, all very sad and unsettling. The subject of one of those announcements was most certainly behind that door. With the majority of moisture evaporated from her palms, Joyce still chose to sweep her palms down her thighs to remove what little residue remained. Joyce moved towards the door. Curling her hands into fist, she tentatively knocked and craned her ear towards the door. "Maya?" Joyce asked softly, not wanting to startle the woman on the other side of the door.

"Oh!" Maya exclaimed as her thoughts were broken and she clambered off the toilet. Her feet landed onto the toilet tissue debris and missed her shoes entirely. Maya shuffled and sneezed to stand up to her full height. Her breathing was somewhat laboured as she had worked herself up into something of a frenzied state. This was now causing Maya to feel altogether confused and unable to coordinate her limbs. So much so that she fumbled with the lock that held the door closed. Eventually Maya was able to slide the catch across, despite her hands feeling greasy from the tears and mucus that she wiped from her face. Pulling the door towards her Maya came face to face with one of the Psychology staff. She knew most of the staff, Joyce included. Becoming part of the school community had been rather scary when she had first started working here three years ago. Now however, being part of the community was a comfort and so many of the staff had offered their support when they could have easily let Maya and her family grieve by themselves. "Joyce. I didn't think anyone was here," said Maya, tugging toilet tissue from the circular holder and using a portion to blow her nose.

"Just popped by," Joyce waved her hands uncomfortably. "Quick dash, else you never get a chance," she added, lowering her hands so that she wasn't doing an impression of impromptu jazz hands. "Couldn't help but overhear. But is everything okay?" She knew the moment that the words left her mouth, that she could have perhaps phrased things differently. "If you would like for someone to just listen, Maya," offered Joyce. "I have about twenty minutes before Year Ten arrive."

Maya's rather fraught and panicked expression softened somewhat. All the anger that currently had her feeling to the brim and half-cocked simmered down a little from its rolling boil of fury. The last thing that Maya had been expecting was the offer of someone wanting to hear about how she was coping.

Her husband was of no use, he didn't speak to her. In fact he never spoke to anyone, not really. Never mind about this, about their daughter and how she was no longer alive. There had been some talk about going to see a counsellor, arranging appointments in the first instance. It had been brought up all very politely at the funeral by a well-meaning family member. Mentioning such a thing had been somewhat uncomfortable at that point, a little too immediate. A little time had passed now, and the idea of talking didn't feel so intimidating. "I'd like that," replied Maya. "Yes, thank you."

"Okay, well," Joyce looked at her watch, having moved her sleeve to check the time. The time limit was true. "How about the social sciences office?" asked Joyce. "It will be empty right now. I can pop the kettle on. We might even have a few biscuits; if you want to pop in."

Maya nodded and even tried to smile. "I'll be right there. I just need to er," she let her sentence hang and gestured to the toilet tissue that littered the floor. She suddenly became a little conscious of her feet being bare. Then there was the dislodged makeup and the sight of her tear stained face that spurred Maya to pass the back of her hand across her nose.

Mirroring Maya's smile Joyce darted her eyes towards the door and turned away to leave. Joyce hoped that they still had biscuits in the barrel that was stashed secretly in the bottom drawer of a filing cabinet. She closed the door behind her and made her way to the social sciences office that she shared with three other colleagues. The whole staff had been saddened by recent events. The feelings loss, grief and anger became that bit more amplified when tragedy hit those with whom you worked so closely that they became family.

Scooping up the unravelled toilet roll, Maya watched Joyce leave. As she lifted the debris up into her arms, she stepped into the rather forlorn looking shoes. The linoleum of the cubicle floor was cold and she didn't particularly fancy being exposed to whatever microbial organisms that might be on the floor. She still felt drained. Perhaps she had come back too soon and there were still things that she needed to work through. Shuffling out of the cubicle, Maya dumped the armful of toilet tissue into a metal waste bin with a swing lid labelled 'push'. From there, she moved to the wash basin. Taking in a deep breath, she turned on the cold water tap to wash her hands. Her make up had taken a hit, foundation was streaked and her eyeliner had not reacted well to the tears.

5 Daniel

When all the colour has gone

There was not enough coffee in the world today, or the perhaps the mug used to drink it needed to be bigger and have more sugar added to it. A black cafetiere sat on the dining table containing enough black coffee to fill another three mugs. Positioned close to the cafetiere was a blue and white saucer of toast. Two slices of white bread that were very well buttered.

The butter had been slathered liberally in an attempt to mask the charred spots that resulted in the bread from having been left in the toaster a little bit too long. A pool of fat had formed in the centre of the slices; the bread was becoming more and more yellow as the butter was absorbed into the structure of the carbohydrate. Such a breakfast was the norm, heavy on the liquid-at least two and a half mugs of black coffee would be consumed-light on the food. The toast was there to soak up some of the liquid and prevent something of a slump before having to do any work. Thankfully, at the moment, the work in question did not involve having to go anywhere or do anything that might warrant being physically overwrought and or expend energy that could be better employed. Such was the perk of working from home when the circumstances allowed.

The commute to work involved exiting leaving the kitchen, and into the garden. To then take a short walk-it took less than three minutes- along the stepping stone path and towards a rather stoutly built building that was termed an office space. So much easier and less painful that having to traverse the city as one of the many sardines packed into a metal cylinder and further suffering the indignity of having your nostrils wedged into a less than pleasant smelling armpit. In addition the cafetiere could be taken to the office without spilling a single drop as might happen when clutching an insulated mug and trying not to scald the aforementioned armpit.

The kitchen looked out onto the garden. Through the bay window you could see the office. A red stepping stone and grey shingle path led the eyes straight towards the building that peeped out from behind a fence of rose bushes. Largely red and pink, there were a handful of orange blooms that punctuated the dark green foliage and golden barb like thorns. During the summer, as you walked down the path you would immediately smell the heady, zingy scent that truly assaulted the senses. By contrast, in the autumn and winter months the bushes took on a rather sinister and skeletal form as flower heads were deadheaded away. The foliage would wither and the golden green stems become woody and brown in being spent.

This morning the bushes were abundantly abloom and a small brown bird appeared to fly out of the closely packed bushes. On its way out, the bird had knocked against a pink headed bloom; causing the petals to take fright and flutter to the ground onto the dark earth of the bed. No doubt the winged creature was headed toward the bird table that was positioned at the half way point on the stepping stone path.

The bird table was another point of observation when unable to focus. From time to time there would be a scene of high drama that might ensue when a duo of magpies would fight over a fat cake or a crafty squirrel would hope to exercise its cunning and shake the bird feeder whilst suspended from one of the corners. There was many a chuckle to be had from such an episode watching creatures both great and small.

Behind the belt of rose bushes was the one storey building with a light grey façade and bright red door that constituted the home office. Next to the rounded frame of the door was circular port hole styled window through which one could look at the back of the house in a direct mirror image of this current breakfast time tableau.

For someone who wasn't particularly green fingered there was still some enjoyment to be taken from having such a green and vibrant outdoor space. From the neatly edges edged lawns to the pathways and beds; there was such organisation and structure. None of it carried out by the current owner, but by a landscaper who had been hired when the house had first been acquired. Hired and presented with a vague plan drawn on the back of a postcard; then tasked with make making the plan a reality.

That had been some time ago, and now a casual gardener had the job of maintaining the garden. He might not have taken much of an interest, but Caleb did. The colour scheme in the borders had caused an interesting drama; Caleb had at one point been in a heightened frenzy, concerned about a very particular range of colour in mind. He on the other hand could not see the difference between one orange flowered shrub and another.

He simply could not face going to the office; or even face leaving the house and he hadn't for the best part of three days. He wanted to stay within the safety of these four walls. Four walls that resonated with memories and helped maintain the illusion of Caleb still being here. He knew exactly how Caleb's day would start, what his routine would be. It was easy for him to mentally picture how the events would unfold. At this time of the morning, Caleb would still have been asleep cocooned within the heavy tog of the duvet that covered their bed. He would be so comfortably swaddled that he would be unlikely to rise for at least another hour and a half. Slumbering and dreaming quite contently until his alarm would go off, his arm would snake out from beneath duvet and his palm then smack flat across the top of the box like alarm clock in hope of hitting the snooze button.

Caleb would then eventually kick off the duvet ten minutes later as the alarm sounded once more and slope off towards the shower. His morning ablutions would involve showering, shaving and singing an aria or two at the top of his lungs whilst under the shower head. He would not hear that today, he had not heard the inability to hit the high notes now for a few weeks.

Sipping black coffee, he felt the memory creep across his mind. The day had started as normal, as expected. He was up early waiting for Caleb to get up and had been listening carefully for the early morning litany of profanity that would come with an assault on the alarm clock as the device screeched its wake up call. It was the aria next; that was the sound he was expecting to hear. He would ordinarily hear an aria or whatever libretto that Caleb had chosen to throw across the pale blue shower tiles.

What he had heard were a clutch of vocal exercises, and then nothing. Absolutely nothing and he had moved towards the kitchen door and craned his neck towards the stairs so as to try and hear the sounds that he was expecting. There was nothing to be heard, not a single solitary sound. The silence was overwhelming and utterly unsettling when routine appeared to have been derailed. Fifteen minutes had passed before he chose to investigate further, and it was at that point that his world fell apart.

He still couldn't think about it in detail; the window occupied by the memory was shuttered closed and he was averse to opening it. Explaining to the medical staff had been difficult, beyond painful. The funeral and with visits by family and friends had made the opening of the window utterly intolerable. Having to relive the moment, frame by frame, as though he watching the same film over and over made the skin on his knuckles turn white and his stomach flip and churn.

Three days ago, Caleb's funeral had been held. A huge event, that was bright, beautiful and wonderfully grandiose. The whole thing was a vivid and opulent celebration of a vibrant and buoyant human being. The whole thing was definitely a celebration rather than being sombre, morbid and a practical full stop at the end of a life. Every element of the gaudy happening had helped beyond measure, the psychedelic splashes of colour had helped to keep Caleb alive in a sense, and be more than just a memory. How he wished that it had not just been one day. The colour that Caleb had splashed candidly throughout his life was now starting to ebb and fade away. Prior to the funeral, the last time that there been had such a kaleidoscope of colour had been at their wedding eighteen months ago. Right now, that was a distant memory that was also starting to fade, and feel as though it had never happened.

Of the two of them, Caleb had been the more colourful, more comfortable in who he was and therein definitely more of an extrovert. His was an infectious personality that whirled and whizzed around as though a tornado; a true force of nature. He would never apologise for having fun, and the whole essence of frivolity zinged through the fibres of his whole being. There was then a deep rooted desire to share that with anyone and everyone.

Even this kitchen with its bright and bold, almost kitsch décor was a testament to Caleb and his kaleidoscopic colourfulness. Perhaps that was why he wanted to sit here and not move. He needed a crutch, something touched by Caleb to bring him some solace and to steady him.

Every corner of this house had been touched by Caleb. As he sat here savouring the hot, bitter taste of a rather expensive coffee, he found himself mentally wandering around the house and remembering where and how Caleb had made his impact. Starting with the front door and with how Caleb had judged its colour and condition not up to his exacting standards. Over the short amount of years that they had lived here together, Caleb had gently persuaded him to sand the door down and repaint it so that the appearance wasn't so weathered and wearied.

To begin with, the door had been a rather dull and flat looking navy. The paint had bubbled and blistered in places, exposing numerous layers of paint and where the paint had flaked off entirely, the original pale grain of the door was open to the elements. He had eventually relented and during the course of a fair weekend, removed the door from its hinges and given it what Caleb described as being a face lift. He had been the one to all the hard work, removing the numerous layers of paint and then repainting the panelled door from scratch. Caleb had leant against the door frame whilst nursing back to back cups of tea and smoking the odd cigarette that formed the basis of his supervisory duties.

He didn't remember Caleb so much as lifting a paintbrush. There had been the odd grimace at things taking a little longer than was anticipated; the only time Caleb had lifted a finger was to point towards a bottle of white spirit when brushes had to be cleaned.

Having been repainted with a gloss rather than a matt finish Navy paint, the door was then rehung. Shiny and gleaming, the door did actually make the front of the house look a little more respectable.

Then there was the cast iron hat and coat stand stood in the hall way. Caleb had found it at a car boot sale. He fallen head over heels in love with its curves of all things and now it was the first thing you saw when you entered the house. There were Caleb-esque flourishes all over that stamped his former presence upon their home. A majority of the alcoves in their home were painted with rich and deep shades of mulberry and aubergine. Paisley print scatter cushions were strewn across the sofa, and there were candles at least three deep in places. Caleb was obsessed with collecting candles in all sorts of colours and with all sorts of fragrances; yet these all sat looking very pretty in very rarely being lit. Caleb had crafted and created a sense of sumptuous comfort and refinement.

Prior to his arrival, both into his home and Daniel's life, the whole house had been a pretty staid affair with the décor being described as perfunctory at best. Caleb had cared for their home, all of his choices were considered, careful and above all gave the impression of their home being crafted to look the way that it did. Every wall bore his signature, his name was figuratively scrawled across each and every one; there was no escaping it. Today there was some comfort in being cocooned within the world that Caleb had created; it was all very safe and Daniel didn't particularly want to escape this bubble.

Right now, Daniel felt lost. He was experiencing a sense of being adrift that the funeral had failed to remove. The day itself had certainly provided a form of closure, finality in that Caleb was physically gone and unlikely to come back. It had however, failed to equip and school him with the means to be capable enough to move on. Daniel didn't know, he couldn't understand if he was ready to move on, if he truly wanted to move on. Caleb had been a whirlwind entering his life and a whirlwind in leaving it. There was a whole heap of emotional debris left behind in his wake that Daniel had no idea how to process, when all he wanted to do was hang on to what he and Caleb had experienced together. Hang on. Daniel didn't want to let go.

Even when preparing for the funeral and trying to decide what clothes Caleb should be dressed in; Daniel had found the process absolutely soul destroying. He had found himself on his knees by the wardrobe, clutching Caleb's clothes and unable to let go. He was desperately hanging on to clothes that had been freshly laundered and had a smell of fabric, but were clothes that he had worn. Each one of the garments had a Caleb moment associated with it. A striped blue shirt that he only ever wore to formal meetings, a greying sweatshirt with frayed cuffs that he took to the gym and even the horrible diamond patterned socks that he loved elicited tears and howls of hurt.

With Caleb's final outfit selected, he had closed the wardrobe as though trying to close the gaping wound that loss had created. He really couldn't face the open wound, a fresh and weeping wound. Watching birds arrive at the table, Daniel's thoughts of Caleb started to flutter and fly away. He would get there. Eventually.

6 Christopher

A boys best friend

His blanket was covered in hair. Black, gold, and white strands that had been shed as Adelphi had made himself comfortable. Coiled up in a heap by the radiator, the blanket looked ready for immediate occupation. Only Adelphi wasn't going to come in anytime soon with his paws padding gently across the wooden floor and his tail wagging behind him. It was no ordinary wag either, but the same speedy rotation that you would expect from a propeller blade.

Christopher found himself looking at the churned up blanket, and mentally visualising an event that he knew would never happen again. This was his daily routine; it had been for a number of years. He would sit here at the desk and behind his laptop; though it had been a desktop in the early years. There would be peering over the screen, where he would be able to look straight at Adelphi and his shiny brown marble like eyes. It was at those points in the day that

Adelphi would move his snout from where he was resting it on his paws, rise from his haunches and pad over towards the desk. A gentle tug at Christopher's legs would suggest that they both take a walk.

Using both hands to lower the laptop screen and switch off the device, Christopher took in a deep breath. A breath that caused his throat to sting; he has shouted and screamed a little more than he should have whilst sat in traffic. Sat next to the computer was a steaming mug of hot cordial that he hoped would soothe away the fierce flaming feeling of soreness.

Lifting the square shaped mug but he handle, he pressed it to his lips and slurped the blackcurrant cordial. Wonderfully sweet with a touch of tartness, the hot liquid travelled down his throat to smooth away the grittiness that came from his vocal cords being over exerted. There was a dual layered uplift. Not only was his throat feeling a little less ravaged but the warmth of the liquid travelling down his gullet felt a lot like a deep hug.

Swallowing another hearty mouthful, he returned the mug to its place upon a coaster. A coaster covered in mug rings and droplets from beverages past. Four inches across, stained and increasingly mottled, the coaster was as souvenir from a holiday taken at a Costa Del Something and many, many years ago. The coaster had served him well over the last few years, and Christopher was not about to retire it any time soon. Swinging his feet forward below the desk, he slid his weight backwards to push his chair away from his desk. As ever, the feet of the chair met with resistance caused by the rug directly below; a measure of protection for the wooden floor. The resistance caused a slightly muffled sound, so much better than the sound of wood being scraped and scratched. At least the wooden floor in here was homely, and not the sort that he forever associated with exam halls and being a student. Moving from his seat, he made towards the radiator and the blanket that sat close by. Bending down to retrieve it, he scooped it up into his arms.

Adelphi's blanket had been warmed by the radiator; he could feel the heat exude from the fabric and towards his arms and torso. Charcoal grey for the most part, the blanket had a tartan pattern with a red and pink running through the checks. Adelphi had formed a very firm attachment to the blanket having first arrived into the family home whilst swaddled within the folds of the woven fabric.

The blanket had stayed with them, when they had said goodbye. Only Christopher had brought it back home and rather absentmindedly thrown it to floor here as though Adelphi would need it again. As though Adelphi was likely to return and hunker down within the folds; that this whole episode was nothing but a dream, a blip in the fabric of space and time. Fumbling around in the fabric, he tried to find the corners. It took a moment, but he soon had two grasped between his fingers and he unfurled the blanket. Part of the blanket fell gently onto the floor before him. There was sudden squeak as a rather well loved chew toy fell unceremoniously to the floor with a thud. Throwing the one end of the blanket of over his arm, he then doubled it over a few times to fold it into a neat square. Clutching the folded up fabric in his hands, he knew that this would always be Adelphi's blanket.

Bringing the blanket close to his chest, he walked out of his office and headed down the stairs. He simply couldn't focus, his thoughts were occupied by Adelphi and the fur ball's absence. Work just wasn't happening, and he already informed them that he wouldn't be turning anything in this week.

Adeplhi was missing, that's what it felt like. Generally, there were noises, and Adelphi made quite a few. Communicative growls and whines that some days would pass for deep and meaningful conversation. Travelling down the stairs, Christopher headed towards the kitchen. His eyes momentarily caught a red flash; Adelphi's lead hung from a hook by the front door. The salience of the colour was a stark contrast against the wall and yet another pointed reminder of Adelphi. His stomach gurgled. A sound that suggested Christopher might actually want to eat something.

Fortunately for him, the 'fridge was located by the kitchen door and he remembered there being a Tupperware box of left over chilli somewhere inside it. Still clutching at the blanket, he pulled open the door and somewhat surprised at how bright the light was inside. Then there was the buzz of the motor that he had never noticed before. Locating the plastic box of chilli on the middle shelf, his fingers curled around it to remove it; the door was closed by the nudge of his elbow. He was feeling rather hungry now, and willed himself to hurry up and eat.

Peeling off the lid, he placed it onto the worktop. Plucking a spoon from the utensil drainer on the drainer by the sink, he also found a bowl into which he emptied the contents of the Tupperware box. Shuffling towards the small dining table, he had his hands full as he sat down. Adelphi's blanket was still ensconced in his arms as he sunk a spoon in the bowl of chilli and heaped it to take a mouthful. As he was about to eat, he realised that there was no sound. No soft thudding of paws across the kitchen floor; no soft grumbles or squeaky whines that Adelphi would make when he too needed feeding.

Looking at the chilli, Christopher felt his stomach flip. The chilli didn't look particularly appetising. He did however need to eat and this was a meal that was the easiest to consume without having to be prepared with a fuss. The fact that it was cold, that was upset him. That was why he had yet to take a mouthful. Rising from his seat, he shoved the bowl into the microwave to warm it through. Perhaps then, the red and orange hues would look more enticing.

Two minutes later-now piping hot-the bowl of chilli was back on the kitchen table. It was a mite too hot, and Christopher was stirring the chilli in the hope that it would cool down. His other hand was still wrapped around the folded up blanket. As he couldn't yet bring himself to think about how Adelphi's life had ended, his thoughts turned to how their life together had started. Adelphi had been eight weeks old when he and Adelphi had first met one another. A black and gold bundle of fur with the tiniest of ears and at the time, what Christopher swore blind was a smile. At the age of eight, he had been entirely convinced that the puppy was smiling at him and looked as though he was plotting mischief. He remembered being sat on the sofa with his legs stretched out before him as he hid beneath a super hero themed duvet. Protruding out from one side of the duvet were his toes, toes that peeked out from a plaster cast. He had taken something of a tumble whilst on a climbing frame at school, and his leg had been broken just below the knee. He remembered experiencing the most dramatic searing pain and had howled in agony. Cuddles from the parents had helped somewhat, but he couldn't help but feel a little sorry for himself as he couldn't curl up properly below a duvet as he watched a children's television show.

As he scooped up spoonfuls of chilli, it was those initial yelps and puppy whines that filled his ears as memories. Engrossed in watching the show, he had assumed that the sounds were somehow related to what he was seeing on the television screen. However, he had then heard his father's voice and the same gentle shushing that was used upon him from time to time. He had heard it often enough, especially when he wake screaming from a night terror.

There had been discussion; as a family they had spoken about having a pet. Both his parents had voiced that they didn't particularly want to adopt a cat. As lovely as cats were or might be within their home; a cat might not necessarily be the best fit for their family. His Mum and Dad had said that they would look into adopting a dog and add another member to their small family of three. Fishing out a rather stringy piece of ginger, Christopher dropped it beside the bowl and onto the table. A lady from the dog rescue home had come to visit, and surveyed their house from top to bottom. She had even spoken with him, and asked how he felt about having a puppy living with them. He remembered the vividness of her pink lipstick and her rather red hair that seemed to have its life zapped out of it. Given how much hair spray had been applied to it the clump of fuzzy follicles looked like a big fat hamster sat on her scalp.

As an adult, he felt embarrassed thinking about their conversation. His words have been typically childlike at the time. He had waxed lyrical about how he intended to play with the puppy, cuddle the puppy, and teach it how to do tricks. There had been excited glee and a lot of naiveté in not being able to fully appreciate what caring for a puppy might actually involve. As an eight year old, he had no real idea of what it was going to be like simply having another member of the family, never mind a furry member of the family.

Sat there on the sofa, he remembered first wanting to watch the television and second wanting to forget about having a broken leg. The squeaks and yelps had become a little louder and it dawned upon him that these were nothing to do with the television show that he was watching. As the noise became louder and the yelping more frequent, he had looked towards the door that was slowly starting to open towards him.

Fixing his gaze on the door, Christopher had been wide eyed in anticipation; his fingers becoming tighter around the television remote. His dad's elbow appeared, and then slowly the rest of him came into view. In the crook of his arm was a grey woolen blanket-that grey woolen blanket-out of which peeked a fuzzy snout, two brown eyes and ears that looked a little too big for such a small face. Nestled in the folds of the blanket, the nameless puppy was cocooned and protected. Its eyes darted around to take in the surroundings. His father walked into the room, with his mum following close behind; both moving tentatively and unsure of how both the boy and puppy might react.

Pulling faces at the taste of a couple of bitter undercooked beans, Christopher pressed his fork into another three to squash them against the side of his bowl. He would persevere and eat the remainder of the chilli. He let his grimace ebb away in remembering the smile that his Dad had worn whilst carrying the puppy into the room. The smile was a special and distinct element of the memory. He didn't often see his dad be that smiley or that animated for that matter.

His dad had worn the brightest, biggest and broadest smile that Christopher had seen. To this day, a smile that had not been repeated. It was a smile, that had taken years off his Dad's a face. That was why it was such a salient and treasured memory. His dad had sat down next to him on the sofa; he had moved over a little to make room.

He had watched the blanket move, wriggle in his father's arms as he felt the hum of excitement in his stomach. Quaking and quivering, the blanket in his father's arms eventually stopped moving and spilled open into his lap to reveal a black and gold puppy who like Christopher, was very much wide-eyed. The boy and puppy looked at each other, eyeballing one another a little nervously. They were both wary and unsure as to who might blink first.

"You'll never guess who we bumped into," his father had said, moving away the blanket to clutch the puppy under its belly and shuffle the creature closer toward his son. "Someone really fancied joining our family."

"The lady said yes?" He had almost squealed the question, his tone and pitch had risen with a sense of jubilation. Looking from the puppy and directly as his dad, there had been an overwhelming sense of both surprise and exhilaration. In his stomach, there had been fizzing feelings that soon become the increased beating of his heart.

His father had leant in, and letting the puppy wriggle, whispered, "She said yes, he's all ours." Once more wrapping his fingers around the puppy, he dropped the four legged fur ball into his son's lap. "And it is a he," added his father, "Rather likes cuddles, lots of them. Your mum and I have already become his friends, perhaps you would like to give it a go. See what happens."

With the puppy clambering around between them, Christopher's duvet was somewhat askew. As small as he was, he did his best to wrap his arms around the puppy. A very wriggly, furry and warm the touch puppy that was resisting efforts to be hugged; the puppy was far more interested in trying to suss out the duvet. Perhaps the duvet was a bit much, as the puppy decided to introduce himself with a flurry of fevered licks and tail that was starting to wag with an increased frequency.

It was only as Adelphi had started to feel his age and the associated ailments that the wag of the tail had become less frequent. It was also the one way to tell what kind of mood he was in. The wag of his tail was effectively a barometer as to whether or not he was feeling sociable at any given point.

Christopher's mum Joyce had watched from afar; she had not wanted to interrupt her son and new puppy as they became met. She had told Christopher as much. She had further told him, during a late night conversation, that she and her husband had thought about this for some time and having a new addition to the family. Nature had determined that Christopher was to be an only child; carrying him to full term had made impossible for her to conceive again. Having a puppy may not have been the same as carrying a human baby, but it would certainly add to their family. Perhaps now Christopher wouldn't be so alone, that was the last thing that she had told him. She had been quite excited that their new baby was a furry baby; four legged and posed some of the same challenges that Christopher had when he was nee born.

Clinking his spoon against the side of the now empty bowl, Christopher then folded his arms to press Adelphi's blanket against his chest. For days, the puppy had been nameless, referred to only as 'the dog' or 'the puppy'. They had been unable to settle upon a suitable moniker for the rag tag fur ball. Eventually a name was plucked out of thin air, and the creature labelled. He remembered being absolutely besotted and wanting to be with the puppy at all times.

By virtue of the broken leg, they had a week together before he hobbled back to school on crutches. His mum had been right, he certainly felt less alone. There had been a definite feeling of sharing his life with Adelphi. He felt as though he had a sibling, a brother; albeit a furry one and one that had four legs and not two. The broken leg could have rendered him entirely miserable that week; but he remembered being happy, positively over bowled. The trauma of a broken leg had been tempered by Adelphi's arrival. Pressing his nose to the blanket, he blinked to clear his eyes of beadlike glossy tears that had suddenly appeared. Two of which dropped onto the fabric. Shiny and reflective, the tears sat for a moment before being absorbed into to the checked weft. He had been able to move his finger and wipe them away, and watched them fade into the grey.

That week had been the start of many adventures. There had been highs and lows, girlfriends and bouts of gastric flu. Adelphi had witnessed hang overs from hell and the sheer ecstasy of cup winning. He had seen it all. Adelphi had been his constant companion and for so many years. Christopher had always tried his best to return the favour. When Adelphi had been laid low with an absolute rotter of an ear infection, they both spent the night lying in a puddle of blankets on the floor in the lounge. There had been an episode of fleas where Man and Dog had very nearly fallen out with one another but there had been persistence in messy shampooing that made things a little easier between them.

Even the odd episode of dodgy doggy poos had failed to strain the enduring bond that existed between them. A bond that was still there, even though Adelphi was not. Hunching over, he could feel his tears flow freely now. Each tear was felt hot, and tasted salty as it travelled down his cheeks. Every now and again, he would feel one dance upon his tongue. Adelphi wasn't here anymore and it felt as though he had no one. No one close enough to hold a candle to Adelphi. No one, who could fill the hole that the fur ball had left behind.

7 Aldo

My baby too

Eleven and a half minutes. He had been stood at the door for exactly eleven and a half minutes, steeling himself to push the door open and to enter the room. The room, and the door to which it led, was her bedroom. It was Millie's bedroom, his daughter's bedroom. For eleven and a half minutes, Aldo had been stood with his palms pressed against the cool to the touch door. His hands were positioned just above a dog-eared poster of Old Harry and his wife. He had been standing, fixed to the spot and unable to exert enough pressure with his palms to push the door open. It had already take him two days to get this far. The door was a final obstacle and he could feel his chest tighten as his heart pulsated urging him to carry on.

Lowering his palms, Aldo pressed his digits into the corners of the rather wearied looking poster. Carefully he pressed each of the corners against the door to affix the image more securely. Greying and dehydrated the adhesive fix that barely held the poster to the door was well beyond being fit for purpose. He made a mental note to change it, replace it with a fresher more pliable fix that would ensure that the poster remained in situ. It would be an awful shame if it were to fall off and away from the door.

The poster had been there that long that the door would look and naked without it. It was an altogether fading image; the blue sky was starting to become green and grey. Around Harry, the sea in its rather placid state was going a little bit murky. A series of splashes across the images documented the many times that Millie had taken a drink into her room and all but hurtled through the door. That was why he was here, partially at least. To check if Millie had left any mugs. She had a tendency to collect them on her desk.

Hearing his heart beat as though it was climbing to a crescendo, Aldo increased the pressure of his palms to push the door away from him. It was just enough for the door to creak and fall ajar. That was okay for Aldo, it was only just open; he could go in now. The barrier had fallen. Whilst the door was closed, it had felt like an insurmountable obstacle of Herculean proportions. With the door open, he could now step into the room with a little more certainty and a little more bravery. Retracting his palms, he nudged the door open a little more with his elbow and then his forearm. Something made him gasp, as he realised that ordinarily he would have knocked and only then go into the room. He hadn't done that today, there was no one the other side to tell him that he could come in. Gulping down the torrent that was travelling from his chest and up towards toward his throat, Aldo put one foot before the other. Using his arm again, he pushed the door open entirely.

What Aldo saw before him was pretty purple and a muted grey. Millie's room was entirely purple and grey in the way that it was detailed and decorated. From the wall against which her bed was positioned, a bright imperial purple that corresponded with the flurry of cushions that sat upon a striped duvet. Curtains that were a shade lighter than the wall and for now drawn closed. Greyness was scattered around with assorted accessories; but there was a different greyness that hung in the room. This bedroom was filled by a heavy and sombre greyness that came from the room being lifeless. Millie had been a spark in human form, filling the room with light. She had thrown joie de vivre as far as she possibly could. Gingerly, Aldo moved his feet and finally crossed the threshold into the room to make his way to the foot of her bed. There he sat, his legs started to tremble and he tried to take it all in. Immediately to his left was Millie's desk, strewn with textbooks, folders and papers. This was somewhat uncharacteristic of his daughter. Everything in the room was generally in its place. Everything was where it should be, where Millie had wanted it to be.

He shuffled backwards with his hands positioned either side of him and ;et the bed take his weight. All he wanted to do was to sit. Sit here, remember and to think. Think of the beautiful vibrant and full of life young woman that had been torn and away from his life. Millie had been his beautiful baby girl, the true apple of his eye and his princess. She had been all of the clichés that you could possibly think of and they were all true.

Glancing over his shoulder and at the brightly coloured wall, Aldo remembered how that the now purple wall had once been a very muted yellow. This room had been Millie's room since well before she had been born. Not knowing whether they were expecting a boy or girl, he and Maya had rather deliberately chosen a neutral colour for the décor of what was to their baby's nursery. The colour had been labelled baby yellow on the tin; fresh, bright and full of promise.

Now a different colour, the wall was adorned by posters. Tacked up with sticky tape, the faces of singers, a couple of sports stars and a slightly bemused looking whale on a motivational poster all looked back at Aldo. Frozen in time expressions beneath dust looked at him searchingly. Asking him, where had Millie gone and why? He could barely understand these questions himself, and those that asked-real people and not those in a poster-he couldn't formulate a response to what they wanted to know. He was unable to speak to his own wife about what had happened, when they might have been united in grief; for him at least, right now it felt as though they were poles apart. He and Maya were barely speaking with one another. The distance between them and the overwhelming feeling of grief left him feeling bewildered.

Drawn into the eyes on the posters, Aldo struggled to pull away his own gaze. Letting out a long pained breath, he leant towards the cushions sat at the head of the bed. Taking a plushy indigo coloured cushion, he slid back towards his original position and held it close against his chest. Enveloping the cushion in his arms, he let his chin sink into the fabric and frills of the stuffed square. The only scent that clung to the fabric was the scent of detergent used to launder the cushions. It wasn't even the scent of Millie that might offer him some comfort and the faintest spark of solace. There could have been any number of different scents that might have belonged to her. As Aldo looked up, what passed for Millie's vanity table came into view. A full length mirror on a wheeled frame; at its feet were an assortment of perfume bottles, make up and other paraphernalia. All of these bottles, had been deliberately chosen by Millie.

"I don't want to smell of coffee though, Dad," She had said one day after work. "I know it's meant to smell nice, but when you spend all day making the stuff, selling it; I don't want to smell like a human coffee machine."

Gathered around the mirror were so many different boxes; an assortment of different colours, and lots of different brands. At first glance, the collection appeared to be entirely feminine, there were quite a number of pink, purple and sparkly red boxes and bottles. In contrast though, there were also nestled amongst these, darker less prettier boxes that weren't so vibrant.

"You have to smell this one, Dad, go on," Millie had bounced into the lounge one evening, waving a grey translucent bottle. "It smells amazing! Go on, try it!"

He had recoiled back a little as she had thrust bottle beneath his nose. "Not bad, it's okay," he has said, wanting to carry on reading the rest of the newspaper article about pensions and how these were no longer worth the paper that they were written on. "Hang on," he had realised that the smell was different compared to the smells and scents that she had exposed him to before. "I've got one like that, I don't need any more. There's no need to buy me anymore."

Millie had cackled as she had turned to walk away. "Didn't buy it for you, Dad," she uttered, a twinkle forming in her eye. "This one is for me."

At the time, he had shaken his head and carried on reading his newspaper. The exchange between them was fairly typical. That was the way they were, their conversations were all over the place. They spoke about anything and everything.

Sliding forwards, he lowered his feet to the grey deep piled carpet and towards the mirror. For some unknown reason, it was positioned at a forty five degree tilt. It gave the impression of his reflection being somewhat off kilter and very askew. Ignoring his own visage, his attention was caught by the streaks and smudges that Millie had left upon the mirror. Across the surface of the reflective glass there were fingerprints that he found himself studying closely. Putting his fingers to the marks left by hers, it felt for a moment as though she was still here. As though all that he had to do was to look up and she would be there right behind him. That he would be able to see her face before him, rather than just his own reflection. On the left hand side of the mirror were five fingerprints. So clear, that he could see the loops and curves in what he could only assume was make up. Pressing his fingers to Millie's fingerprints, Aldo realised how much bigger his hands were compared to hers. The span of his digits shrank as pressed his fingertips against the echo of hers.

Just over two decades ago, he had walked into this room with Millie in his arms. Two days old and wrapped up in a yellow crocheted blanket made by his mother-in-law, Millie was introduced to the room that would always be hers. He had stood not too far away from where he was now, and he had pointed out each and every single part of her nursery. Her cot-which was now stowed away in the attic as Maya refused to get rid of it-had been pine; the mattress covered with multi-coloured ducks. Suspended above it had been a noisy, gauche and almost psychedelic mobile. At the time, the mobile was state of the art and the must have of the season. Everything had been coated in a box fresh newness, shiny, positive and pregnant with promise.

The bundle that had been brought home with such pride had grown and rapidly from her initial birthweight of six pounds and eleven ounces. Still clutching the indigo cushion, Aldo turned around to survey the room. From being the nursery of a babe in arms, the room had undergone so many changes as Millie had grown up. A bright yellow nursery had given way to a warm orange room belonging to a toddler. Then there was the pale pink of a the teenage years that was accented with fuscia, if he remembered correctly. The sort of hot pink that smacked you clean between the eyes.

"Daddy, it's broken," Millie had sounded so distraught, as she had ran towards him. "Fix it for me, please," she has said waving a glittery wand. Her face had been a picture of abject disconsolation. The wand topped by a glitter star, was altogether battered looking and rather bent out of shape. It truly was a sorry sight with the star precariously hanging on by a single, fragile looking thread. In one hand, Millie had the wand; in her other hand was a roll of sticky tape.

Aldo had pulled the six year old Millie into his arms and they had sat on what at the time was her 'big girl' bed. Together, they had painstakingly fixed the wand using the sticky tape that Millie had been waving.

"How did this break, Millie?" he had asked, as she supplied him with a steady stream of sticky tape.

"Troll ate it," Millie had replied, watching the repair process intently. "Or tried to," she had added, handing over sticky tape.

Aldo remembered laughing to himself. Millie always made him laugh and with love. That had been his whole world; sat there with Millie beside him, dressed in a pink leotard, a netted tutu and sparkly purple ballet style pumps. Millie was his little girl, and only child. She was the centre of the whole universe for him and for Maya. And now she was gone. A smile of reminiscence had bloomed across his face and slowly it started to fade away as he felt his stomach flip once again. There had been the teenage years, years that were not too distant in his memory. It was at that point, that the pastel pink and fuscia had been replaced by the purple and grey.

"Your Mum has sent you some tea," he had stepped into the room carefully, not wanting to trip over the dust sheet that covered the rather new carpet. His entry had disturbed some of sheets, and he dragged the fabric back towards the metal gripper that marked the gap between the bedroom and the landing. Aldo had then not known where to place the mug that he carried, so held onto it between his palms. He watched silently as Millie painted the wall purple. A rich, royal and resplendent colour was soaked onto a roller and being moved somewhat expertly by Millie across the wall using an extendable pole.

"I can do it," she had said, glancing over her shoulder. Some part of him knew that she had clocked on to what was going through his head. "I already put tape up there," and she had flexed a finger at the masking tape where the wall met with the ceiling. "I checked online how to do it. It's fine."

Aldo had nodded and forgetting that he had her tea, he had taken a slurp from the mug. Feeling a little as though a spare part, he remembered being immensely proud. He was proud of how Millie had painted and decorated her room entirely by herself. Financed the whole venture too, having spent the summer working in a coffee shop and taking all the hours that she could. The only thing that she had conceded defeat on was the washing up of all the paintbrushes and rollers. Aldo could forgive that. If he washed and dried then, that would allow for him to be part of the process. He was not ready to let go; even then, with trivial matter of paintbrushes. What he had had to do and somewhat gritted teeth was to watch Millie get on with what she wanted to do and to do things her way. It was only when things went pear shaped that might seek his assistance.

Sobbing and with a nose full of bogey, Millie had called him and in a panic. He had found it quite difficult at first, to understand what she was saying. Eventually, after much coaxing and reassurance, Aldo was able to get a street name from her. Two o'clock in the morning, and still in his pyjamas, Aldo had driven to Talbot Street to meet her. Millie and Joel had left a club, and had been trying to get a taxi. Only the two of them had run into trouble and into a street mugging. Joel had been liberated of his wallet and was now sporting scars that made his otherwise quite timid appearance look rather battle proud. Millie had lost her 'phone, along with the contents of her handbag.

It was only through the sheer fluke that Joel had enough change in his pocket for them to use the one pay phone on the street that was still in commission.

Aldo had noticed how Joel had watched rather uncomfortably as Millie had curled into his arms.

"Lipstick, Millie," Joel had said rubbing the scratches upon his face. "Hopefully, it's not the right shade.

"But my 'phone, and cards," she had started to shake and sob, and was hanging on for dear life.

Shushing and trying to sooth his daughter, it felt as though he had been transported back to the early days. A throwback to when Millie was newly birthed and entirely helpless. He had been as frightened then when she had been tiny as he was now post street mugging and Millie a grown adult.

Letting the memory of that rather cold morning fritter away, Aldo turned his attention towards Millie's desk. That was why he had come in, to check for glasses and he could see two. Throwing aside the cushion that he had been holding onto as he stood by the mirror, he moved towards the desk. Aldo had been aiming for the head of the bed; only for it to bounce off the rest of the scatter cushions and fall to the floor. Curling his fingers around the tall and slender glasses, he peered inside of each one. Both were empty, with nothing growing inside and trying to make an escape so that it might be termed a bio-hazard.

Aldo took one last look around the room; just to

double check. Every inch of this room was infused with Millie, with her essence and all that made Millie their Millie. All around him, the walls hummed with his daughter's presence. Her laughter, tears, words and energy were imprinted onto everything. She was not gone yet, that he was sure of. As he turned to leave and looked passed the door through which he had entered, he knew what he had to do. He needed to speak with someone, about Millie, about everything. Maybe not Maya, not yet, but someone and soon.

8 Michael

Pieces

Who knew that nursery furniture could be so fragile? Surely it was only a baby that was supposed to be so delicate and not the objects built to surround the child. Struggling to calm himself down, Michael was positively incandescent purple with rage. With his back against the wall, he was crouched in the corner of the nursery. In one hand, Michael held a stuffed elephant by the ears. The fingers of his other hand were curled around the brown neck of a fairly potent, fairly fiery and incredibly heady bottle of home brewed beer.

The room was supposed to be a serene sanctuary; the nursery of a defenceless child. Right now, the room was a tableau of rage without rein. A near violent scene had unfolded here, and it had all started with the changing table.

Already a little worse for wear having downed two fairly strong bottles of beer, Michael had somehow stumbled up the stairs. Groping in the dark for the light switch, the door had been poked open with a foot that only just registered the message from his growling and extremely intoxicated reptile brain. Had he been sober, he might have firstly not missed and taken two attempts to kick the door. Second, used enough force to make the door swing on its hinges. Michael had cambered towards the changing table as the bulb hanging from the ceiling turned on and cascaded light into each and every corner. A light that was altogether a little harsh as an appropriate shade was yet to be selected and applied. Pricking his eyes, the brightness of the light heightened his state of disorientation.

Pulling at the table by a corner, Michael dragged the wheeled unit towards him before pushing it away with brutal force. Tipping on its coaster, the changing table met with no resistance and capitulated to lie on its side. The motion of the changing table had already caused its drawers and contents to jump ship as it were and now baby paraphernalia was scattered across the floor. With the stricken prey on the floor, Michael had raised the bottle of beer aloft and slammed it upon the table. Deliberately and repeatedly, Michael exerted his full weight onto the frame and drawers with a furious flurry of blows. He was determined to fracture the frame in as a many pieces as he could. It was only when a piece of broken plastic scrapped across his leg that Michael stopped pummelling the table.

His thirst for destruction was not yet quenched; Michael moved towards the cot, above which an elephant theme mobile was suspended. Wrapping his fingers around a few of the characters, Michael wrenched the mobile from its moorings and threw it towards the door with all of the force that he could muster. Having grasped the entire mobile between his fingers, his digits throbbed from having had such a firm grip and this only went further to infuriate him. Thrown against the door in a heightened fit of fury, the mobile had thudded against the wood and the elephants clattered onto the floor under the influence of gravity. In a state of disarray and something of a puddle on the floor, the colourful herd of plastic elephants was something of a sorry sight.

Audibly drawing in breath, Michael turned and towards the cot. Putting his bottle safely aside, he used both hands to grapple with the cot. All he wanted to do was to tear the thing apart. Michael pulled at the bars on the side and managed to snap a couple in the middle to then hurl them away with a flick of his wrist. Dismantling the bed was a lot harder than he had anticipated and it hurt. His already throbbing fingers were starting to protest with increased intensity. Staggering back and unable to commit any further barbarism towards the cot, Michael found himself stumbling over a Moses basket. Reaching for the wicker and feeling its coolness, Michael put some effort into picking it up, throwing it with full force across the room and towards the stenciled wall. The wicker basket landed heavily and lay stricken as though a capsized tugboat. Having felt the full force of the Moses basket, the dog eared stencil that had been hanging onto the wall decided that that enough was enough. Breaking free of its dried out moorings, the stencil relinquished its place upon the wall and fluttered noisily towards the basket by which it had been unceremoniously assaulted.

Michael had watched with his mouth agape as the stencil had descended. By now the red mist that had blinded him and caused the unrestrained destruction was starting to lift and float away. The hot heat of being bereft, being caught up in the moment was starting to cool and gave him some clarity as to what he had done. Wiping a palm across his forehead, his fingers pushed away cold beats of sweat; Michael felt his focus change. His trance like state had been broken and slowly, Michael scanned the room to survey the extent the damage he had caused. All of it broken, destroyed and contributing further to the feeling of having been punched in the gut.

Shaking his head, he picked up the bottle that he had

tucked aside. Close to it was a stuffed elephant that he took into his hand. Slowly and steadily, Michael drew himself into a corner. He was cold and shaking as he crouched towards the floor. Then, it dawned upon him; he a destroyed it. He had destroyed the nursery.

Unsteady in his crouched position, Michael pushed his feet across the deep pile of the carpet to sit. Stretching his legs out ahead out him, he clutched at the bottle still to place it upon his thigh. Then there was the plushy stuffed elephant that he drew close towards him and onto his stomach. Broken and battered, the carcass of the cot before him was a rather explicit demonstration of what he had done.

All of the time and effort that had gone into making it was all wasted. The cot was undone and destroyed. The damage, the sheer carnage caused most certainly irreparable. Two bars that had been broken and snapped, lay tossed aside. Both were fractured and looked woefully forlorn. Seeing all of the bits and pieces disgorged from the drawers, Michael felt another level of agony and devastation. What he saw in front of him was a mess, caused entirely by his own hands and in moments. Faced by the result of his angry action, Michael could feel himself sobering up somewhat. In the pit of his stomach, there was the sensation of a swirl, made quicker by the gassy bubbles from the homebrew and making him feel worse. Michael had hoped to find solace getting blind drunk and with fairly rubbish alcohol. Yet what it had done was to amplify an already bad situation to make the experience even more unbearable.

For the moment, he could not move. Michael was fixed to the spot with no energy to spare. What energy and inclination that the alcohol had provided was now spent; there was very little if anything left in the proverbial tank. He was exhausted, having ridden on the crest of an alcohol induced wave. Rubbing the ear of the fluffy elephant, the sensation was that he was exhausted by everything; he was exhausted by this whole experience. There were repeated losses, being so close and on so many occasions. All of the hope that he had was torn up and scattered to the winds.

This was it. He didn't want to do this again, he simply couldn't. Michael winced slightly, as bubbles bounced around his insides and with an increased frequency. Biting the inside of his cheek, Michael's bottom lip was starting to tremble. As the bubbles bounced harder, he could feel the warm surge of reflux travel and heat his chest. It was towards his chest that he moved the fluffy elephant, as though placing it there would magically quell the reflux away. Taking in a deep breath helped warmth abate a little. It was bad enough that he had physically broken all of the bits in the room. To then decorate the carpet with a barrage of projectile vomit-was in his mind at least-a step too far.

Plus they had fought today. For the last few days, all that they had done was snipe at each other and bicker. Barbs and ingratitude had been exchanged and only further added to the grief that existed between them. That was another reason why he was bordering on inebriated; the moonshine offered some warmth and solace. Michael felt that he if drank enough of the homebrew perhaps then things wouldn't feel so raw; drinking the beer might also help heal the figurative wound that with their bickering seemed to be picked open just as it started to scab over and heal.

Pressing the rim of the bottle to his lips, Michael once more took a large mouthful. He was drinking from the bottle as though he was on auto-pilot; Michael had spent many hours and over years practicing. He really didn't realise how easily he was getting towards the bottom of the bottle. Soon the liquid inside would be all gone and he would no doubt want another bottle. As Michael realised, his brows knitted together and he placed the bottle a short distance away from his knee and onto the carpet.

He would drink no more of the liquid. The beer wasn't particularly pleasant and no longer offered him the succour that he so desperately sought. What it had offered Michael was oblivion. Alcohol the sanitiser, wiping everything out and akin to novocaine. It numbed away pain and made you comfortably numb.

There had to be a balance and as he hugged the elephant closer, Michael wondered what that might be and how they might achieve it. He was tired; tired of feeling the flaming heated agony and anger of loss. The alcohol induced autopilot was the perfect antidote and antithesis to his current state of being in complete agony.

Sat there surveying the damage, Michael's thoughts were as scattered as the broken furniture. There was however the base underlying urge to get through this and over this fatigue. His tiredness was all centred upon waging a war against constant grief, disappointment and loss. A war, that left him feeling less than whole. To be whole again, seemed a state so far away and unachievable. To be whole, for the wound he felt so keenly to heal over. For it to scab over entirely, and not picked open daily.

Drawing his legs towards him, he shuffled a little side to side and rose to his feet. Under the influence of a potent brew, the immediate sensation that he underwent was that of the room spinning. His response was an involuntary rocking back and forth whilst trying not to be sick.

Holding out his hands to gain some buoyancy against the feeling of seasickness, Michael did his best to stabilise himself. He really didn't want to fall over in what promised to be a rather comedic fashion; he could just see it happening. His centre of mass would tip him forward, and he would land in the depths of the deep piled carpet face first. His son's stuffed elephant dangled from his hand by its trunk, looking rather sorry for itself and as though it felt it was for the high jump.

Like everything else in the room, there was a small danger that the stuffed elephant may well be thrust aggressively towards a wall in another fit of fury. Michael did however keep a hold of the stuffed animal and it swung side to side like a pendulum. He was determined not to drop it, when so much had already slipped through his fingers. In his head, the plan was becoming perfectly clear. All he had to do was make sure that the message to start clearing up made it from its current germ-like state within his brain towards his alcohol infused and uncoordinated awkward limbs.

"Michael?"

He had been about to lurch forward; the sound of his name being called, caused him to snap to his right. Dressed in creased and crumpled slate grey jogging bottoms and a matching somewhat age wearied sweatshirt was Sophie. Retracting his outstretched limbs, he drew them close towards chest. Turning to face her, he slowly made his way towards her.

The sense of auto-pilot was back again as he felt her fingers curl around his hands. And her feet had moved so that they were no positioned between his. He could only imagine that it looked an odd, slightly strange image as he dropped his head to look at their feet. Michael's own toes were a nude, naked, fleshy pink; hers were speckled with the remnants of nail varnish that had proven too stubborn to be removed in a hurry.

As he looked up, Michael thought about what might say. His brain was still altogether rather addled as Sophie settled her eyes on his. Grey eyes, that he noticed were tinged pink and under the darkness of feathered eyelashes. Sophie's eyelashes cast shadows across the stripe of freckles that stretched from the sockets of her eyes and all the way across the bridge of her nose. He had tried to count them once, only to earn an elbow to the ribs. As she curled her arms around him to envelop him, Michael let out a breath. There were no words, no sound. All he could was a sense of steadiness as Sophie propped him and stopped him from falling to his knees. There didn't need to be any words. Not even one.

9 Caliope

Growing pains

Every now and again Nandini would look up from her knitting and watch them. Her eyes would rise up from the dual coloured panel and she would gaze upon the faces of her two grandchildren. From the confines of the conservatory, Nandini was able to take in the full panorama of her garden. At the centre of the panorama were Caliope and Koby stretched out on a Paisley patterned sheet and basking in the sunshine that had made something of a surprise visit. Having purled one row, Nandini turned her panel over to take in the sight of Caliope sitting up and crossing her legs. It seemed that in a blink of an eye, Caliope had changed from being a doughy ball faced babe in arms to a young woman with the whole world at her feet. Nandini tutted and shook her head as Caliope's shoulders had started to burn and a pink hue was starting to form. Nandini herself saw no reason to be half dressed. In her mind there was never a good reason to wear such a thin vest; a vest was supposed to be a bit more substantial and went towards protecting you against your death. However, Caliope as headstrong as she was, had an answer for everything and largely answered only to her father.

Nandini knew her place. The role that she occupied was that of being a grandparent. She saw it all, said nothing but felt everything and with intensity. Her expression may have betrayed her thoughts as she saw Caliope look back at her directly. The teenager waved tapered fingers, the nails of which would otherwise be described as being well polished. However, with recent events the coat of pink nail varnish applied to them was chipped and the nails themselves were somewhat bitten to the quick. Having waved back, Nandini watched her granddaughter thread her into a pale blue t-shirt and tug it over head to then smooth it down. For now, Nandini's concerns were assuaged away and she returned to her panel to knit the next row.

Seeing her grandmother return to her knitting, Caliope let out a deep breath. Her shoulders sagged down and she winced at how much the movement hurt. She had somewhat underestimated the strength of the sun, and could feel an intense circle of pain where she had forgotten to apply sunscreen. Her grandmother had been right; the sun was rather strong; Caliope made a mental note to not tell the old lady how right she had been. Turning her head to her left, she looked toward her brother as he lay upon his side. Koby had his hands folded beneath his head and looked quite happy in having fallen asleep. Caliope watched him carefully, and smiled at the shadows cast below his eyes by his eyelashes. Whilst she might have paid well above the odds for mascara that might lengthen, thicken and curl her eyelashes; Koby had all three traits that a woman might kill for and all without trying.

Sat here and lying next to him, there was one thing and one thing alone that Caliope could not understand. How was it, that all of her friends would rant left right and centre about their siblings. In some cases this would be rather vociferous and detailed description of a younger sister, the patronising dissent of an older brother; this was all a contrast to when she and Koby actually got on with one another.

Caliope couldn't remember the last time that they might have come to blows, had a verbal sparring match or had to call upon a responsible adult to be a referee. She really couldn't remember; as far as she was aware, they were fairly tolerant of one another. There was never any drama. Especially now, given what had happened, Caliope was more than a little glad they were able to share the same air and not brain each other. Reaching across, Caliope freed a stray dandelion seed. Powered by the gentle breeze it had landed onto Koby's crown of dense, mousey brown hair. Freeing the orb and letting it rest a moment on her palm, Caliope made a silent wish. Parting her lips, she blew it gently away and into the air.

Having felt a shadow as Caliope loomed over him, Koby snapped one eye open. His sister's movement had briefly interrupted the direct landing of the sun's rays upon him; this had disturbed the enjoyment that he felt of having the warmth against his face. He was trying to make the most of the sunshine, it was not often that it appeared and with such brightness. Sliding his palms from beneath his head, Koby unfurled himself from his curled up sleeping position. Sitting up, he opened his other eye; he had briefly looked like the sailor pop-eye, even down to the gurning expression that was always worn by the cartoon character.

Mirroring his sister, Koby also crossed his legs and tried to become less uncomfortable. It was possible to feel the lumpy, bumpy, a slightly damp law beneath the patterned sheet upon which they were both sat. There were a handful of small damp patches dotted across the sheet where moisture had transferred from the blades of grass below and onto the woven fabric of the sheet.

Caliope looked at her brother as she held her hands

clasped in her lap. He was changing so quickly and she half suspected, that Koby himself did not realise how quickly. The process could not have been any easier with-And there it was. She could not bring herself to even finish the thought. A thought that was so cold and heavy that it felt as though it was a block of ice. A block of ice that was sat between her ears; so cold and heavy, it was sat so silently with no danger of it warming up and melting away. The steely coldness caused Caliope to knit her brows together, with her eyes feeling too hot to open.

"You know, it all going to be okay," Koby moved his hand from his lap and placed it gently upon Caliope's. He could feel the coolness of her skin; the sun had been unable to stretch that far. For as long as he could remember, his older sister had always had cold hands. Rubbing his thumb across the back of her hand, Koby's immediate thoughts were to warm her hands up. "I was thinking," he said quietly, shuffling forwards and a little closer. "If Mum was watching us, just like Dadima," Koby's eyes darted towards where Nandini was sat in the conservatory. "What would she say, do you think that we'd be sat here doing nothing?" he asked, the smallest of smiles travelled across his face and making his cheeks dimple.

On the outside, he could try and smile. On the inside however, it was a different story. A small hot ball of fury bounced around still and didn't feel as though it was getting smaller any time soon.

Still Caliope's brows were knitted together and with her brother's question, they knitted a little tighter as he had taken her hand. She didn't care much for the sweatiness of his fingers, but knew that he meant well. That, and at this moment, they were both a little lost and in need of some comfort. Suppressing the urge to flinch and recoil at his touch, Caliope gathered his hand into hers and curled her fingers around his. She shuffled her bottom as the bumpiness of the lawn meant adjusting her seat from time to time. Caliope coughed for dramatic effect, clearing her throat to hypothesis what their Mum might have said. "You really think," started Caliope, adopting an imitation of her mother's accent, complete with clipped edges and shortened vowels. "That if you are sat there, that your rooms will tidy themselves? Koby, sweetheart, there are three glasses sat by your bed. I am sure they are growing fur. Move them. Thank you."

The very mention of his name, the way in which the emphasis had been placed upon the last syllable had stung. Caliope's attempt at an impersonation had caused Koby's smile to dissipate away. The flush across his cheeks that was caused by the sun was now replaced by something entirely different. That little ball of heat and energy that had been bouncing around and against the walls of his gut; this small whizzing ball had had now travelled to his face. There it had imploded, and was now starting to streak. The flushed hue of warmth was being streaked by hot salty tears that stung sun scorched skin. Koby sobbed and uncontrollably; he was struggling to catch his breath and he could feel his rib-cage tighten. Every inch of him now felt cold, heavy and increasingly numb. Everything that up until this point Koby had been holding in was now gushing out unrestrained. The trigger had been simple; the way in which Caliope mimicked their mother and said his name. All because the pronunciation had been almost exact; it was all too much.

Two things made Nandini look up from her knitting. The first was the staccato sound of rain drops falling onto the roof of the conservatory. The sound was unexpected, as she remembered hearing the weather forecast on the radio this morning; Even though it had been in Punjab and given by a local Asian radio station, there had been no mention of rain. The forecast had mentioned that there would some clouds, but generally the outlook would be bright for the day. Nandini tutted and dropped her knitting to her lap. As she looked up, she saw that Caliope and Koby had moved into a tight embrace. Their motion had been a smudge in the corner of her eyes as she had been counting stitches.

For a moment, Nandini did not move and simply watched. She observed just how much Caliope was like her mother, how closely she held Koby towards her and leant her chin against his head. Nandini could feel her heart thud, causing her to place her hand to her chest to quell the uneasy feeling of not knowing quite what to do. To her, Caliope and Koby were still babies: the two children were young, innocent and unaware of what the world around them held for their futures. Now they would have to grow up a little quicker than the two of them might have thought. Caliope and Koby would have to realise too early what it meant to have lost a parent, to have lost their mother. The rain was still falling; the sound was less staccato now and with a fixed, rhythmic beat the radio drops fell against the tinted glass panels of the roof.

Frantically bundling up the sheet, Caliope huffed at how their moment of togetherness had been quite literally rained upon. A brief window, where they had been able to share their sadness had been smashed and its shiny splintered fragments littered the space between them. Gathering the damp, patterned sheet into a ball, Caliope tucked it under her arm. With the other arm, she led Koby towards the conservatory. His hand was still warm and little wet now from the rain, but still carried some heat. Caliope pulled Koby closer towards her as they walked in step. She noticed how gawky and awkward his movement was. Even though they had each other, one thing was very clear to her.

They had to speak to someone, someone beyond their family; someone who was different and at a distance. There had to be someone that they-she and Koby- could speak with, that wasn't so directly involved in what had happened, and might help them. Help them both to negotiate what they felt, why they felt this way and help them to heal. Opening the doors of the conservatory, Caliope shoved the balled up sheet into Koby's hip to usher him through.

As she had watched his face crumble, Caliope had remembered what her Psychology teacher had said. Theirs had been the briefest of conversations, but Mrs. Hardcastle spoken about counsellors and how part of their role was to listen to you; counsellors could help you. She would have to pick her moment, to run it passed Koby and may be even their dad. She had no idea if it might help, if it might work. Caliope would hold out for the might and the possibility of yes. Yes, that it might help and could help them to heal.

Koby was attempting to run his hands through his locks that were now pressed against his scalp. As his fingers met with resistance, he pulled something of a face as he felt altogether uncomfortable. Firstly, he was wet through and was dripping onto the faux cherry wood laminate that was the flooring of the conservatory. A cluster of droplets had appeared just in front of his left foot and somewhat irked him.

Secondly, he had once again let himself go. He had let everything go and found himself being propped up by Caliope.

He watched as Nandini had got to her feet and was fussing around them both. Koby hunched up his shoulders as his grandmother tutted and huffed whilst patting him down with her hands. As though that would miraculously dry him off, Koby couldn't find it in himself to stop her or resist. He could hear her telling them off and in a surreal combination of English and Punjabi. The English, Koby could understand quite easily, the Punjabi elements were a little less clear. He was however, able to get the gist of what she was saying from her aggravated tone and increased pitch. As overwhelming and intimidating as it was, his grandmother's fussing was somewhat comforting and settling when everything else seemed so jumbled and askew.

Having wrapped her arms around the bundled up sheet, Caliope could feel the dampness. The sheet was now doubly drenched having been their seat upon the damp lawn and now soaked by greasy raindrops. As she watched her grandmother fuss around Koby, her focus sharpened with new thoughts. Here was their grandmother, fairly robustly built, effected by nothing but old age and its associated ailments. She could only just imagine what Nandini might have been like as a younger woman. The wiry grey hair that was woven into a plait and hung between her shoulder blades would have been thick, glossy and completely raven black in colour. Caliope had seen a couple of photographs of Nandini in her younger days, and was able to imagine a younger version of the lady before her quite perfectly. Younger and probably near in age to her Mum. Pressing the ball of fabric closer to her chest, Caliope did her best to imagine how her Mum might have looked at the same age that Nandini was now. Might she have also fussed over Koby and in the same way? Might she have frogmarched Koby, as Nandini was now, towards the kitchen and flung a towel at him so that he could dry himself off? Might have, could have been, it was a whole world possibility. Could, have and been.

10 Matthew

In your shoes

Plumes of white smoke twirled and turned from the end of the cigarette that was glowing orange as it burned. Tapping the end to remove the burned out tip, Matthew pressed the cigarette to his lips and drew in the menthol mix that was probably lining his lungs with tar every time that he took a prolonged drag. Up until now, he had been good. Eight months had passed and giving up had been good. The combination of will power, assertive and being otherwise occupied had made the process of ditching the devilish delight a little easier. Then his grandmother had died and there had been a seismic shift with his will power crumbling away like a stale digestive. His thoughts were no longer focused but, derailed. With no appropriate distractions, the habit was back.

Leaning against a gazebo that had clearly seen better

days, Matthew had been focused on the deep brown fence that separated this garden belonging to his grandparents Lilly and Albie, and the one belonging to the neighbours. A set of three chaffinches were sat on the fence panel as though three ladies waiting for the bus to a lunchtime session of bingo. He could not remember the last time that he had stood, been still and just watched the world go by.

Feeling the prick of the rose bush that grew up around the gazebo, Matthew rubbed his arm where his skin had been caught through the fabric of his shirt by thorns. The thorns were rather vicious, a small dark bloom appeared on the thread of his shirt from the attack. He pulled a face as he saw the bush was entirely loaded with thorns. Some of the pink flowers were dying back, and he could see hundreds and hundreds of thorns on the woody stems that snaked around the gazebo. Triangular and curved thorns, that had he been paying attention, would have served as a warning to not stand so close.

Matthew took one last drag from his cigarette with his eyes closed. Once the cigarette was spent and had been smoked up until the filter, Matthew held it pinched between his fingers and with a flick of his wrist it was thrown into a large and rather weather beaten terracotta flowerpot. It was a practiced manoeuvre. Lilly had hated the idea of smoke hanging around her living room. If he was to smoke, he could do it outside. She had no tolerance for what she described as a filthy habit, and here he was. Just like when she had been alive, flicking filters into the pot really was now a habit. A habit that was so well formed that could probably aim and throw the filter tip with his eyes closed. He was about to light up again having removed a packet from his pocket; his fingers were already curled around a lighter. Yet his thoughts of further practicing were disturbed by words being shouted from the other side of the fence.

A creak and thudding signaled a heavy door hitting against a door frame. Then there was the sound of wood scraping across concrete and then another thud. There was enough noise to cause the chaffinches to fly their perch and the fence panel shook in vibration.

Matthew's window of silent reflection and general broodiness had been well and truly shattered. Returning the packet of cigarettes to his pocket, he moved towards the fence with his fingers still curled around a lighter. Putting his fingers to the top of the panel, Matthew registered how tall the panel actually was. As a child, the fence had seemed insurmountable. A mountain that he failed to climb each and every time he had sent his ball flying over and into the garden next door. Now and many years later, the fence panel was only just chest high. Matthew was able to look direct over it and into the garden next door quite easily. Resting his elbow on the fence panel, he saw that a wooden chair had been thrust against the panel and was now saw amongst some brightly coloured shrubbery.

"And why slam the door?!"

Matthew's attention was immediately drawn away from the abused garden furniture. He focused instead on the elderly woman stood at the large looming doors. She was dressed in what he knew to be traditional Indian clothes; her pale scarf hanging from her shoulder, where it was being tugged at by a gentle breeze. In all the time that Matthew had been visiting his grandparents, he had never heard the elderly next door neighbours raise their voices loud enough to be heard over the fence. There had been laughs, screams and boisterous noises made by their grandchildren, but never this.

Noticing that she was being watched, the woman waved at Matthew. "Hello, Matthew," she said as her face softened a little. "You talk with him," her hand wafted towards the teenage boy who stood not too far and appeared to be in something of a sullen mood. "He's in a funny mood," she added, closing the door with both hands and going back into her house.

He saw that the boy's expression was akin to face like thunder, but wasn't too sure as how to he might deal with it. Matthew had been poised to wait back at Nandini Anand; she had lived next door to his grandparents for longer than he could remember. Given how brief her appearance had been, he didn't get to wave back at her and was now focused on the teenage boy. He knew the teenager quite well, almost as well as Nandini. He said nothing as Koby moved towards the fence through wet grass that glistened with recently fallen raindrops.

"Funny mood?" asked Matthew, using Nandini's words; he was curious at the expression. Over the years, he had watched Lilly and Nandini have many a conversation over the fence and he had always listened in and intently to the nativised variation of English that Nandini spoke.

Koby gave a rather nonchalant shrug of his shoulders, as his expression remained rather sour looking. He didn't look as though he felt particularly sociable. "It's nothing," said the teenager, the arms of the chair that he had thrown earlier were gripped tightly beneath his fingers. "Just Dadima being her usual Dadima self. Everything is always such a drama," added Koby, his gaze fixed firmly upon the chair.

"Been a lot of those though, dramas and recently," Matthew commented. "Lots of drama has happened on this side of the fence and your side. The whole house is so much quieter without Lilly, and don't even mention the cake." Matthew laughed quietly, hoping that it would help break the tension.

The mention of cake caused Koby to move his gaze from the chair and towards Matthew. "Cake," he said quietly. "It would have been Mum's birthday tomorrow, and she liked cake. She liked proper birthday cake. It had to be birthday cake that was always home-made and with jam and sugar on top. There's one in the kitchen-not home-made, though-think Dad bought it, think he forgot-" Koby paused, and his brow furrowed, making his expression now look a little pained rather petulant.

"That explains the funny mood, I supposed," Matthew nodded as though a penny had dropped. "I'm sorry, Koby, I didn't think. There was always cake, and well, you know." Now it was Matthew's turn to feel slightly uncomfortable and he fiddled with the lighter in his hands.

Shaking his head, Koby sighed and moves his hands away from the chair. Cold and wet, there as film of raindrops that had transferred from the brown stained wooden chair and onto his fingers. Rubbing his palms together, Koby tried to rub his hands dry before giving up and wiping them across his jeans. "I don't know how you are doing this either," said Koby. "I can't imagine Dadima not being here. I really don't get it. She's been a bit sad," he looked over his shoulder, to see Nandini sat in the conservatory with her knitting spread across her lap. "Not just about Mum, but she won't even mention Lilly. Didn't realise how good friends they were."

"This fence has a lot to answer for," this time Matthew laughed properly. There was no awkwardness in his words. "Pakoras-them onion bhaji things-being passed over at Diwali. Those were good pakoras," he added nodding in approval.

Koby also nodded in agreement, a smile almost appearing upon his face. "Not too spicy, are they, Mrs. Anand?" he couldn't help but parrot Lilly's response to much of the food that found itself being passed over the fence.

"Not too hot, no!" returned Matthew, shaking his head. He couldn't but help smile either. The tension and heaviness between them had well and truly lifted. "Lilly actually liked them. She thought they were really quite tasty. Exotic, even," he said tucking his lighter into his pocket, before crossing his arms. "I can understand why she is sad, Koby. Two people that she was fond of and close to, they're no longer part of her life; with both of them leaving quite close together and in a short space of time. It's not easy, but it is okay," nodded Matthew. "And it's your Mum's birthday?"

Koby nodded, shuffling his feet from side to side. "Yep," he took a deep breath before carrying on. "It all feels a bit odd, especially as she's not here. Normally, we'd be celebrating. We might all have gone out, had dinner somewhere, and birthday cake. But now, after everything, it feels odd. She was supposed to be here. So that we can celebrate her birthday, have a good time. Instead, instead we're all miserable, unhappy, and just thinking about Mum. About Mum being-"Koby could hear his tone rise and his cheeks felt as though they were getting warmer. He couldn't say it, couldn't say that his mum was dead, that he wanted her to be here and alive.

Not interrupting, Matthew had listened and watched the teenager as he stood a little beyond the fence panel. He could see and hear that Koby was grieving. To him, this was perfectly within reason. What the teenager in front of him was experiencing, was in essence the same gamut of emotions and thoughts that he was also experiencing. The key difference was that they were dealing with things in different ways. "You still could," he offered gently. "You could still celebrate and mark your Mum's birthday. Might be a little different, a little harder, but it is still her birthday. You can still eat the cake that your Dad has got." He had added the last part in an attempt to be supportive, but it also echoed his own thoughts about cake.

Koby had cast his gaze downward again, and was now looking at the grass beneath his feet. Covered in glossy raindrops, the blades of grass glinted in the light. Shuffling his feet, he watched as his movement caused a flurry of drops into the air. "I suppose," he said quietly. "What about you," asked Koby, he wasn't even looking up towards Matthew on the other side of the fence. "I'm not the only one skulking outside by the fence."

"No, no, you are not," Matthew spoke as he absent-mindedly scratched his ear. "Same as you, I guess. I didn't and couldn't imagine Lilly not being here. It is different and without her being around. It's hard for me, but I can't even begin to imagine what it might be like for my Grandad. He and Lilly, they were together a long time; they were married for a long time." Matthew turned slightly, and through the kitchen window he could see the slight figure of Grandad pottering around in the kitchen. Turning back to Koby, Matthew gave a slight shrug. "We both look for her from time to time; it's all a bit strange really. No one ever tells you, what might happen when the people who mean the world to you go away and will never come back."

"I keep waiting to hear my name," said Koby as he slid his hands into his pockets. "To hear Mum ask me where my kit is, or did I do my English homework. I hate English," he spat the words out as though they tasted sour. "I just can't do it, it makes my brain hurt. Mum would help me, or at least point me in the right direction. Asking Dad, well it's just not the same. It's bad enough that he has to take me to rugby training; he doesn't have a clue."

Matthew had decided that he would have another cigarette, and slid a packet out of his pocket. "Maths or rugby?" he asked . "I don't get rugby, myself. As for English, I like it simple." Sliding a cigarette out of the packet, he held it at his lips. Finding his lighter, he cupped his hands over the cigarette and watched the flame kiss the tip.

Nudging the wooden chair before him, Koby also hit the shrubbery next to it and caused a further cascade of raindrops. "Both. But rugby is the worst and will be the worst," replied Koby. "Just not his thing either. By going, I know that he is trying to help. He's trying to make things better. Mum actually liked it, she liked to go and she'd proper get into it." As he looked up, Koby's eyes were momentarily bright and gleaning. "Mum would be standing on the touchline, shouting and screaming at the scrum. That was what she did. Dad, well, he just watches with his arms crossed and waits for it all to be over. Two different people, I guess." Koby's shoulders sagged into a shrug and once more his expression was that of a bereaved young man.

Breathing out clouds of white, Matthew had his lips pursed together. "That's how I feel about Lilly's home-made cakes. Hers would win any day and hands down over shop bought ones. I even made one, just so that I could remember what it might have been like. I just wanted to have Lilly around even if it was in the form of a cake. Nothing else quite compares." He held out his hand and tapped ash off the end of his cigarette. "It is still very early, and things are still fresh, Koby. This is going to take time and for all of you." Matthew's eyebrows darted towards the conservatory where Nandini was back at the doors.

Taking the hit, Koby craned his neck over his shoulder to see his grandmother standing on her feet. "Tea, Dadima?" he asked, wondering if she was about to tell him to come back in.

"Rain," replied Nandini, pointing towards a grey cloud that just appeared in the distance. "But yes, you come in, make me some proper tea. Come on," she added, beckoning him in. "You'll get wet. In, please," she urged, as yellow bangles jangled at her wrist.

"I'm coming, hold on," Koby told his grandmother before turning back to Matthew. "Rain," he said, "And tea. You're wanted too," he flexed a finger towards the window behind Matthew. Albie was stood looking at them both and tapping at the glass.

"So I am," Matthew waved at his grandad, and then flicked his now spent cigarette into the time honoured target of a flower pot. "Make sure it's proper tea, Koby," he said turning away.

"And don't forget proper cake, Matt," Koby also made his exit, and they both departed in opposite directions. The grey cloud burst to shed its load, drenching the garden and filling the cigarette butt filled plant pot.

11 Christopher

Words on a page

He had tossed and turned. As he tried to sleep, his had churned up the bedclothes. No matter how much he tried, he could not get comfortable. No one side was comfortable enough for him to sleep. He was tired; Christopher was tired of feeling exhausted. Flinging away covers; he dragged himself forward and swung his feet to the floor. Everything around him was shrouded in a grainy darkness. As he squinted at his 'phone on the bed side cabinet he found that it was three in the morning.

Clutching the device in his hand, Christopher rubbed his eye with his free hand. He remembered coming up at eleven, perhaps there had been a moment where he had entered the twilight zone and briefly. Christopher planted his 'phone back onto the cabinet and sat for a moment to savour the silence that filled the room. He was awake now, alert and somewhat energized. His eyes adjusted to the darkness to focus upon a pile of clothes sat next to the wardrobe in something of an undignified heap.

There was only one thing for it. To write and to help those thoughts escape; perhaps process them and alleviate the strangled sensation that he was currently experiencing. The sensation that clung to his mind, his skin, and his very being since Adelphi had fallen asleep.

Pressing his palms against the pale blue sheet that covered a rather firm mattress, Christopher pushed himself up from his seated position and onto his feet. With his eyes still adjusting to greyscale darkness, Christopher negotiated a path through the vast array of things that lay scattered across his bedroom floor and out through the door. Letting the door stand wide open in his wake, he wandered a short distance across the landing and into the room that by day served as his office.

This was a room that he had shared with Adelphi whilst he pretended to work. Work that was generally punctuated by Adelphi's request for them both to take a walk. Flicking on the lights at the switch on the wall, Christopher's gaze travelled towards the spot where Adelphi would sit and in the folds of his blanket upon the floor. A conditioned response, still so immediate through years of practice. This was a habit that was probably going to be very difficult to break.

With no Adelphi sat there waiting for him, Christopher shuffled towards his desk and the chair tucked in neatly beneath it. The chair had a cold surface that was slippery beneath his fingers. Christopher had to curl both of his hands around the back of it to drag the chair from under the desk. The chair gave something of a soft groan as Christopher lowered himself into the cushioned seat. Dragging his feet across the floor, he pulled himself and the chair closer towards the curved edge of the desk; so close to the work surface, he felt safe and there was a sense of security in being so close and sandwiched in so tightly.

Splaying his digits across the close laptop that sat in front of him, Christopher's brow knitted together and felt tense as he concentrated. He was concentrating on the thumping beat of his heart, the tightness of his dry throat and the whooshing of blood in his ears. Beneath his fingers, the surface of laptop was cold to the touch and pregnant with the possibility of what he might write as he raised the screen.

Patiently, Christopher watched the machine whir to life, boot up and present him with a home screen. For now, he would draft up the assorted thoughts that occupied him and plundered his peace by robbing him of shut eye. He did not trust himself at these small hours to write and press publish immediately.

To press publish when he was done, felt a little rash. Christopher's aim was to simply deliver his brain of all that currently felt crammed within. A blank document was raised, casting a blue tinged light across his fingers as they rested upon the keys; fingers that were poised to pounce upon the thoughts that all being well would escape from confines of his consciousness.

'I couldn't tell you what it means to lose a goldfish. As a child, I never had one. I was never that child who on finding a dead fish in a tank, asked their parents to explain what had happened to poor Fishy. I didn't have a goldfish; what I did have was a puppy. A wet-nosed, four legged fur ball who really was a boy's best friend.

Note the past tense. I had a puppy.

The puppy, became a dog; grew, in the same way I did from babe in arms, to infant, gawky adolescent and to a grown up. Alas, the dog, he is no more; Man, does it hurt.

His name was Adelphi. The fur ball, my grown up puppy has been gone for less than a week and I miss him. I miss him more than I may have missed a goldfish that ended its life bobbing up and down a fish tank. I miss my best and I feel as though I am going a little mad. I can't sleep, that is for certain. I'm sat here writing this in the middle of the night when I should be sound asleep and adventuring in the lad of nod. Only I keep seeing his face and every time that I close my eyes and try to drift away. There are no barks, no whines; there is no scratching noise of paws against the door. Adelphi is no longer here and it feels altogether strange.

Let's face it. He had been around a while. I couldn't have been more than seven, perhaps eight when Adelphi and I first met. Adelphi had just turned twelve, so you could argue that the old boy had a fairly good innings. By and large, that was fairly good going for Adelphi. In dog years, he was fairly well seasoned. In human years, he may have just been headed for a teenage crisis of some sort. Adelphi had always been around, man and boy. He was also my Mum and Dad's second child, my four legged baby brother. Neither one of them, took exception to the four legs and fur. Mum had another child to mother and to kiss all over. Dad may have been happier than most at being able to throw a ball and for it to be returned in a fairly timely fashion. He really was my furry little brother, that is the only way it all makes sense to me.

Twice in two days, I have gone to feed a dog who no longer exists. I was going to pop out to the shops to get some milk, and as I left my hand made a well-practiced grab for his lead by the door. It took me a while each time to realise what I was doing. Even then, it felt as though I was doing something that I was meant to be doing, and nothing out of the ordinary. It is, after all, something that I have been doing nearly every day and for years. The second time, I sat on the stairs holding on his lead and that was when it hit me. Adelphi is dead.'

The last sentence may Christopher stop typing. It was just as hard reading back what he had had written, as it was sitting on the stairs having the thought. He focused at three words that had just typed, the cursor flashing on screen looking way too excited given the words. The three words made his stomach hurt, his eyes prick once more and his head hum with the gravity of it all. Moving the cursor to the top of the page, Christopher carefully read through the words that he had typed. He tried to absorb each and every word, turning over the phrases silently in his head. Sliding his fingers back across the keys, he resumed typing. He was not done quite yet, with the creeping feeling of a little more still being in the tank.

'It is not often that I have had to make a difficult decision. In Adelphi's case, the decision wasn't so much life changing as life ending. His life was to be over, and I was the one responsible for that decision. After everything that Adelphi and I had been through, deciding to put him to sleep was one of the hardest, gut wrenching and heart rendering decisions to make. It was however, the only decision to be made. The vet stressed that all things considered, Adelphi was important and the quality of his life was crucial to Adelphi being Adelphi. To put Adelphi to sleep-send him across the rainbow bridge, to borrow the phrase that my Mum tried to comfort me with-was by far the kindest and most loving thing to do. It was not a time to be selfish, not really. Adelphi really was the most important-I want to say person-person in all of this. He was so much more than just a dog. I cannot even begin to imagine how this sort of decision might be made and if at the centre of it was a human being. This was all about Adelphi.

With Adelphi gone, there is a horrible great big black hole left behind in my universe. A horrible big black hole that is grief and I have nothing to compare it to. I still have grandparents. Remarkably, they are far from doddery, frail and infirm. Losing Adelphi is the first major bereavement that I have experienced and it has taken until I am adult for it to occur. As an adult, I feel broken, lost, as though I am at sea without my best friend.

I could not even tell you how a child might have processed this, least of all the dead goldfish that I mentioned before. A goldfish is probably very different; a goldfish might be easily replaced with no questions asked. I don't think for one moment that Adelphi should be replaced. That dog was very unique. I understood him, and I know that he understood me. I guess that is why I feel the way that I do, plus it is only a matter of days since it happened. Everything feels very raw and very immediate. I couldn't tell you how I might feel tomorrow, the day after or next week. It is impossible for me to think that far ahead.

There is yet to be a funeral, a proper send off for Adelphi. All that remains of him is his ashes, a selection of squeaky toys, a lead and his blanket. Once he was put to sleep, things moved rather quickly. That window of twenty four hours is a very pained, very blurry space in time. I have no yet decided what I might do with Adelphi's ashes. Ashes that are sat contained with a grey urn in the cupboard beneath the stairs. For the moment, that is where they will stay and until I arrive at a decision. That is all I have physically left of Adelphi, his ashes. There is no wet nose, four legs and a wagging tail. Those ashes are Adelphi still. Adelphi is all there, from paws unto powder.'

Letting out a contained breath, Christopher stopped typing.

For now, some of what he was thinking and feeling was out and on a page. He had put into words, part of what his brain was trying to process. There was some relief in that, Christopher could feel the tightness around his shoulders slacken off a little. His head also felt a little less full of white noise. His eyes were still sore and he rubbed the hollow of his left eye with the heel of his hand. Displaced and coating his palm there were freshly formed tears. Perhaps now he could asleep, if only for a little while. The sheer heaviness of being tired, grieving and trying to think was horribly overwhelming. Saving his words, Christopher powered down the computer.

There was a definite desire now to go to sleep; rubbing his eyes he made his way out of the room. He would sleep and may be in the morning, he would check in with his mum. It was her that he had called straight after Adelphi had gone. She had listened and said nothing as he had sobbed his sobbed his heart out and over the 'phone. In those immediate moments, the only person that Christopher had wanted had been his mother

12 Daniel

A shared grief

The sills were grimy, as were panes of glass in the windows. Covered in sediment and generally just a bit weathered, the curved bay windows were in need of a good and thorough clean. Using two fingers, Joel rubbed circle in the dirt that covered the glass in the hope that he might be able to see through a little better. Whilst the curtains were drawn back, Joel could see little that might indicate life beyond the window and within the walls of this semi-detached house.

Peering in through the glass, the room with its northerly aspect was dark. He could just about make out two mugs left idly upon the mantel above a faux fire place. Moving away from the window, he moved towards the letter box. Joel had already pressed the doorbell, jabbing at it in frustration as there was no immediate response. He had now opted to knock on the door, and rapped a curled fist against it. Joel then rattled the letterbox for good measure.

Standing on the hessian welcome mat, Joel ran a hand through his blonde hair. This was hair that took forever to revive and made to look presentable. In its unmanipulated state, the strands of hair were baby fine and lacked volume; it was entirely flat and lifeless, with little or no character. A number of products and a significant amount of time was appropriated on a daily basis for his hair to be fit for duty and worthy of public attention. Having disturbed his crowning glory, Joel sank his hands into the pockets of his dark denim jeans and waited.

He waited with a sense of uneasiness and he looked intently at the door and mentally willed it to open. Joel listened, and for anything that might indicate and confirm life beyond the entrance. A couple of minutes passed and there was nothing. Once more he rattled the letterbox, this time with a little more force. As the letterbox creaked in protest, he bent down to prize it open so that he could look through and down the hallway. Drawing breath, he readied himself and yelled. "Are you in? It's me, Joel," his tone was rather terse, given his current mood. Still he studied the hallway, and his gaze darted towards the staircase in anticipation.

Then came the sound, he heard it quite clearly. The sound of a door thudding open as it hit a wall. After came the sound of feet falling heavily on the stairs and thudding down the hallway towards him.

"Yes, I'm coming, hold on!" A second man had tumbled down the stairs and was approaching the door in an equally agitated fashion. "I heard you, whoever you are, and the first time," he all but growled.

Daniel had thundered down the stairs as he pulled a blue t-shirt over his head and threaded his arms through the sleeves. He had rushed out of the shower and was barely dry; this had made getting dressed a little more difficult. He had pulled on his shirt, but it inside out. For the minute, that was irrelevant and had rather escaped his attention. As he opened the door, droplets of water trickled toward his shoulders from his mousey brown hair and spotted the fabric of the t-shirt where they were promptly absorbed by the natural fibres.

"Okay, what was it, that was so-" Daniel drew the door open towards him to see his nephew standing before him. "Joel, it's you. Please, come on in, young man. How are you?" asked Daniel, standing aside to let Joel enter and pass as he held out his hand.

"Did you fall in?" asked the younger man, momentarily waggling his finger at his uncle's wet-look hair before he shook the proffered hand. "No wonder you weren't able to hear me shouting. I'm not bad, thank you," he added stepping into the hall to take the door from Daniel and close it behind him with a gentle click of the lock. There were two things that struck Joel. Firstly, the colour of the door, he had never paid attention to it before. He distinctly remembered it being a different, another colour. The current colour-navy-was rather sober; miserable even and quite dull given who lived here. Secondly, the weight of the door felt strange too as he moved it towards the frame where it had clicked closed. Joel snatched his fingers away quickly as the door moved away from him. The last thing he wanted to do right now was to get injured and lose a few digits.

"I'm okay," he replied, letting out a deep breath. "How about you, how are you doing? Mum sent me-to you know-check in, see how you were."

Daniel shook his head at his nephew. Gently he places his hands upon Joel's shoulders to shepherd him towards the kitchen at the end of the hall way. "Of course she did. Typical of your mother, sending a boy to do a man's job," said Daniel. "Leaves me all sorts of voicemails, sends her son, but won't come here and see me herself. Here, do put the kettle on," directed Daniel having ushered Joel towards the worktop where the kettle was located. Sat next to it was a washed and cleaned cafetiere waiting to be used.

"I was sorry to hear about your friend, Joel. What was

her name, Millie?" He sat himself down onto a chair, exhaling deeply as his arms sagged to his sides. Today, Daniel had managed to make it to the shower. The best part of two days has been spent curled up in a duvet with occasional trips to the kitchen. The two days had been solitary and soulless with countless cups of coffee that lubricated the eating of stale Danish pastries. Taking a shower and having a shave had taken something of a supreme effort. However, seeing Joel here made it all a little more worthwhile. Joel was the first human being that he had spoken to in a number of days. The messages that had been left by his sister really didn't count. There was nothing human or endearing about messages left upon an answer machine.

Joel emptied the kettle and turning the tap at the sink filled it with freshly drawn water. He was well aware of how Daniel was very particular when it came to making coffee. The joke being that his uncle was something of a coffee snob and able to smell out a badly made cup of coffee at a hundred paces. Daniel himself described it as being a connoisseur rather than a snob; this was probably not the most appropriate time to be discussing semantics.

"Millie, yes," answered Joel, flicking the lid of the kettle closed and planting it firmly onto the base that was plugged into a socket at the wall. "It's been an interesting few days," commented Joel. "Not sure what was worse. In the first instance to have seen it all actually happen in front of me. Secondly, then having to describe it all to the police and in detail." Reaching a hand towards the kettle, he depressed the switch on the base of its curved handle. He had forgotten to turn it on and it took the absence of a low hum to make him realise. "Not just the once either, but several times." Joel shook his head a little as he leant back against the worktop. "Over and over," he added, slouching and sliding his hands into his pockets. "I swear, at one point I did think I was going a little mad. All those questions and having to answer in so much detail. Everything had to be very specific; bits and pieces of information."

Daniel was nodding as he rose to his feet. "Don't remind me, it is an awful experience," he said moving towards a cupboard and removing two mugs. "I don't envy you experience at all." He placed the mugs next to the cafetiere, briefly running a finger around the rim of one of the mugs. "Being asked the same question over and over again; you end up feeling as though everything that you had seen, remembered was systematically being worn away. So many questions, and question after question. There is nothing in between to let you draw breath or anything."

"Sometimes in a different order," said Joel, pulling open the fridge. There was a bag of coffee in there somewhere. His movement had been instinct, force of habit as he had done this quite often in the past. There it was, on the second shelf tucked into the back corner and lurking by something quite questionable in a Tupperware box. Wrapping his fingers around the cold, smooth surface of the packet Joel dragged it towards him and out of the fridge. It felt quite light in his hand; Daniel could quite easily exist on this stuff and little else. "Questions as to how everything happened, but having you describe it in a different order, from someone else's perspective. Just to get a good picture. I saw it, felt it all happen. It was all horrible," Joel's lips twisted into a grimace of disdain and he handed his uncle the packet of coffee. "To describe it over and over, each and every moment flaming well prolongs the torture really."

As he listened to Joel, Daniel heaped the dark, chocolate coloured ground coffee into the cafetiere. "Any news yet on the driver?" he posed, leaning against the worktop and watching the kettle continue to boil. It had been over filled and still had a short while to go.

"Caught by the traffic police, two minutes down the road," Joel answered. "Driving erratically, would you believe. Erratically!" huffed Joel, tutting sharply. "Never mind just killed someone," his tone and his hands flew from his pockets and into the air in visible anger.

As the kettle finished boiling and with a click, there was a barely concealed scoff of disgust from Daniel. Drawing the cafetiere closer to the kettle, he picked up the kettle to pour in the hot water. "Least of their problems, driving erratically," commented Daniel. "At least the driver was caught. You've been in touch with her parents, Millie's Mum and Dad?" he asked as he depressed the plunger and let the coffee brew. Pulling out drawer, he selected a teaspoon from the tray. They could probably both do with a spot of sugar as the teaspoon was dropped into a mug.

"Yeah," whispered Joel slowly moving away and towards the chair that Daniel had sat in before. "I don't know what to say to them or how, so it's a bit…difficult," he spoke quietly, as though reflecting what he might say. Sitting forward, Joel started to fiddle with a stack of coasters. "But any way," he exhaled, sniffed to draw breath in and then looked at his uncle. "Mum sent me."

Daniel arched a brow to look at Joel whilst he poured freshly brewed coffee into mugs. "So you said," he stated. "Sugar?" he asked, sliding his foot out pivot just in case but holding a mug towards Joel.

"No," replied Joel, taking the mug towards him and plucking out the teaspoon. Instead he handed it back to Daniel, who taking it dropped it into his mug. "She's been fussing and flying around. Guess she must have just wanted me out of the house."

Daniel had picked up a jar of sugar and now sat adjacent to his nephew at the kitchen table. Unscrewing the jar, he used the spoon from his mug to scoop out two teaspoons of sugar and dropped them into his coffee with a plop. Setting aside the jar, he stirred the sugar in the liquid. "Maybe," ventured Daniel, "Your Mum thought that misery loves company. If you are miserable, I am miserable, we can both then be miserable together. The added bonus for your lovely mother is that she gets to check in on me and not get her hands dirty. Cheers," he smiled as he raised his mug aloft. He was feeling a little less annoyed with his sister and glad that Joel was here with him.

Taking the hint, Joel held up his mug to clink against Daniel's. "I should probably ask then," he said pressing rim of the mug to his lips to take a small sip. "Whether you are okay? I should have asked before, sorry."

Resting his elbow on the edge of kitchen table, Daniel pressed a curled fist against his cheek. "There are bad days, there are good days," came the quiet and measured reply. "After two fairly crappy, rubbish days, I can say that with some confidence. I got out of bed today, even got to the shower despite the fact that you rang the doorbell incessantly. That got me down the stairs. You do have your uses, young man," he half smiled with the last sentence. "Haven't spoken to any, seen anyone in days." Taking a mouth, Daniel was starting to feel a little more settled.

"Avoided Mum's messages," Joel chimed in.

"Quite," Daniel retorted. "She means well. Might not have got on well with Caleb, I know. She does still care, and that does matter. I know that much. I'll call around eventually. Just need to get through the next few days somehow. Caleb and I, we had plans for our anniversary. It would have been two years and only four months since Caleb…" he let the sentence hang; there was no part of him that wanted to turn a possible good day into bad. He was tripping over the word; even now it was too difficult to pronounce.

Blowing into his coffee, Joel looked up as he heard Daniel's voice trail off. "Anything in particular?" he enquired, slurping more coffee and on purpose to try and provide some light relief. His brow furrowed as the coffee was a still a little hot and he had now scalded the roof of his mouth. Joel swallowed a little quickly, and then pressed his tongue to the scalded skin, The resulting expression across his face suggested that he might have sucked half a lemon, given how much he had wrinkled up his eyes. The mug of coffee was thudded down onto the table in protest; he would wait and let it cool down. The coffee could wait awhile, Joel wanted to hear what Daniel had to say.

"Florence," replied Daniel. "We had planned it a short break, scheduled it ages go," there was a dismissive wave of the hand as he spoke. "And then obviously it had to be cancelled," he pulled his shoulders up to shrug and looked into his coffee. "Would have been nice, Florence, Rome was on the list too," he shook his head sadly. "Just wasn't meant to be."

Folding his arms, Joel looked at his uncle and his brow was still furrowed somewhat. "You could still do something," he offered. "I know it's only been four months," continued Joel, shuffling in his seat and sitting a little further forward. "And that it all feels really very raw. But do you really think that Caleb would want you sat around and at home, being a misery? Caleb was all about fun and games, remember." Joel's shoulders sunk as he pressed his lips together after a deep sigh. He rather hated the feeling of having to walk on the proverbial egg-shells. Sent here by his mother to check on his uncle, he felt compelled to coax Daniel out of his self-imposed seclusion from society. "You're not exactly a modern day hermit, Dan."

Moving his eyes from the salt and pepper set in the centre of the table; Daniel looked up and at Joel and said, "Joel, I know what you are trying to do, and thank you. But I am okay," he blinked to compose himself, able for the moment to keep his tone level.

His nephew meant well, that was abundantly quite clear. "I will get through this," he said sitting backwards and hooking a finger around the handle of his mug. "I'm fine."

"Pfft, and I'm from Ulan Bator," exclaimed Joel as he unfolded his arms and threw his hands into the air. "No, no you're not. Other than the funeral, other than the odd trip to the supermarket, you've been here. Mum's called you and incessantly. Every time that I've popped 'round, we've had a fight-always a fight-to get you off the sofa," Joel spoke hurriedly, and now blinked his eyes wide open. He focused his watery blue eyes ardently upon Daniel. "And I am exhausted fighting with you, with no more ideas as to how I can better support you. Get out of here may be, take a couple of days away. May not Florence," said Joel. "The seaside," he could hear himself getting more and more riled up. "You could plan a trip to the lakes, whatever you might want to do. But do something for a change of scenery. Ashes!" Again, Joel appeared to have light bulb moment. "Weren't you going to scatter Caleb's ashes?"

"Stop," Daniel got to his feet suddenly whilst clutching his mug and moved his chairs backwards. Scraping across the floor, the legs made a screeching sound as they moved. "Changing the scenery is one thing. Yes, I can understand the need to get out of here." Daniel moved towards the cafetiere that was still sat on the worktop. "His ashes. Caleb's ashes. Not there yet, Joel. It is still too soon," he said looking over his shoulder as he poured more coffee into his mug. He had managed to drink three quarters of it. What remained in the mug was almost cold. "I need a little more time. I can't let go just yet."

Feeling a little as though he were a small child who had just been told off, Joel pouted. He also gave something of a small shrug of resignation. "Just don't go all Miss. Havisham; Mum said you might. She's a bit worried that you might, and well, it just wouldn't be very you."

Daniel let out a throaty laugh as he looked at his nephew. The sound rather surprised him; he had forgotten laughter. He could not remember the last time that he actually had cause to laugh. The analogy did rather bring a smile to his face. "Miss. Havisham was jilted, she was not widowed," said Daniel, turning back to his coffee and inhaling the heady aroma. "I can see her point, and I take it graciously. I will not be turning into Miss. Havisham," he returned back to his chair at the kitchen table. "That would be very dramatic, very Caleb, that. You can tell your mum that; I am sure that she would take it the wrong way."

Joel nodded in agreement as he smiled broadly. "Would be very Caleb, yes," he said laughing at the thought. "There would be flounce," he added.

"Lots of flounce," agreed Daniel. He was starting to feel a little better, the laughter helped shoo away greyness. "I'm glad that you came, Joel. That we didn't fight this time. I don't mean to start fights, I really don't. It's nice to speak to someone. Not easy, but thank you."

Nudging his mug towards Daniel's, Joel clinked his against it and even winked. "A pleasure; you are after all family. What else would we do exactly, hmm? Maybe you could talk to someone, other than me. Someone a little better at, at the whole grieving thing; just a suggestion," he said carefully. "But you know."

"And you," posed Daniel and pointedly. "You'll talk to someone as well, about your friend. About Millie. You've barely said two words and about her, and you were rather close. So let's turn the tables a little." Picking up his mug, he watched Joel across the golden rim. "We're both on the same train line, Joel; we just happen to be at different stations. Do you really think that I want to be where I am?" he asked, taking a mouthful of coffee. Hearing his own words out aloud, it actually struck him as to what Joel had done and was trying to do in being here. His nephew had been one of the first to check in on him in those first few days of his loss. Here Joel was and in a similar position. "Talk with Millie's Mum and Dad, Joel. Chances are that they need you as much you need them. I suspect they have left you a fair few voicemails, just like your mum has been doing."

As he sat there and with his hand wrapped around a cool mug of coffee, Joel looked at his uncle and realised. His mother really was trying to kill two birds with one stone in having sent him here. Both he and Daniel were grieving for different people but their experiences were really quite similar. Their process might have been different, but Daniel was showing Joel just how much they had in common. What Daniel was doing and in the kindest way was turning back towards him everything that he himself had said. With Millie only been gone a few days, everything really was disjointed and he did feel as though he had rather blocked everything out.

And so they would sit awhile. More coffee was to be made; there would be an attempt to make sandwiches only for the cupboards and 'fridge to be bare. It would be at that point, that they would agree to go find a café and have a fairly unhealthy brunch. But not before Daniel realised that his shirt was inside out and had to change it. Standing at the door, Joel waited for Daniel; he looked out down the street and had to do a double take as a woman walked away towards traffic lights that had only just turned red. For a moment, that could have been here, and for that moment she was still here.

For Daniel's part, as they ate he felt a sense of gladness. Sat in the café with Joel, he wasn't going to actually tell his Joel that he was right. Right about a change of scenery being just what he needed. He would tell him later, when the time was. Coffee was served, and he pulled a face that declared it to be awful. For that moment, being outside and beyond the Caleb-coated walls did something of a trick.

13 Joyce

Lend an ear

Being so far from the main staffroom, the Social Sciences office was something of a departmental bolt-hole far away from all other departments. Equipped with a microwave, a small 'fridge and a kettle, the office had all the necessary and required amenities for the staff. Joyce had filled the kettle and even located the biscuits barrel. Peeking inside, she was somewhat gladdened by the fact that were actually a handful of jam and cream biscuits inside. There had been a few dramas where biscuits had been necessary, only for the barrel to be barren.

As she waited for the kettle to boil and for May to arrive, Joyce heard a quiet vibration coming from her handbag. Scooping out her 'phone, her brow creased as she tapped at the touch screen. It was unusual for her to receive calls and messages whilst as work. The vibration had signalled a message from her son Christopher. It was fairly general, the general gist that he would check in with her at some point, and he wanted to know if she would help with Adelphi's things. Joyce felt a pang of sadness for both her son and his dearly departed dog. She tapped back a reply in the affirmative; suggesting that he pop by and both her and his father over a cuppa. Returning the 'phone to the bag, she saw that kettle had boiled. Next, she located both the tea and coffee as she had no idea which Maya prefer.

Maya had tidied up her toilet cubicle as quickly as she could. To compose herself, she had splashed cold water lightly across her face, hoping that it would get rid of the tearstains. Luckily, Maya had her handbag, and at the bottom of it was a small round compact of pressed powder. Passing the soft sponge lightly over her cheekbones and jaw, Maya did her best to cover the tracks of her tears and look a little more presentable. Sliding the compact back into her bag, she took a moment to look at her reflection. Her make up mask had slipped somewhat. To get through the rest of the day the mask would have to be adjusted and put back into position. Talking with Joyce could help for that to possibly happen. Clutching her handbag at her hip, Maya made her way to the Social Sciences office.

Gingerly opening the door, Maya peered around it.

"Joyce?" she asked tentatively as she scanned the room from left to right before spotting her in the far corner.

"Tea or coffee?" asked Joyce, holding a jar of coffee in her one hand. Pinched between the thumb and index finger of the other was a rather screwed up triangular tea bag. "And we have biscuits too. Come on in; I'd close it too. Students have a tendency to spot you and there goes your five minutes of peace before change over."

Maya entered the office and closed the door behind her. "Tea, thank you," she said clutching her handbag closer and for comfort. She was hanging onto it for dear life, lest this be one more thing that might be lost.

As she poured hot water over the tea bags, Joyce darted her eyes towards two chairs nestled in the alcove that she could call her own in a shared office. "Year ten shortly, so I have a few minutes-fifteen-before they turn up and destroy the peace," she said looking at Maya with a gentle smile. "Sugar?" she asked, bringing the mug of tea over to Maya as well as a re-purposed jar of coffee that now contained coarse granulated brown sugar. A spoon was already in the mug, just in case. With the tea handed over, Joyce retuned toward the kettle to make her own drink.

Unscrewing the lid of the coffee jar, Maya scooped up

a heaped teaspoon of the sugar and stirred it into her tea. "Thank you, and for this," said Maya, as Joyce sat in the chair next to her. "For offering to listen," she added, blowing into her tea to help it cool down. In reality, blowing out a breath helped her feel a little less anxious. "I thought it was only the kids that came to see you. In the office, a couple of them have mentioned coming to speak to you from time to time."

Setting her tea onto a coaster in the shape of a brain, Joyce nodded. "Generally, yes," came the reply pushed the coaster back a little from the edge of her desk. "They might pop in, wanting someone to talk to; to listen to them and in a safe place. It's part of the pastoral support system with the personal tutors. Sometimes there's the safeguarding angle, I can listen but I can't keep any secrets."

Working in the office, Maya knew of safeguarding and also pastoral support systems that the school had recently put into place. "But you don't do counselling now do you?" she asked, her voice quivered with a spot of tentativeness.

Reaching for her tea, Joyce shook her head. "No, I'm afraid not. I listen, but I'm not a trained counsellor," she said taking a sip. "If a student comes to me with something beyond what I have to offer, then I have to signpost to someone who can help or the direct them to the pastoral team. Are you looking into counselling?" queried Joyce, aware of the recent bereavement that Maya had experienced. "Many people find it useful, especially with concerns such as bereavement."

Maya inclined her head slightly, giving her a look of uncertainty. Thoughts of counselling had crossed her mind, that much was true. It was one of many thoughts, all of which were clamouring for attention in her head. Pressing her mug to her lips, she took a mouthful of the sweet liquid. She found herself looking intently at Joyce and trying to think how the woman opposite might feel about all that she had experienced.

How might Joyce, a different person to her, process and deal with the loss of a child. She was happy to sit and silently pose questions, did she have children. Maya pursed her lips to ask that very question, only for gaze to move and across photographs that were stuck to the wall above the desk. Letting the heat of the mug of tea warm her fingers, she just couldn't speak.

Joyce had watched and let the silence hold in the space between them. She had observed Maya, how she had gone to speak and having seen the pictures on the wall said nothing. The silence that existed was gentle, linking two mothers; the difference being that the one of them was bereaved and recently at that. Joyce didn't know how that felt for her personally, but sat here close to Maya, she would do her best to try and understand. "Being back," said Joyce. "So soon after Millie's accident. Is that what you wanted to do, Maya?"

"I couldn't stay at home," replied Maya, "Not anymore. All cooped up and pretending that everything was okay, safe and as though nothing had happened." Pausing to draw breath, Maya then bit her lip as she felt sharpness behind her eyeballs that was accompanied by the warmth that was a tell-tale sign of tears approaching. She audibly gulped away the ball of tenseness that had gathered in her throat and continued. "Pictures," she said, picking up a hand to point at the picture of Joyce and a boy that she assumed was Joyce's son.

"Memories of Millie fill our house. Then there are the cookie," Maya tutted as she pronounced the last word. "There are cookies-raspberry and white chocolate-sat in the biscuit tin that she had bought for her Dad and I. They have been there ages and I couldn't bring myself to get rid of them. They've gone stale and soft. Then, then, Joyce, there is her room," Blinking, Maya freed a tears that escaped and attached themselves to her eyelashes. "I can't go in there. I sent Aldo in and to have a look-" Breaking off, Maya sniffled and sobbed, clutching her handbag into her lap.

Joyce listened still and carefully, not yet offering a

rejoinder to what Maya was saying. Instead, she opened a drawer beneath her desk and took out a rectangular box of tissues. Plucking out a couple in something of a paper plume, she offered them to Maya.

Not uttering a word, but gulping away sobs, Maya took the proffered tissues into her hands. She fiddled with the thin paper and absent mindedly folded it neatly into squares as she tried to catch her breath. "And he didn't say anything," continued Maya as she delicately dabbed the folded up square of tissue to her lower lash line. "He has said even less than normal," Maya moistened her dried lips with the tip of her tongue, before taking another mouthful of tea. "I wish, I wish that he would just say something. Something rather than just wander around in silence. I can't bear it."

Glancing at the white clock balanced rather precariously on a filing cabinet, Joyce double checked how much time she had left before year ten arrived. There was still some time left, as she posed a question. "This has made things more difficult, talking, having conversations?" she asked gently. "You must have been very close, with it being just the three of you."

"Aldo and Millie, they were very close," Maya answered. She almost smiled as a memory budded in her mind and started to form and flower. "I remember her being younger, smaller. Dressed in a pink fluffy tutu, with purple glittery ballerina pumps and just playing. She had broken a wand and she asked Aldo to fix it for her. Millie was Aldo's princess. She was my baby too, and I wish," Maya broke off to blow her nose into the folded tissue. "I wish, that he would talk to me," she drew in breath sharply, setting her teeth on edge a little.

"Sounds as though Millie was very much loved and by both of you," said Joyce looking into her tea, "This sounds a very difficult time for you," she said as her photographs came into her eye line. The one that caught her attention was that of Christopher and Adelphi; she could have sworn that Adelphi was grinning. "Losing someone that you love, losing someone who is very important to you and a big part of your life is a very difficult, challenging experience. Plus the thing is, Maya, people grieve in different ways. We are all very unique, as is the way that we process the world. How would like this to change, to get him to speak with you?"

Pressing her lips together, May also close her eyes as she shook her head. "No idea," she said opening her eyes. "If he can't talk to me, maybe he should speak to somebody else. Maybe I should too, speak with someone who isn't Aldo."

"Counselling," Joyce commented whilst sipping her tea and remembering what Maya had asked earlier.

"Could do. Sometimes speaking with someone who is at a distance is really very useful. It helps us to develop strategies that might help how we relate to those closest to us. And what you have described, the feelings, the memories; immediate as it is, there is a lot that you, Aldo might want to process that could help you both grieve. And this is process, there is no quick fix. What you have experienced, a counsellor might call it a traumatic life event. What you are feeling, thinking, is what would be expected as a response in this situation."

Maya rubbed a thumb across the tissue that she had folded up. "Traumatic life event," she repeated, "Certainly was," nodded Maya. "We've never had trauma, as a family. Not really."

"Counselling could be useful and for the both of you," offered Joyce. "You know, there might be school provision," she said moving her chair a little closer towards her desk; she peered at the school directory that was pinned to the wall amongst an assortment of pictures, posters and notices. "Support for staff, as part of an employee assistance programme. Speak with HR, it would all be confidential," she said looking over her shoulder. "And would definitely be more than me offering to listen." Joyce glanced at the clock again. "Not sure if this has helped. Year ten should appear soon."

Catching the movement of Joyce's eyes, Maya

horridly took in more of her tea. "Oh, you did say," she put her empty mug aside and smiled. "And thank you, for letting me have a moment. It's been hard to well, not explode and at everyone. It has helped," Maya said quietly as she got to her feet.

Mirroring Maya's movement, Joyce also stood as she held onto her tea. "You're welcome. My door is always open. Take your time," she commented. "It will take time to heal. Speak with HR, they will do their best to signpost and support you."

Maya nodded in acknowledgement and pulled the strap of her handbag up her arm and tucked into place upon her shoulder. "I will, but I could do with going home first," said Maya. "Thank you, and for the tea," she added, departing through the door.

As she watched Maya leave, Joyce couldn't help but feel a pang within. She really couldn't imagine what her colleague was going through. Christopher was a little older than Millie, and she could barely remember life before he had been born. Finishing her tea, she braced herself for the imminent arrival of her students. She would try and be there for Christopher when they saw each other next. Whilst Christopher was very much her human child, Adelphi had a very special place within their family.

Some part of her was able to understand and appreciate what Maya might be feeling and experiencing. When her son had called and to tell her about Adelphi, Joyce had listened to her sob; listened as he barely managed to choke out his words. The last time that she heard him cry and like that was when Christopher had been a small boy. It was at that point, that she had wanted to leave work go find him. She had been immediately transported decades into the past when her son had been vulnerable, saddened and wanted no one but his mum. Only Christopher had rejected her offer, he had blown his nose and rebuffed it. A trivial thing and he changed his tone within seconds, telling her that he would be okay; he would call later.

It had been days since he had checked in. However, now that he had sent a text message, she felt a little better, a little reassured. With students lining up in the corridor, Joyce adjusted her frame of mind to shift from mum towards teacher in loco parentis.

14 Lydia

In the mood for swing

All she wanted was an answer and for the moment there was none forthcoming. There was nothing in the affirmative or even the contrary negative. In not having a direct answer, there nothing to quell the deep rooted anxiety that was a tight knot in the pit of her stomach. Lydia just wanted to know whether or not they had something to focus on. It was an altogether curious feeling, as she had everything riding on there being a positive outcome.

There was no part of her that believed that she even consider the answer being no. In her mind, all she had to hear was yes. Nudging her car door closed with her hip, she depressed the button on the fob of her keys to activate the alarm. Tucking the fob into her crossover bag, she slung it over her shoulder whilst grasping tightly at another set of keys. These were a spare set for Lilly and Albie's, Matthew had the other set and the keys allowed them both to come and go as they wished. There was no sign of his car at home and he had yet to return to work. She deduced that he was probably spending time with Albie before resuming routine and normal life. Turing the key in the door, Lydia was mulling over in her mind that her timing probably hadn't been the best. Proposing marriage to Matthew and less than thirty six hours after his grandmother's funeral could have waited a while. Now they were circling each other with uncertainty, as though two tom cats who might engage in a duel or wanting to wrap each other up and in a deep hug. If only he had given her an answer, then this might not feel so much like a stand-off.

Closing the door behind her, Lydia almost jumped as the silence of her thoughts was shattered. Her thoughts were shattered and thrown askew by the sound of what she assumed was a trombone. There were more, more instruments and their sound travelled down the hall a short distance from the hall. With her curiosity piqued, Lydia moved in something of a hypnotic trance towards the sound of trumpets and a saxophone combining for a quick beat section of heightened rhythm. Ahead of her, was Matthew standing at his grandparent's dining table and flicking through manila brown paper dust covers. She hung back a little to watch Matthew slide out the shiny vinyl records; each one was slid a little so that he could peer inside the packet before sliding it back. For each one the label was exposed in the centre of dust cover, some were brightly coloured and in contrast to the cover.

Lydia watched for a least a couple of minutes, the record continued whilst she did. The music gently ebbed away the time provide something of an interesting soundtrack. There were quite a few records strewn across the table, as though waiting for their turn to be played upon the turntable that was currently occupied. Despite the odd squeak and click, the music had a wonderfully crisp quality that was almost ephemeral and made it hang in the air. Lydia smiled and bit the side of cheek as she imagined quavers and crochets filling the space around Matthew's head as it bobbed in rhythm. His toe was also tapping and that was even more surreal to watch.

The music wasn't entirely alien to her; Lydia had had known Lilly and Albie play their records often. The turntable would be positioned in the corner on a small table and the music would filter and float around the house behind conversations and general milling. She had never heard the records played like this and at this volume. It sounded much more alive, vibrant and full of feeling compared to when she had heard it before, played discreetly and at a lower volume. Watching Matthew tap his feet, Lydia couldn't help but imagine a brass band standing by the fire place, with the sax players swaying back and forward to keep time to the music.

"Lydia?" Matthew had turned around and was stood in front of her with mouth a little agape. "Hellooooo?" he repeated her name a few times before she snapped out of watching the imaginary brass band.

She was somewhat taken aback as she blinked back into reality. Her face was frozen with the expression of complete blankness. Lydia had been lost in the deep recesses of her imagination, with a swing band, a parquet floor and lots and lots of dancers. Dancers who swooshed and swirled around the floor dressed in dressed with full petticoats and looked as though they were gliding on air. "Swing," she whispered, the word was barely audible as it escaped her lips and it came out rather mangled.

Coughing and putting a curled fist to her mouth, she sighed and looked at Matthew again, this time with something of a less spaced expression. "Swing," Lydia repeated. This time she repeated it a little more firmly and a lot louder. "What are you up to?" she asked, moving passed as the music stopped and the arm of the player moved across the turn-table as it was released from a groove.

"Erm, just playing," replied Matthew, picking up a record.

Lydia dumped her bag behind the turn-table to take Matthew's hand and picked up another record. "May I have this dance?" she asked quietly.

"Dance, here?" Matthew was somewhat incredulous as put down the record that he held and was dragged to the middle of the room.

"Here," nodded Lydia, and very firm in her reply. She took a firmer grasp of his hand and pulled him into hold. There was something somewhat unnerving about this, and she only just knew what she was doing.

"Music might help," laughed Matthew, departing briefly to the player and moving the arm back into place. "Okay, where did you have me," he said returning back to hold.

"You'll have to lead," said Lydia, she didn't dance per se, least of all ball room. She did however know that Albie and Lilly were able to, and often talked about how they used to go to dances. Lilly had described the evocative sounds of the swing bands being played; sometimes there would even be a live band. She remembered Lilly going positively dreamy eyed over the descriptions of dresses, hair styles and the soft swooshing of petticoats across parquet floors. "You do know the steps, don't you?" asked Lydia, her eyes narrowing in query.

Matthew squinted back at her, his expression didn't look altogether hopeful. "Hold on a second," he said, letting going of her hands and digging his 'phone out of his pocket. Tapping furiously as the touchscreen and poking around the internet, Matthew eventually found something to help. Videos of how they could dance, and have a go at doing jive to the music that they had started to play.

Shoulder to shoulder they watched; they watched the clip several times. Matthew had to return to the player a number of times to reposition the arm and re-start the music.

Eventually and rather impatiently, Lydia tapped Matthew's hand and dragged him to the middle of the room. "Okay, Okay, I think I got it. Let's give it a go," she said, gliding him into hold and putting his 'phone onto the table. "And straighten up, don't slouch," Lydia half tutted as she threw her own shoulders back and straightened out her spine.

It was hearing the pulsating sound of the brass and drums that caught Albie's attention. The opening bars with the rise and fall of the saxophone heralding in a swing band immediately transported him back a good sixty years; the sound that had wafted into the kitchen as he had made tea for him and Matthew. Setting the tea cups down upon kitchen table and followed the crochets and quavers that cascaded invitingly towards him. Each and every sound was a musical breadcrumb that urged him to move in their wake and towards the lounge. He knew this piece of music backwards, all three minutes and thirty seconds of it. As it flowered towards him, Albie could feel the years shift around him.

The ivory linoleum of the kitchen gave way to the honey hued rectangles of parquet floor. It was sometimes in the forties, the war wasn't over yet and swing was king. Slowly but surely it was all coming back to Albie as the music played. He couldn't have been more than twenty, Lilly was a shade younger. They had just started courting, both were unsure if Albie might be called up and soon. He was eventually, and like many others; there was a huge amount of trepidation with Albie being a reservist. The war was changing the world and beyond the happy, heady ear of the dances in the local hall, it was becoming an increasingly scary place to live in.

Lilly had pulled Albie to his feet as the trumpets had sounded and was dragging him towards the centre of the floor. He remembered almost skidding across the floor, his shoes squeaking in protest as he moved. His last pair had given up the ghosts and he been forced to mix up an assortment of coupons just to get this pair. He wanted to get a good pair of shoes, to take Lilly dancing and impress her. She loved to dance and he had asked her to come with him to tonight so that he could forget. Albie just wanted to spend as much time with her as he could, and forget that they had such little time left together. The newsreels were becoming greyer each day with carnage on the continent; spending time with Lilly helped to forget all that.

Albie had been all fingers and thumbs as he was finding it difficult to lead. He didn't mind dancing, but the jive had him bumbling around whilst trying not to step on Lilly's feet as they moved to the rise and fall of the music. Tonight there was a band, rather than the usual case of vinyl on the player. It might not have been Glenn Miller's Army Air Force band, but the pulled together band of musicians were doing a good job of playing as though they were the real deal. 'In the mood' was steaming through the air as Lilly half lead around the floor and moved them both with the strains and pulses of the band.

"You'll have to learn how jive," Lilly had pulled him closer and spoken into his ear.

He had got a waft of violets, not resisted being pulled in and nodded in agreement. He would have done anything for her; all she had to do was to ask. At that moment, Albie could not even imagine his life without her. Sooner or later, he would have to gain the courage to tell her.

"Watch out," Lilly had tapped his shoulder and turned him away from a couple that were headed straight towards them. A couple in full flight as the petticoat of a skirt nudged at Albie's leg and they swung out of the way to avoid a straight on collision.

Albie had waved at the couple; the woman gave a garnet smile back as her blonde locks bobbed and bounced with her motion. She was beautiful, quite striking actually. Not as beautiful as Lilly, he had thought and returned his gaze towards her.

"Marry me," he had said at the end of the song as the trumpets sounded. His words had got a little lost with the crescendo and he had no immediate indication of whether or not she had heard him.

"And again!" Lilly pulled him around again to avoid a further would be collision. She waved this time, and at someone she knew. This woman was had darker features; her hair hidden within a red and white scarf that was pinned and knotted tightly into place upon her scalp.

Albie was convinced that Lilly hadn't heard him. It took him a while but he would ask her again and just before he left. With one thing and another, they would eventually tie the knot; Lilly was hell bent on teaching him to jive and properly. There would be children and a grandson.

Albie had moved and towards the lounge as he had reminisced. Once there, he lowered himself into a chair by the door. He was yet to be spotted by Matthew and Lydia and as he sat quietly he watched them dance. Watched them move awkwardly around the lounge whilst trying not to elbow each other or knock something to the floor. He and Lilly had done the same thing, and so many years before; watching them, it might as well have been him and Lilly.

There was however, something that didn't quite sit well with him. Albie had noticed that for the last few days, there seemed to be something not quite right between the young couple. He wasn't going to pry, and that was probably Lilly would have stopped him from doing. She might have also told him to hang on if he was going to ask; Matthew had a tendency to chew on something and share it with him and Lilly when he felt it was right to do so. Albie smiled as Matthew clipped Lydia's ankle and subsequently caught a playful elbow to the ribs. Matthew and Lilly had spent so many afternoons sat in the kitchen and putting the world to rights over tea and cake. He himself had listened, nodded in all the right places as Lilly offered their grandson words of sage advice.

"Turn the other way!" Albie called out, leaning forward in seat before deciding to stand. "Turn the other way, Matthew."

Matthew's head snapped towards the sound of his grandfather's voice. No sooner had Albie spoken, was he headed straight towards him and Lydia. "Grandad, how long you been there?" he asked; he was ushered aside and found his hand being removed from Lydia's to be replaced by Albie's.

"Long enough to see that you weren't doing it right," Albie's rejoinder came as he took Lydia's fingers into his. He patted Matthew's shoulder and nodded towards the turntable that had once again fallen silent.

Laughing quietly, Lydia was compliant as Albie took her hand. She noticed that he had something of a glimmer in his eyes; a sparkling glimmer that been absent and for such a long time. It had been dulled and disappeared during the time that Lilly was ill, and here it was making a return. The return of Albie's glimmer made Lydia a feel a little more positive and before she could blink, the music was back with the band in full swing. It wasn't long before Lydia found herself being lead around the small square space of the lounge. She was mindful that she was still something of a novice; yet Albie lead her with practiced ease and at a speed that was contrary to his advanced years.

Charged with keeping the music playing, Matthew ensured that the arm was moved back onto position every the track ended. He was still a little perplexed. Firstly, he was surprised by Lydia deciding to dance and here in the lounge. Secondly, he was taken aback a little by how quickly his grandfather had moved; the older man seemed to have gained something of spring in step and his confidence had become bolstered.

As the finals bars played and the rhythm moved towards trumpets, Albie started to slow down. His smile faded a little as he felt his feet become a little heavier. "Lilly, I have to slow down," he all but whispered. "I am not as young as I was."

Lydia would have been forgiven, to have misheard. Only she hadn't, Albie had definitely called her Lilly. She nodded and slowed down so as to bring them both to a stop. She look passed Albie and waved at Matthew to stop the music. As the music subsided with a scratch, Lydia led Matthew's grandfather towards a chair.

"You would be a fool to let her go," said Albie, waggling a finger towards Matthew as he settled back into the chair. "Whatever it is between you, that's got you avoiding each other, drop it," he pronounced the last two words heavily, his hands landing with a thwack upon his thighs as though in emphasis. "Especially, Matthew, as Lydia didn't think twice about jiving with you."

Lydia exchanged a knowing look with Matthew. She didn't expect for them both to be rumbled, and had thought that she had been doing a good job of disguising things. However, as Albie had clearly clocked onto something, her unease was subsiding further. So much so, she pulled out a chair from beneath the dining table and sat alongside Albie.

At this point, Matthew knew. Knew that Lydia was going break the heaviness between them; she was going bring Albie up to speed and about her proposal. Albie was right; they had been skulking around and avoiding each other. He had a feeling that he was about to be ambushed and he wasn't too sure whether he would be able to do anything about it.

"You tell him, Albie," said Lydia, looking over her shoulder at Matthew with an arched brow. "I did ask him, only he didn't give me a straight answer."

"About jiving?" posed Albie, looking at his grandson.

"To marry her," sighed Matthew, as he lifted the arm of the turntable and removed the disc from the deck. "Kinda caught me off guard to be honest," he muttered, casting his gaze downward towards the discs that littered the table.

Albie's brow creased, and his mouth turned down at the corners as he looked back the woman sat close to him. "Lydia, I asked Lilly twice; she didn't hear me the first time, 'cause of the trumpets," he said waggling a finger at the turntable. "And good for you," he continued, taking her hand into his and giving her fingers a gentle squeeze. "For having the courage and asking him; it's not easy to do, I assure you. Lilly would have had you being a gentleman,

Matthew," Albie looked at his grandson rather tersely, fixing him to the spot with a heavy gaze. He couldn't help but chastise him.

As Matthew stood before him, he looked a lot like he had done when a small boy and about to be told off for something. "The first time, Lilly didn't hear me. And when I asked her the second time, I remember being so nervous that I wet a shirt straight through just thinking about it. And when she said yes," he grinned as he spoke, his face had lit up and his eyes were glinting once more. "I wondered why I had got all het up for. Oh, I was making tea!" exclaimed Albie. He had forgotten all about it as he travelled through his memories of Lilly. "Lydia, don't suppose you would stick the kettle on, Matthew and I were about to have one. You get one too. Tea pot and cups are still on the side, actually. Whilst you do that, Matthew, I need you upstairs. Some of Lilly's things still need a good home."

"Can do, certainly," agreed Lydia, releasing Albie's hand. "Any cake floating around," she asked, rising to her feet and turning towards the kitchen.

"On the side," Albie half shouted as she departed. Then he turned to his grandson, and remembered that they were both old enough. He was too old to use force, and Matthew was a grown man. Albie shook his head in disbelief and dismissed the thought of shaking Matthew to his sense.

Matthew arched his brows, he knew that look. It was the look of Albie willing him to make the right decision, to make the right choice and be mindful of the consequences. The look that told Matthew, that if he made the right decision, then they would both be laughing. He remembered Albie giving him the look throughout both his childhood and his adolescence. Thankfully, it had appeared rather less so far during his adult years.

Feeling every one of his accumulated years, Albie staggered to his feet. He growled a little at the sound of squeaking and popping joints. This was a musical score that was increasingly more frequent and definitely frustrating.

Matthew moved quickly and towards his grandad; the idea was to provide some support, and his hand was poised just in case.

"Oh, stop," tutted Albie. "I'm old, yes, but I am not dead yet." There was a little burr in his voice, and his face had contorted in discomfort. "Upstairs, you go on. I shall follow," he gave Matthew a gentle shove and hung back a little. He would move on and in his own time.

Matthew knew better than to argue; Lilly and Albie both had a stubborn streak. Slowly, but steadily he moved the stairs, he looked over his shoulder once or twice to make sure Albie was okay.

"In there," said Albie as they arrived at the top of the stairs. He inclined his head towards the second bedroom where Lilly had spent her last few days. The room had been tidied since, the bed changed and remade. All of the assorted medical machines that Lilly had needed had been returned. He shuffled passed Matthew and pointed towards the bed.

"Sit down a moment," Albie patted his grandson on the shoulder as he edged passed.

Matthew did as he was told and took a seat on the edge of the bed. It was softer than the hospital type bed that Lilly had been in. Covered by a brightly coloured and floral design cover it looked a livelier too. He sat with his hands placed either side of him on the curve of the bed.

Albie himself was headed towards a walnut wardrobe. The sort of wardrobe that was no longer made, with a distinctive grain across the door and art deco inspired curves. Unlike modern furniture, it was rather robustly made and didn't have the same expiration date as something made from cheap chipboard and stapled together. With a deep click, the door opened towards Albie; his reflection cast onto a mirror on the inside of the door. On the left was a rather cavernous space that was filled with Albie's suits that hung from a brass hanging bar. The right hand side was compartmentalised and covered with a glass fronted door with bevelled edges. He opened the door and revealed a selection of small boxes and jewellery, all neatly positioned on the shelves within.

"Knowing Lydia, she will ask you again," Albie turned slightly towards Matthew whilst searching the compartment. "She is not the sort to just give up," he added as he located a red square box.

Holding the box between his hands, Albie ambled towards Matthew at the end of the bed. He prized the lid open and sat next to his grandson. Albie placed the box onto Matthew's knee and carefully so as to safely balance it. His own knee was a little wobbly having danced and also climbed the stairs. The ascent up was becoming increasingly more difficult. Inside the box was a black velvet covered foam pad, resting on top of which were pair of earrings. At the centre of each was a ruby surrounded by diamonds. Below the earrings rested a pendent that matched them.

"Don't make her ask you twice," Albie stated quietly. "I suggest that you get in there before she has a chance to regroup and try again," he put a finger to the box as it looked as though Matthew's knee was about to go as wobbly as his. "There are bits and pieces that will go to your Mum and Dad. Lilly wanted these to go to Lydia, and she left some instructions."

Matthew had been fixed upon the box as it rested on his knee; he tensed up a little, hoping that the box wouldn't fall off and onto the carpet below. Slowly, he turned his head towards Albie so that he might listen and carefully to the instructions.

Albie moved his finger towards the pendent, the knee was definitely wobbling. "I never had the money to get Lilly a diamond ring, and it was years before I was able to get these for her. Use the diamonds, to make, buy-whatever you want-get Lydia a ring. Make sure that Lydia has diamonds, Lilly stressed that. The rubies, you can do whatever you like with them," Albie slid his arm across and tapped the box closed.

"Tea!" Lydia's voice bounced up the stairs and broke the moment.

"Coming!" Both men chorused having had the same thought at exactly the same time.

"Box clever," Albie told Matthew, adopting a conspiratorial tone. "Quick," he said hearing feet upon the stairs. "Pocket," he added, jabbing a finger into Matthew's arm as the sound of feet got louder and closer.

Lydia appeared at the door and leant against the door frame. "Tea's done," she said with a smile; though she did think for a moment that the two of them looked as though they were up to something.

Using his hands to raise himself up, Albie puffed out his cheeks. "I'll pour shall I?" he said to Lydia, shepherding her back down the stairs. He glanced backward over his shoulder at Matthew, willing him to secret away the box that was currently tucked in below his knee.

Pulling out the box, Matthew held it between his thumbs and index fingers. He really did feel rather ambushed. At the same time, he knew that Albie meant well. To be sat here and with Lilly's jewellery was intensely overwhelming. Lilly and Lydia had got on well, and they had become very close. More often than not, they would spend a great deal of time plotting and conspiring about him. It varied from persuading him to have a hair-cut, get a new suit or bending his arm over something simple. For Lilly to bequeath these items to him and Lydia was really very important. Now all he had to do was follow Albies's and Lilly's instructions. 'Woe betide,' he could almost hear Lilly say, 'If you do not.'

15 Nandini

Soul food

Red and blue, a striped sock fluttered in the breeze. Alongside a singlet, it was pegged to one of four lines on the spinner and had been left behind when the rest of the laundry had been taken down. Both the sock and singlet were spotted with raindrops and starting to become darker in colour as the moisture was absorbed into fabric. As Raj closed the door of the conservatory behind him, he caught sight of the forgotten items and briefly closed his eyes in frustration.

Tucked under his arm was a white plastic basket, on the rim of which a film of raindrops had formed with some failing to hang on and sliding to the wooden floor. Looking at the spinner, Raj could see that whilst he had rescued the laundry from initially quite light drops of rain, it was falling faster now and in were visible vertical streams descending to the ground. Seeing the clothes heaped in the basket, Raj pressed his teeth into his bottom lip. With the bulk of the laundry safe and indoors, he was in two minds as he tried to decide whether the two items were worth salvaging.

"You left two!"

The shrill sound of Nandini's voice suggested that his decision would be made for him.

"Move, I'll get them," she said, bustling passed him and through the door. "Everything wet," Nandini told him, looking over her shoulder at her son as she walked through the rain and towards the spinner. She had moved as quickly as she could, and as the rain fell faster her clothes became splattered and wet. Nandini's cardigan was absorbing raindrops, changing from being grey in colour to almost black; her scarf billowed in the breeze from her shoulder and she snatched at it with her hand to settle it back to her side.

"Mum, leave them!" Raj protested and tutted quietly as he held the door open and immediately felt the sharp impact of cold rain upon his skin.

Clutching the sock and singlet towards her bosom, Nandini shuffled back towards the conservatory to step up and in. "You just left them," she said dumping the items into basket that her son still held onto. "Only two things and you left them. That's Koby's sock," Nandini waggled a finger at her son before looking at her feet. "My slippers gone wet now," she huffed loudly; her slippers were indeed a little soggy. Lifting up her one foot she tried to shake away the raindrops and left a splodge of footprint behind on the wooden flooring.

"Could have just left them," Raj muttered, sounding a lot like a belligerent child. He grimaced at the large pile of damp clothes that now included the sock and single that he had been prepared to abandon.

Nandini threw her son a look, a look that suggested a definite disdain and disagreement with his statement. "And waste the energy drying them later, just those two things. No," she said shaking her head and reaching for the basket. "Tea, please," she added as she shuffled off and away.

"Tea," whispered Raj, letting out a pent up breath in relief. Tea he could deal with, the tumble dryer less so. He followed his mum as she moved away, hoping that she wouldn't lead him to the kettle.

Nandini had shuffled off through the lounge with Raj in two. She left him in the kitchen and carried on beyond into the utility room where both the dryer and washing machine were housed. She knew that Raj was perfectly capable of taking down the washing; the issue came with loading the tumble dryer. This was clearly a step too far, and a job that she and Rachel had long since decided to take up between themselves rather than leave to Raj to be done reliably. Nandini's brow furrowed as she stepped downwards onto the grey concrete floor of the utility room. There was a horrible, soggy dampness beneath her soles that made walking uncomfortable. Before she got to the machines, she paused and lifted her feet out of the very wet slippers. She groaned softly as her feet felt the coldness of the concrete in the lean to utility room. The coldness of concrete underfoot was marginally better than wet feet.

As she walked towards the tumble dryer, foot prints were left in her wake and marked her route. Toes held tightly together with the gentle curve of yet to fall arches. Nandini planted the plastic basket upon the worktop that rested across the top of the washing and tumble drying machine. She stooped to open the door of the tumbler dryer, and at her wrist gold bangles jangled as they hit plastic and metal. With the door open, she pulled out the filter and balled up the lint and threads that accumulated in the netting.

Pressing the ball onto the worktop, she slid the filter back into place. Her hand moved towards the damp and heavy clothes in the basket, she pulled the whole thing towards her so that garments would be easier to grab a hold. Scooping up damp clothes-a couple of shirts and the abandoned sock-Nandini tossed them into the drum of the dryer.

It had taken time for her and Rachel to work out a routine for their daily life. There had been clashes at first; the idea of living with an elderly mother-in-law had been a challenge for them both. Throwing two socks into the drum, Nandini felt a pull of memory that harked back to when Rachel and Raj had been newly married; the atmosphere in the house had become somewhat tense. For her, having her son and daughter-in-law living with her was not unusual. She was traditional in herself, this was custom and practice for as long as she could remember. Nandini herself had lived with her own in-laws before coming here and to a different country to that of her birth.

Being in a different country, had however made her think and she had never pressed the issue with Raj. In all honesty, she had expected him to move out in the same way that his peers had. She was more than aware that the generation that she was part of, needed to move with the times. Nandini had been quite glad when Raj had gone away to university; there were lessons for him to learn, and he needed to stand upon his own two feet.

Compared to her contemporaries, the wives and mothers who like her had travelled over decades before, Nandini prided herself on being a little more progressive and forward thinking. When Raj and

Rachel had married in a riot of colour that was an Anglo-Indian amalgamation, she had felt more than just happy.

It was the sound of her stomach grumbling and the thought of chappatis that made her bottom lip tremble slightly. Even though it was years ago, Nandini hung onto the memory, prizing it tightly in her chest as though it was a precious jewel that she could not bear to part with. She remembered being in the kitchen, preparing dough so that she could make chappatis. She liked them, so did Raj. For her, they were a staple accompaniment to most meals.

Nandini still liked to cook, to prepare food and the dishes that she had been raised eating. The same dishes that Raj had been raised eating, and more often than not had been part of the food parcels she would send with when he came back home on visits from university. Raj had moved back, married and Rachel moved in too. Cooking became a different experience at that point, and there were clashes in cuisines in the early days. Rachel was intrigued; the Indian food that she had heard of, eaten in restaurants was different. She became curious as to how Nandini prepared it, how it was all so different. Curious and intrigue summed up this entire memory.

Nandini had put a colourless plastic mixing bowl onto the worktop, and sat next to it was a pint glass of water drawn from the tap. Into the bowl, she had heaped grey white flour that she needed to make dough. Her hands were covered, dusted in flour that had been scooped out of a box that sat in a cupboard to the right of the stove. She had turned on her heel to move towards the sink where she had left a tea towel. It was then that she caught sight of Rachel peering around the kitchen door. She looked as though she was skulking and had not expected Nandini to be in the kitchen.

Rachel had blinked with her mouth agape. Nandini had mirrored her daughter-in-law's actions, and she remembered feeling a strange sense of anxiety that fizzled in her stomach. They were still quite new to each other then. They had certainly met each other before the wedding, and got to know each other a little. Now they were sharing a house, but there was still a heavy sense of unfamiliarity and deference that led them to tentatively circle each other from time to time. Standing there in front of her with one hand pressed to the door, Rachel looked as though she wanted to say something but couldn't decide what or how.

Nandini had picked up the tea towel, unfolded it and rubbed the fabric over her hands as she smiled at her rather nervous looking daughter-in-law. "You okay?" she had asked, folding the tea towel into a neat rectangle and draping it over hands. She was asking to be polite, to be civil to her son's wife. Yet the woman who stood before her, with grey-blue eyes that were dull with worry and caramel coloured hair that felt to her jawline with a curl, looked as though she was in need of a hug or a hand to reassure her. Nandini had stepped forward, Rachel had done the same. They were stood face to face and looking at each other rather searchingly.

Moving her gaze from Nandini, Rachel had looked at the mixing bowl and then back at Nandini. Her lips had twitched, pursed to move and giving a glimmer of white teeth. A look of enquiry had formed on her face, the look of intrigue and curiosity.

Nandini failed to realise at first, her head inclined slightly to the side as she tried to work out what had Rachel so worried. There was no part of her that wanted Rachel to be a stranger in her own home. They might have come from different cultures and therein different worlds, but with Raj they had something in common.

"For rotis," Nandini had said. "Chappatis," she added for clarification. She turned a little towards the mixing bowl sat upon the worktop. "I tried to teach Raj," Nandini had sighed heavily as she turned back towards Rachel. "But he made them wrong, left them raw in the middle," she said shaking her head.

"Well," finally Rachel spoke. "May be," her tone was rather uncertain. "May be, I could…."

It was then that the penny dropped for Nandini. "Yes," she nodded, pressing the folded up tea towel to her hip and moving towards the mixing bowl. "If you have a look," Nandini continued, beckoning Rachel to come and join. "Maybe he won't get it wrong. Can you help me, please?" she asked, putting the tea towel aside.

By the mixing bowl, Nandini stood shoulder to shoulder with Rachel. Together they made the dough, making a well to start and adding water to the flour. Mixing it to form soft dough, from which they could make chappatis. Nandini had gone through the process slowly; she was used to doing so quickly and largely without thinking. Everything was described in detail as she gathered up flour and water with her fingers. Nandini had been impressed by how Rachel had taken it all in and eagerly, asking questions as they moved onto pinching balls of dough between their fingers to then roll out the chappatis.

It was in that hour, that the heavy sheet of icy awkwardness that had lain between them was well and truly broken and allowed to melt away. Sharing the process with Rachel had felt like the right thing to do, to make things easier with no sense of distance or awkwardness. They would do this again, make the dough and roll the chappatis. There would be times when the dough would be awfully hard. It would be a dense, unpliable mass that would make rolling difficult and double up as a work out for their arms. At other times, the dough that they formed would be a wet, sticky and stretchy ball that was far too elastic to use. There was frustration, at chappatis rolled out too thickly and being raw in the middle. Nandini saw burned fingers that caught the heat as the tips were yet to develop resistance to hot metal. They ate miss-shaped rotis that started off round and regular, only to develop modern art edges. Edges that didn't matter, the rotis were always made so lovingly that the shape became inconsequential.

Raj had been a little surprised. Some part of Nandini believed that Rachel was glad to know about food, making it and sharing it. Nandini had enjoyed it, showing Rachel how to roll out the chappatis, stretching them and flipping them over to cook them through. Rachel had picked it all up so much quicker than Raj, that much was certain. Before long, Rachel asked about other things. She had wanted to know about dishes which were easy to make, that she could have a go at making. There was genuine curiosity, a desire to know and understand a world that that she viewed as being different to her own. There had been pitfalls and positives, burned chappatis and slightly raw potatoes. It had all helped to bring mother-in-law and daughter-in-law together.

Nandini bundled the last of the clothes into the dryer, and then took a crumpled up piece of tissue from her cardigan pocket. The tissue rustled as she dabbed and pressed it against each eye in turn. There were other memories too that also made her eyes water and sting. Eyes that ordinarily were so dry that she had to use liquid tear. This deluge of actual tears was uncomfortable as she blinked them away. Her normally quite placid and stoical expression changed as she muffled sobs.

Nandini remembered that Rachel had suffered with morning sickness whilst expecting Caliope. Infusions of ginger and mint had been lovingly prepared to soothe away the feelings of nausea. Rachel had even tried to pick up a few words and phrases of Punjabi. There had been a few times at family events where some of Nandini's less liberal peers had spoken of Rachel in hushed conspiratorial tones that had left them both feeling uncomfortable. When Rachel had shared this with her, Nandini had coached her a little. This coaching had allowed Rachel to answer their mother-tongued barbs in almost pitch perfect rejoinders that had made Nandini very proud to call Rachel her daughter-in-law. She was however more than that, much more.

In Nandini's mind, Rachel was her daughter and that was it. She had lost her daughter, Raj had lost his wife, Caliope and Koby had lost their mother. All that they had was now just memories, and memories that felt so far away in time and space.

Passing a palm across her cheek, Nandini swept away a clutch of tears that had streamed away from her eyes. Rubbing tissue across her palms, she once more dabbed it at her eyes and more firmly this time to allow all her tears to be dried away. She could hear Raj move in the kitchen over the sound of a boiling kettle and clinking mugs. She truly missed Rachel and she knew that she wasn't alone in that feeling. They were all still grieving: her, Raj and the children. As she drew her tissue away from her eyes, she saw that one of Koby's socks was once more left behind and languishing in the bottom of the plastic basket. Opening the door, she picked it up with the tissue still in her hand and lobbed the sock inside. As the door closed, the machine re-started and hummed. Its song was a bass line of socks thudding rhythmically against sides; a song that Nandini knew well.

Plus, she had no Lilly to talk to. Lilly was gone too, and Nandini sobbed once more, muffling her sounds with the tissue pressed to mouth. This had been hard, losing two people that she cared about, so quickly and so close together. She gave up on the now very damp tissue, and tugging at her sleeve wiped away her sobs.

Letting out a long breath, Nandini realised that she had not cried like this and for years. She had not cried at such length and felt so hurt since her husband had died. Even then, Nandini had cried alone, with no one knowing. Not even Raj had seen or heard her cry.

Not then, or at any other point. She wasn't supposed to, to cry or be seen crying by others. Grief was always private, this was a family matter and no one else needed to know.

"Mum, your tea's-" Raj had appeared at the door and was momentarily taken away. "Mum, you okay?" he asked, stepping forwards a little as he held a mug of tea for her.

Nandini's thought processes were jolted askew. "Yes," she half yelled, half exclaimed and furiously wiped away tears. Nandini glared at her son, not so much in anger, but trying to brook tears that might still fall and freely. "Am fine," she sniffed and blew her nose into the woe be gone tissue. Clearing her throat, she took the mug from him and padded past through the door into the kitchen. Feeling his heavy gaze upon her, she pressed her tissue into his palm. The tissue she could hand over and easily, the feeling of loss not so much.

16 Death

Destroyer of worlds

It was the scent that got Gorbind. Perfume that clung to the chunky knit mink coloured scarf as it was placed delicately into an evidence bag. There were other items, harvested away from the deceased. The body of whom had been placed with gentle reverence upon autopsy room table. Her dignity was preserved by a light weight pale blue sheet and he watched in silence as it was drawn up and over her face. His first thought was that of a sleeping angel, lying in repose in between missions from The Almighty. His second thought had been of his own daughter, his little girl; he could not even dare to think of a world where she did not exist. Gorbind made a mental note to hug his daughter a little closer when he clocked off later.

Even now and after a good few years on the job, seeing dead bodies lain out so cold filled him with a sense of heavy unease. All he could do was to paint on a cold exterior that gave the impression of being barely human. This allowed him some distance to do his job as best he could. The downside was the joke amongst his colleagues that he was in some part android and without feeling. He was here to get a few more details. There was a witness waiting at the station, a friend of the deceased young woman. Gorbinds heart missed as beat as she was being taken away to be placed into cold iciness of storage.

It was down to Gorbind to interview the witness and get a picture of the rather tragic events that had led him to be here.

He was about to leave and through strips of colourless plastic that hung at the door when something else caught his attention. Sat on a grey metal tray was a pair of glasses. Thick framed and fashionably so; the one lens was fractured and corresponded to the deceased eye being an oxidised red mess as the socket had caved in. Sat next to the tray was another bag, containing a duffel coat that must have been a little damp. With evaporation, vapour had misted up the bag as it cooled. Rubbing a palm across his stubble clad tense jaw, Gorbind centred himself to leave. He still had his daughter and he held onto that fact within his hard. A couple of colleagues had been despatched to the young lady's parents to deliver the news that every parents hoped that they would never hear.

***

Joel was starting to feel cold. His dark woollen coat was sodden through and through and felt heavy against his shoulders. Yet, removing it so that he might be rid of the damp and warm up was the last thing on his mind. All that he could think about, all that he could see in his head was Millie. Millie lying in the road and getting wet as the rain lashed down. Then there was the sound that felt as though it was playing on loop in his ears.

It started with the thunderous roar of an engine, the sound of a souped up Subaru. Added to that was the shocked murmurings of pedestrians as the high street came to a stop. There had been a screeching of wheels, sharp and piquing his attention. Then there was the thud as Millie met with the car, quickly and violently. It hadn't registered at first, Millie been silent. She had made no sound, no screaming. There were no cries as she was tossed aloft and then fell to the ground in a crumpled heap onto her side.

Fixed in his seat and lost in his own world, Joel's train of thought was derailed by movement. A beige plastic cup had been set before him upon a scratchy looking piece of paper that could only just call itself a napkin. Joel blinked himself into a more cogent state. The man responsible for placing the cup before him moved away and positioned himself behind the table that sat between them.

"It was two sugars wasn't it?" asked Gorbind as he draped his coat over a chair. He had gripped onto the jacket firmly, and held the garment by its firm and fleshy fabric shoulders. "You might want to warm up a little," he added as he pulled out the metal chair to take a seat.

With his sleeves rolled up to his elbows, Gorbind splayed his fingers across the sheets of paper that were required to record Joel's statement. In anticipation, a biro with a chewed up cap sat between his digits. The ink was half way up the barrel and would probably only last long enough to do the job. Details were important, so the pen had an awful lot to do in committing what Joel recounted to the page. The testimony that Joel provided would be critical, if the woman that Gorbind had seen on the table was to receive justic. Realising that he had sat down rather uncomfortably and was slouching in his seat, Gorbind moved his elbows back a little and sat upright in a more attentive position.

Joel nodded and silently took the rather flimsy plastic cup into his hands. Heat plumed in white tendrils from the surface of the liquid and he took some comfort from the heat that radiated through the plastic and towards his cold palms. He felt the heat hit his cheeks as he took a mouthful of the tea and could taste the sweetness from the sugar. The two sugars did little to disguise the origins of the tea. Vending machine tea was never going to be a symphony of liquid joy. It would do, and for now. As poor quality as the tea might be, it would help to warm him up.

Gorbind picked up the black biro in his left hand. With his other hand, he positioned the sheets of paper diagonally in front of him. Curling his elbow so that the pen was poised, he looked up and at Joel. "Just a few questions, Joel," he stated gently as he held the young man's gaze. "Take your time and give me as much detail as you can as to what happened. First thing that we need to do-and I know you that you are probably feeling a fairly shaken-is to find out what you saw, and from start to finish. I'll try and keep up, and when you finish, I'll ask you any questions that I might have," he said tapping the end of the now uncapped biro and leaving two inky dots on the page before him.

Letting out a breath that felt as though it had been trapped for an eternity, Joel looked into his tea. The redness of the liquid betrayed the fact that this cup of tea had not been made by a human but by soulless machinery. For the moment, this didn't quite feel real. This all felt like a dream. What he was about to say, it felt as though he was going to be telling a story, a fairy tale. "We'd been in The Bird Cage," started Joel.

"A few of us had gone in, after lectures, just to have a quick drink. Only Millie was a bit stressed out, something to do with a lab practical. She wanted to go home. So we left, and I was going to walk her home. It had only just started raining. I did ask her about taking a taxi, but Millie wasn't interested. Walking it was then." Joel paused to hold the cup tighter in his hands. Hands that still felt cold as he curled his fingers around the beige plastic.

"We didn't get far down the road. As far as Obi's the newsagents," he continued, removing a hand from the cup to waggle his index finger. As though that would somehow make the location clearer and provide the detective who sat across from him a window into what had happened. "I needed some milk, I wanted milk," said Joel. "I drink that much tea and I've run out. I told Millie, that I was going in. She said to carry on, and that she'd meet me on the other side of the road. The traffic lights are just a little beyond Obi's. Say another fifteen thirty metres maybe."

Gorbind listened. That was what he would do for the moment. With his elbow curled around the paper, he continued to write what Joel was saying and in Joel's own words. "Go on," he said, looking up briefly. "Did you go in?" he asked, returning back to the writing that was crawling across the page as Joel spoke.

"I was about to," Joel gulped and momentarily passed the tip of his tongue across his lips. The thin skin felt taut and cracked in places. "I'd told her, that I would catch up, and that was when I heard it. A car roaring as it travelled down the street and towards the traffic lights. It sounded though it was speeding. Going way, way, too fast. Way too fast for a high street that is never busy. Anyway," stopping, Joel took a sip of the tea in the hope that it would help quell some of the anger that he felt rise inside him. "Millie had stopped at the lights, they were changing. I remember looking away, and then seeing it. The car was getting closer and it was zig zagging as it was headed towards the lights. Millie was about to cross, the lights had gone red. The lights were red and Millie had stepped out. She didn't even get half way. I heard a screech, then a bang."

That was where he had to stop. Joel put the cup down onto the table, a small amount of tea splashed onto the surface as he pressed his hand to his chest. His heart was racing, beating so horrendously fast that he could feel waves of nausea pass over him. Joel took in several long draw out breaths so that he might calm down and get rid of the sick feeling. Still the sound of screeching tyres filled his ears and combined with the beating of heart to form a crashing cacophony.

Gorbind was alerted by Joel's rising tone with its heightened sense of immediacy and trauma that was amplified by recounting what had happened. The pen that he had been writing with had fallen from his fingers and he had leant across the table to mop up the small puddle of tea with the thin paper napkin that he had set down earlier. Sitting back, he let his gaze settle on the fair headed young man opposite. He made gentle eye contact to indicate that he was here with him, and listening still and paying attention to what was being said. It would take more than a splash of tea to derail things. "You mentioned the weather. Rain had started to fall, and the road," said Gorbind, "The road doesn't normally get very busy, so the car was going faster than expected," he looked down towards the words that he had written and was poised to pick up his pen again.

Joel nodded and picked up the cup of tea. This time it was about the story, as the detective repeated what he had said. He was able to think about the context. "Definitely raining," Joel uttered quietly. "My coat was getting stupidly wet as it fell, as it got heavier. There is no way that the car would have stopped safely and in that," he exhaled softly, causing the surface of the tea that remained in the cup to ripple. There was little milk in the tea, no skin had formed and the liquid dimpled easily.

He could feel that this coat was still wet, still so heavy against his shoulders; this, combined with the sound of Millie meeting metal made it feel as though he was being thrown back into time as and when the accident had happened. "It didn't stop, it went straight at her. Millie was caught on the bonnet; it was still going before she was thrown off and away. It didn't stop, drove straight off. And I couldn't move," he looked at the detective who had now stopped writing and was simply watching and listening to him speak. "She was thrown across the road, and I just couldn't move."

Storytelling and recounting continued and for a short while longer. Gorbind had continued to listen, asking questions and reflecting Joel's words back toward him. He had asked Joel to change the order of the events, to describe what other witnesses might have seen. He had done his best to keep Joel calm and focused; the young man had just witnessed a traumatic and tragic event. Yet his words, his testimony was fresh in his mind and best retrieved early.

Human memory was fragile and falsifiable, so nothing could be left to chance or until later. Gorbind had made his best efforts to not serve up a relentless barrage of questions whilst discharging his duty to gather evidence and facts accurately. As long as he got all the fact, the driver of the blue souped up Subaru would get what was coming to them.

As he watched Joel leave, he saw his colleagues in uniform bring in Millie's parents. Ashen faced, they both looked dazed; their whole universe had shaken and the centre of it torn out. They had been brought here to be filled in with how the investigation was progressing. Hanging back as they entered a room close by, Gorbind was able to blend into the background. The driver of the car that Joel had described had been accosted and was now being detained in a custody suite. As he watched the couple disappear, he thought of his own little girl. She was barely three years old and her whole life was stretched out ahead of her. For Millie's Mum and Dad, that would have meant a hundred thousand opportunities.

Opportunities that had been snatched away and were nothing but dust washed away by raindrops. All gone, taken away from Millie and because of an idiot behind the wheel of a souped up Subaru. Gorbind bit his lip in frustration and realised that he had folded in half the beige plastic cup from which Joel had drunk badly made tea. Crushing it further, he threw into a waste paper bin sat next to a door. Under his harm was Joel's statement and it was to be shared with the rest of the investigation team.

***

The room was filled with an eerie, heavy silence. That was the most noticeable thing; a complete lack of sound. That was what had first alerted him to something not being right. There had been the expected noises, of people to-ing and fro-ing. A whole symphony of noises with his voice, Sophie's voice, the voice of the mid wife and the consultant who had appeared. Sophie had been screaming, shouting at him, at the mid wife and at any one who was there and could hear her anguished cries. He had no idea, no idea as to what Sophie was physically going through.

She had decided to do this standing up. After hours of lying down on the bed and being altogether uncomfortable, standing up and at the end of the bed was where Sophie wanted to be. Michael was stood behind her, feeling very much like a back seat driver whilst trying to be a cheer leader. He wanted to help; but all that he could do, all that Sophie allowed him to do was to hold her hands. Rather that Sophie was holding onto his and with a hot, sweaty, vice like grip. At first, maybe they had both wanted comfort and had sat curled up together. Now, here he was standing there, so close and with her in this moment; Michael wasn't about to go anywhere. They were in this together, and they would finally get to meet their baby.

They both knew that it would take time, neither one of them expected this to be quick. All they wanted was their baby, they were prepared to wait. It had taken them this long to go through a pregnancy full term; this was however starting to feel a little like torture. There were already concerned brows, quiet whispers and wary nods of the head as things had plodded on slowly over the last twelve hours. This wasn't going to be simple, not by any length of chalk.

By the time that she was standing up, he knew that Sophie was ready. She must have known that it was time. There was no letting go of his hands. Michael had no idea what was going on, what was happening to his wife and to his baby. All he could see, was the midwife kneeling before Sophie, all he could hear were alarms straddling the sound of Sophie's screams. Amongst all of that, there was a splash. Blood and amniotic fluid fell to the ground. Then, then there was silence.

He felt that Sophie had let go, as though it had been a reflex. His digits felt angry and aflame at being held so tightly. Slowly, he clasped his hands together over his stomach. As much as his fingers were pained and throbbed, he knew that Sophie had gone through something so much worse.

They both listened. Listened and waited to hear that sound. The one sound, that no matter how fast the world revolved around them, they wanted to hear and were waiting for with baited breath.

There was only silence.

He could feel the weight of the long, drawn out silence and it was overwhelming.

There was no sound; he started to realise that it might not come. A sound, that he and Sophie were destined not to hear.

They would not hear it today, they probably would never hear it. All of this buzzed around his head, as the baby was taken away. He turned his head towards his wife, who had collapsed into her bed and like him watched the midwives take away their child.

He could still hear nothing. The silence so drawn out, that it felt for Michael as though his soul was slowly being torn from his flesh. A quiet uncomfortable hum had filled his ears and was travelling towards his brain. There, the sound had become a disturbing and disorientating buzz that set him uncomfortably on edge. He had stepped away from Sophie as she was aided back to her bed; there was still some pushing that had to be done. He stood there, trapped in the middle of a vortex as the room seemed to spin all around him. Medical staff were rushing around in the bloody soiled scrubs and making awkward eye contact.

Michael staggered backwards, his feet un-coordinated but mobile enough to carry him out of the delivery room door. As he tumbled out, Michael felt his stomach lurch and its acidic unsettled contents travelled up his gullet to land in a puddle upon the duck egg floor before him.

This was not how it was supposed to end.

He remembered almost falling to the floor, only to be scooped up by his father and into strong, unyielding arms. He was there with Michael's mum, as well as Sophie's mum. They had arrived with such excitement, and they had quickly got to their feet as Michael exited the delivery room. Michael sank into his father's arms. He was a wearied boy whose entire world had been torn up into the tiniest of fragments. Soaked in tears, any hopes that he might have had were fluttering away on the wind. He couldn't speak, he couldn't breathe. Unable to stand upon his own two feet, Michael howled out in agony.

The group of parents had taken him away. For a brief time he and Sophie were separated. He had gone home, and into the nursery where he started to grieve. Everything in the nursery had been positioned and poised for a new beginning. This was supposed to be a new chapter, but now everything in the room only to make the pain that engulfed his whole being feel that bit more intense. His parents had effectively babysat him, and Sophie's mum returned to her daughter overnight.

It was morning before he and Sophie were together again. Together they sat, wrapped in each other's arms as they sobbed. Together they cried and felt their hearts break in almost perfect synchronicity. Together, he and Sophie clutched at damp tissue and wiped away one another's tears. They held each other close in the grip of a dark and foreboding vacuum that had sucked away all the joy and happiness that the universe had finally promised them. In one another's arms, they started to grieve and mourn the loss of their beautiful baby boy.

He was most certainly beautiful.

They had both asked if they could hold their son. Speaking with the mid wives felt altogether strange now, there was no live baby who they might go visit in the nursery. They seemed to know, with sympathy and empathy etched across their faces. The midwives in the room were not exactly strangers; they had become friends and experienced the ups and downs with him and Sophie in every immediate aspect.

So the two of them had gone to see their little boy, and in the chapel of rest but in a room entirely different. It could have been a waiting room, only it had been repurposed and made more comfortable with a suite of well upholstered chairs and glass coffee table. On his return to the hospital, Michael had brought with him some clothes that had been stored in the nursery. It was in these clothes that the little boy was dressed, and swaddled in a pale yellow blanket that had been crocheted by one of the grandmothers.

Michael sat with his hands curled in his lap as he

watched Sophie cradle their sleeping son. He watched as she cried, and her tears fell upon his angel-like face. He sat silently beside her, as she wiped away the single solitary tear that had landed on their son's nose. Michael pressed a finger against his own cheek, as Sophie smoothed down their baby's tufty dark hair. He could no longer hold back the guttural groans as his wife smothered the sleeping child with kisses.

It was all too much for him to take. As his son was placed into his arms, Michael was shaking and almost violently. It took several moments for him to steady himself; his tremoring subsided as he felt the weight of the child nestled into the crook of his arm. The sleeping form was his child, their baby. This child had meant a whole spectrum of hopes, fears and new beginnings. All of these were now gone, all had disappeared and in a heartbeat with no reason given. The midwives had been at a loss, saying only that these happen and often with no clear reason.

Sophie had put her arms around his shoulders, as though that might help steady him and stop the shaking. He could feel himself calm at her touch; settle as he felt her close and his son in his arms. She was there and with him. This was their grief, their loss and a shared bereavement. They had each other, and they would get through this together. As he sat there, he could see what might have been. The three of them together, and a family.

They must have been sat there for an hour, and just the three of them. Michael didn't remember saying anything, as he concentrated on holding his baby close and tried not to drop the sleeping child. All that he could do was to look at the closed eye lids, with the tiniest of lashes that were only just visible. Very carefully and feeling very scared, he moved the folds of the blanket to find his son's hand. For a few moments, Michael held on to the tiny hand in his to marvel at the fingers, the nails and the fine lines on the palm. A future written across the soft skin that was no longer going to happen; lines that could have told a story of adventure and excitement. Slowly, he returned the hand into the folds and bundled up his baby boy.

Later there would be certificated. At last, the child would be identified and given a name. Samuel Sachin James. Male. Seven pounds and eight ounces. Born asleep.

***

His mum smiled at his father, she didn't say anything. The woman lying before him in a bed, couldn't say anything, not any more. He remembered that smile from when he was a boy; it was a special smile that she saved only for Albie. This was a special smile that in happier times would have been followed by a reassuring squeeze of his father's hand. It may have even been followed by a delicate kiss upon his cheek. Today, right here, right now, all that Lilly had to give was that smile. Lilly smiled at her husband, and Albie smiled back. His smile was forced and interrupted by the tip of his tongue wiping away a tear that was caught on the edge of his Cupid's bow lips. She smiled and slowly turned her head towards the window.

David lowered his eyes as he sat on an ottoman on the other side of the room. He was watching this as though it wasn't real. He was watching this as though it was a schmaltzy version of 'It's a Wonderful life' and he was being forced to watch it against his will. David was utterly transfixed as his arm pressed harder into the pillow that he had clutched toward his chest. Behind the pillow, he had felt his heart race and reach a crescendo as Lilly had smiled, turned her head and breathed her last. He had gasped too, and moved his fingers towards his dry chapped lips. His mother had just died, and right before his eyes. It was all over. Lilly was gone.

It was only fifteen minutes earlier that he had observed Matthew say his goodbyes. The little boy that Lilly had doted upon was a grown man who had sat on the edge of her bed with his tears streaming and his voice breaking. Matthew had walked in gingerly, his movement was painfully slow. As he had appeared at the door, David had seen Lydia-more specifically, the back of her-disappear back down the carpeted stairs. Some part of him had expected Lydia to come in, stay with Matthew. Lilly had something of a soft spot for Matthew's girlfriend. The rest of him knew and understood that Lydia was more than aware of how much grandson and grandmother meant to each other. With that, he could rationalise that Lydia had not abandoned Matthew but given him the space that he needed to say goodbye.

He had been barely able to keep it together as he gazed upon Matthew bidding his grandmother Adieu. Closing the door behind him, Matthew had walked towards his grandfather and placed a hand gently upon a shoulder that finally sagged having been resolute for so long. David had noticed that; his father always sat up right in something of a genteel fashion. As Lilly had become frailer and spiralled in deterioration, Albie's shoulders had started to droop.

Albie had shaken his head as Matthew had moved passed him and sat himself down onto the bed and between his grandparents. Matthew's hand had moved towards Lilly's, and David saw that his son's eyes had become a little wider and in fear. His eyebrows were raised, and David recognised the look of a scared little boy. He could feel his son's unease, something that he had not felt and for such a long time. It was not a look, that as a parent, he really wanted to see or to feel his son be so scared that it hurt.

With his body sat heavily on the ottoman, David

found himself unable to physically move. All he wanted to do was to move toward his son and throw his arms around him. His deepest, strongest feeling as a father was to pull Matthew away and protect him. The same feeling that he had experienced when Matthew had been a small boy and they had gone to feed the ducks. Matthew had strayed a little close to the edge of the pond and his immediate reaction had been to hoick away the boy before he tumbled into murky waters.

There were no ponds today or ducks; there was woman, who for both of them was incredibly important and she was about to leave them both forever. David feared her absence, and what it might mean for them both. There would be a loss, of her love, care and her very existence would come to an end. He could not stop this from happening, protect his son from what may happen; this was something that they both had to experience and both would feel.

"There will always be cake, Grandma," Matthew had said, gulping away sobs. "I promise you, that there will always be cake, and never any rice pudding." There had been a sharp sigh, his voice trembled and finally broke. "No rice pudding," he continued, wrapping his hand around hers; Matthew was visibly distraught as his tears flowed freely.

For David, it was torture to seeing his little boy have his heart broken. As a parent losing his own mother, this was all too much.

Shaking his head, Matthew couldn't say anymore. He tugged his sleeve around his hand and passed it over his eyes, with his face glistening with tears. Matthew rose from the bed, his gaze cast downward and he left the room without further ado.

His wife had sat next to Lilly after, said her final goodbyes as well before coming to sit next to him on the ottoman. Things were changing by the minute; the end was soon upon them all. Together, they watched Lilly leave.

In a stony silence, the three of them had sat whilst the palliative care nurse did her job and double checked. David had watched her every move, and eventually there had been a nod of confirmation. There would be procedures to be followed, all sorts of medical things to be arranged. His father had shuffled his chair closer to his now eternally sleeping wife. David couldn't make it out clearly, but Albie whispered gently to his wife as he delicately moved the fine white hair that had fallen across her face.

"I have to tell Matt," David had whispered, turning briefly to his wife and rising to his feet.

She had nodded and stood up next to him. Hand in hand, they had left the bedroom and travelled slowly down the stairs. Holding each other's hand, they held each other and fought the feeling of falling that now cloaked them. David had stopped just short of the kitchen door; he took in a deep breath as he saw Matthew sat at the table through a gap between the door and the frame.

For a moment, Matthew was a small boy, sat at the head of the table dressed in shorts, a jumper and with his feet clad in cobalt blue sandals. David must have seen his son sit there hundreds if not thousands of times before. It just felt wrong. In the three seconds that it took for him and his wife to enter the kitchen, he reminded himself Matthew was now a grown up.

Matthew was no longer a small child, and he could no protect him from what might hurt him. David stood inside the kitchen, and his son met his gaze. From the corner of his eye, David saw Lydia's tapered fingers curl around Matthew's hand. He went to speak, pursing his lips together, only he found himself unable to speak. He was unable to squeeze a single solitary word from his vocal cords. Instead, he broke away his gaze from Matthew and walked towards his son at the head of the table. Before he knew it, David was being held up by his son and the roles had been somewhat reversed. In his ear, Matthew whispered that everything would be okay. The very same words that he had used to console his Matthew were now being used to console him.

The illusion of watching a film was now broken. As

Lilly had turned her head, the pin had been stuck into the figurative balloon and it was all over. As David tried to breath, he couldn't even hang onto his smile. Matthew must have let go a little as he found himself being lowered into the chair that Lydia had vacated. He was now well and truly beyond the feeling of watching a film; now he could feel the realness as Lydia filled a kettle and he could hear the sound of running water. Matthew stayed close, pulling his chair closer and wrapping his arm around his shoulder.

Lilly was gone, her smile had disappeared. The mother that David had loved and so completely had left him; she would not be coming back.

***

There was going to be a bill; the invoice would arrive in a couple of days. For now, he wouldn't worry about the cost or how everything might be paid for. Right now, all that he could think about was Adelphi. The last few days had been supremely difficult as Adelphi had become slower and slower in his movements. His whelps and whines had become sharp calls of pain. When he had stepped across the landing and found Adelphi lying prostrate and unable to move, a deathly clarion call had sounded. Christopher had lowered himself to his knees and stroked Adelphi's fur between his ears in efforts to soothe him. Adelphi had looked at him in bewilderment, as though asking what was happening and why. Christopher shuffled his feet and moved closer to Adelphi so that he could scoop him up and into his lap. There were more sharp whines and audible sniffles, all pulling into focus how poorly the dog was and tugging at Christopher's heart strings to make things feel altogether more grave.

As he took Adelphi into his arms, it struck him how small and thin Adelphi had become. Gently shushing Adelphi, Christopher ran his fingers through the dense black and gold fur that was now shot through with silver. Coarse as they were, the silver strands gave Adelphi a glow and shone in the light.

There was only thing left for Christopher to do and for his best friend. To make the call, to then discuss things with the vet had been one of the hardest things that Christopher had ever had to do. He had remained stoic on the 'phone, his voice had been level and matter of fact as he kept calm enough to make the appointment and discuss the arrangements. He had been sat on the stairs when he had called, his hand trembling as he held onto the 'phone. Adelphi lay across his lap looking directly at him. His usually shining and bright eyes were had become dull now and looked increasingly pained. Wrapped up in his blanket, Christopher had made the difficult decision to take Adelphi to the vet's practice.

Driving there, Adelphi had been positioned carefully across the back seats on fluffy cushions removed from the spare room. He drove slowly over the three and a half miles between their home and the practice. He deliberately took the path of least resistance and the one that didn't involve any roundabouts or speedbumps. These were Adelphi's last few miles and as he drove, Christopher and Adelphi both cried in almost perfect unison.

This happened all the time and to other people. Other people would go through this. Cats, dogs and other animals would come here and complete their journey in this world. So much so, the vet had tried to make this easier; a fairly inconspicuous door labelled the rainbow room identified the space where friendships and relationships could come to a safe and meaningful end. It was through that door that Christopher carried Adelphi, a nurse followed with the pillows from the car tucked beneath his arms. For now, Adelphi had gone silent with his snout buried deep within the folds of his blanket. Christopher could feel the heat of Adelphi's body radiate towards his arms; he could also hear his own heart beat quickly and more intensely.

Beyond the grey door, Christopher slowly walked into a room furnished with a sofa and a handful of well stuffed and brightly coloured bean bags. A window on the far side looked out onto a neatly organised garden filled with shrubs that were dotted with clusters of small blooms. Next to the window was a second door, and it was through this door that the vet arrived. She had brought with her, the necessary bits and pieces for Adelphi to leave. It was this that caused Christopher to yelp himself and to hold Adelphi that bit closer. His noise must have been loud, as Adelphi stirred and whined in response.

He didn't fancy the sofa, and there was just something about the bean bags that made them look more comfortable. "Might be nicer if we had those," he said jutting out his elbow in the direction of the bean bags. He didn't want hand Adelphi over or drop him, this was his best friend. "Somewhere in the middle," he added, only to look at his feet and realise that he had already gravitated toward the centre of the small room. It wasn't as dreary as he had expected. The window, through which the garden was visible, was large enough to bathe the room in natural light. This day had started quite grey; the clouds had now started to lift and sunshine made the blue sky a little brighter. When he and Adelphi had exited the car, there had been a freshness in the air that the blue sky had disguised somewhat. He remained standing as the vet and nurse worked together to drag two bean bags toward him and Adelphi.

Kissing Adelphi's snout, Christopher held onto him firmly and lowered himself down into the bean bags. He was conscious now of the physical sensation, the way that he himself drew in breath and the rise and fall of Adelphi's chest. Looking up at the vet who had stepped aside, Christopher gave a silent nod.

The signal; this was the time.

The vet and nurse readied Adelphi, Christopher concentrated on the dog in his arms. He quietly shushed Adelphi, and continued to gently scratch fur between his ears. Adelphi's ears were no longer standing to attention at a jaunty angle; these were ears that Adelphi had long since grown into.

Watching the vet and nurse depart, Christopher sharply drew in breath. It was just the two of them now, just him and Adelphi. They had been boy and dog, man and dog; they had been friends and family. Sat here and with Adelphi, he knew exactly what was going to happen. The vet had shared the details before hand and gone into some depth. There had been a lengthy description of how Adelphi would go to sleep and leave. Christopher had chosen not to watch the mix be injected, he had looked away; now he could feel the drugs take effect as Adelphi relaxed in his arms. Barbiturates, that was what they used and with anaesthetic.

Adelphi was warm in his arms, and he gently moved his palm into the folds of the blanket and to where he assumed Adelphi's heart was. His own was beating fast and made him aware of the cold sheen of sweat that had formed across his forehead. Trying to ignore his own heartbeat, Christopher wanted to focus on Adelphi's. The beat was steady at first, like his own would normally be; he could feel the thudding vibrate through flesh and fur. Adelphi's heart beat was deep and earthy, with no discernible gap between thuds. Perhaps Adelphi knew, and this had scared him just as much as it scared Christopher.

It was when the gaps between the beats started to become distinct, that Christopher pressed his teeth into his bottom lip. It was also becoming more difficult to feel the beat through Adelphi's fur, with Adelphi starting to feel a little lighter in his arms. Tugging the blanket closer, Christopher felt his embrace become tighter. He didn't want to let the fur ball go.

Adelphi had all but stopped moving, and he couldn't see his chest rise and fall anymore. He could also feel that Adelphi no longer felt warm, his arms felt so much cooler. He tried desperately to wrap Adelphi up tighter and tighter within his blanket to help preserve some of the warmth. His friend was leaving him; he could feel Adelphi pull away. He held in his own breath, but Adelphi let out his one last time and was gone.

Christopher howled into the blanket, his face pressed against Adelphi's to soak the now silent snout with his tears. He had lost his friend, his fellow and faithful playmate. He felt alone in that Rainbow room, bereft and completely heartbroken. He didn't hear the door open behind him and before he knew it, Adelphi was being taken from him and out of his arms. Christopher kept a hold of the blanket, and balled it up tightly against his chest; he shook his head when asked by the vet if they should keep it. Shell shocked, he left the practice to sit in his car. He must have sat for half an hour, with his head resting on the steering wheel. Feeling the puddle of salty tears across and those that had fallen onto his knees, he sat back with a pained sigh.

Wiping both of his hands across his face, he then rooted around in his glove box for his 'phone. Switching it on, he made a call to his mother. Through sobs and strangled sobs, he told her about Adelphi in a teary, pained stream of consciousness. Christopher talked and let everything out, everything just poured out from the bottom of his heart. His mum offered to come find him, but he refused as he loudly blew his nose. He wanted to be alone, he might call later. He eventually hung up, all that needed right now was to simply tell someone. Now, he wanted to be alone. Turning the key in the ignition, he drove off and took the same route that he had taken to get here. As he drove, he glanced in the rear view mirror as though by habit. There was nothing there Adelphi, wasn't there.

***

In a rivulet of red, blood intermingled with soap and travelled towards the plug hole and away from the mass of wet, curly dark hair that was pressed against Caleb's scalp. The stream was the brightest red that Daniel had ever seen; the water had become vermillion and frothed as it gurgled out of the shower tray. This was the scene that greeted him, with something quite fatal unfurling as he had waited down stairs for the sound of Caleb singing. He had been waiting exactly fifteen minutes before deciding to come up here. The absence of sound, the lack of high notes being stumbled upon as Caleb's voice failed to reach them had told him that all was not well.

He had knocked, even though the door was ajar and he could the shower run. The compact bathroom was full of steam and a film of moisture had descended upon the mirrored cabinet above the sink. Daniel had a called out Caleb's name as he threw open the door with his shoulder. Something told him, shouted at him in his head that things really were not right.

There he was, Caleb lay slumped across shower tray and face down. A red star burst on the side of the cubicle suggested that Caleb had struck his head there first and also on the edge of the shower tray as he had fallen. In falling down, he had forced the cubicle door open and lay with his arm stretched out toward Daniel.

Tripping over clothes and a towel, Daniel all but flung

himself to the floor and next to Caleb. Water was continuing to cascade from the shower head, and he must have lain there for a good five minutes whilst sweeping his hands through the water to try and determine where the blood was coming from. With his hands covered in blood and soap, Daniel felt his chest tighten. He had to get help. Sliding away, he stepped into the shower tray and turned off the shower.

Without the sound of the water, there was a cold silence. A steely, deathly silence as Daniel in his panicked state tried to rouse Caleb. Caleb's eyes were open, but were dazed and vacant looking; his tongue lolled to the side of his jaw and his colour was becoming paler. Daniel side stepped again, this time covering Caleb with clothes and a towel. He dragged Caleb away from the tray and into the recovery position.

"Ambulance," he told Caleb. "I need to call an ambulance. Just hold on, Caleb, please. Hold on," he sunk to his feet and kissed his husband's lips as he ran a finger across the apple of his cheek. "Ambulance," he whispered, getting back to his feet and running out of the bathroom. Thundering down the stairs, he lifted the telephone from its base in the hallway. It fell from his fingers and to the floor with a thud. Daniel was scared, angry and unable to process everything that was going on as his hand trembled. Picking it up from the floor, he dialled triple nine with shaking fingers that had to be jabbed sharply onto the button. Clutching the 'phone to his ear, he ran back up the stairs in something of a heavy daze. He returned to the bathroom, and lay next his husband as he told the operator to send help.

"He's not saying anything," Daniel all but screamed, "And I'm trying, he said, his fingers pressed to Caleb's neck, "Trying to find a pulse, but I can't. I can't find a pulse."

Soon enough, the ambulance arrived. The attending paramedics bundled Caleb out with David in tow; they left the house with sirens blaring and blue lights flashing as the ambulance sped across the city. It didn't take long to arrive at accident and emergency, and Caleb was handed over to the medics. All Daniel could do was to wait behind swinging doors; he grasped at the hair on his head, and tried not to pull it out. He felt as though he was hurtling through waves of agony as his stomach flipped and his heart beat frantically. Eventually, he was shepherding away by a healthcare assistant who wanted to ask Daniel some questions, get some details and persuaded him to go with him and get some coffee.

"I just want to know, is he awake?" asked Daniel as he was escorted away. Looking over his shoulder, he felt his heart break and into a thousand, splintered pieces.

Forty minutes passed. Forty minutes during which time Daniel had paced up and down the relatives room with a beige plastic cup of vending machine coffee. He had slugged away the contents, and now absent mindedly had started to fold the cup up in his hands. He was about to throw it away into a waste bin by the door, when a doctor clad in blue scrubs came in.

Daniel looked at the doctor a while. His face wore that expression that trainee doctors must have spent hours practicing at Med School. This was the look that was prefaced with a deep breath to steel them as they focused and looked you in the eye. Then came the parting of the lips, and the words 'I'm sorry' would tumble out in a perfectly prosaic way. It was a phrase said so often, that its edges have worn away and the phrase becomes neutral and inoffensive.

"Please don't," uttered Daniel, moving towards the waste bin and dropping in the folded up cup. "He can't have," he said shaking his head and moving towards a plastic grey chair with a blue fabric cushion. Sinking into the seat, Daniel curled his hands into fists and rested them on his knees.

Now he would hear the speech, the condolences. A standard boiler plate set of words describing what had happened. Describing, how for the last forty minutes the medics had fought to save his husband's life. This was a difficult time; yet there was an opportunity to help others. Caleb was on the organ donation register, had he been aware of this, and had they discussed what the options were.

His world was in tail spin, and they wanted to know about organ donation.

"I want to see him," said Daniel as he slowly uncurled his fists. His hands hovered in the air above his knees and were shaking. "I want to see Caleb. I want to see my husband."

Caleb might as well have been asleep, zonked out and not waking up anytime soon. His lids were drawn down over his caramel brown eyes. Daniel stood at the door and took in the sight of Caleb lying in repose with a blue sheet folded at his broad shoulders. Slowly and rather awkwardly, Daniel put one foot in front of the other and moved towards the wheeled bed. Placing a hand delicately to Caleb's hair, he found that the locks were still a little damp. Gently, he swept away strands of curly black brown hair from his eyes, and leant forward to kiss Caleb for the last time.

"What am I supposed to do without you?" he asked as he rearranged the folds of the sheet at Caleb's shoulders. "Would it have hurt you, to have given me some warning? After everything, all that we have been through; to tell me that you've had enough and your leaving me. That's just plain rude, sweetheart. You know that things just won't be the same without you, don't you?" Daniel spluttered into tears, and had to hold onto the bars at the side of the bed to prevent him falling to his feet. Things were definitely going to be different, and he had no idea how he might deal with them.

It was late afternoon by the time that he arrived back home. Whilst at the hospital, he had made a few calls to family, friends; those that really mattered were given the obligatory call. He was brought back home by his nephew; Joel had been despatched his mother to pick him up and look after him. A duty that his nephew took altogether very seriously as he made Daniel a strong coffee and further insisted upon ordering take-away. Daniel didn't have the energy to protest, and as Joel ordered food, he dosed his coffee with what was easily a triple measure of rather expensive brandy. He zoned out as Joel wittered on, nursing his coffee whilst feeling uncomfortably numb. Caleb had gone and taken all of the colour in their life together with him.

***

Thirty four minutes past seven. That was the time at which his world was paused. Up until that point, all that had happened occurred frame by frame and was snatches of real life as he knew it. It was at that twenty-six minutes to eight when reality ground to a halt. They had known this was coming. They had known for at least four months, and ever since then there had been plans made for everything. Plans for after this point were altogether uncomfortable, and he didn't want to think about them. His mum would suck her lips closed; shake her head as she closed her eyes to avoid the topic entirely. The in-laws were only marginally better, tutting and wringing their hands in overwhelming discomfort.

He had tried to talk with Caliope, but she wore that 'bunny caught in headlights' look every time he or Rachel tried to talk about what might happen, and afterwards. This then made talking to Koby even more difficult. Koby was still so young and in so many ways; Rachel would have wrapped him up in cotton wool with bubble wrap just to make sure that the blow was adequately softened. Raj found it difficult to speak with his son anyway, and then there was this.

So he had left this with Rachel, she had spoken to Koby. She had spoken with him a few weeks back, when she was still able to walk; they had both gone out for ice cream and been gone for most of the day. When Raj had asked, Rachel told him that they had talked, cried; Koby had asked so many questions. Some of them had been relatively simple and she was able to answer them easily. Others had challenged her to tears and she hoped that Raj would clarify things when the time came. Clarifying terrified him. He had no idea how to cope with the kids and without

Rachel.

He had got caught up in their last embrace; there was one last hug. Rachel had asked for him come closer and to hold her. All Rachel wanted to do, was to get warmer. She was covered in layers of blankets; her shrunken form was completely cocooned and swamped, but still she felt cold and shivered. Koby had pulled a face that suggested he was uncomfortable with such public displays of affection as he sat on the other side of the room.

Caliope was sat next to him, and elbowed him sharply in reprimand. Both of them had been pulled of school a few days ago. That was when the frame by frame development had started to jump and skip. Things had changed; he and Rachel both knew that this was the point of no return and this was how their life together was about to end.

Telling the kids had been far worse than he had imagined. There had been counsellors, support workers, the school too; all trying to help and be as supportive as they could. A few of the counsellors here at the hospice had spoken to him about how the children might react, both now and after they had given him some advice on how to support them. That helped, a little but not entirely, in getting some clarity and comfort. His mum had arrived, alongside Rachel's parents. Raj could not for the life of him imagine what that car journey must have been like.

Knotting the end of her scarf in her hands, Nandini gestured for Caliope to move further down the sofa and sat down beside her.

Raj was nestled alongside Rachel and had threaded his arms around her shoulders to draw her close. She was already dozing in and out of consciousness, and looked as though she was fighting the urge to fall asleep. As he kissed the top of her head, Raj wished that he could make this all stop; he wished that he could turn the clock back a year and re-write the history of abnormal cells being discovered.

All Raj wanted to do was turn back time and magic away all the pain, the drama and the tears. All the scans, biopsies and consultations could all go to the seven circles of hell, and stay away from the woman that he loved. He couldn't do that though, there was no way that he could change anything; he and Rachel had fought about it, screamed and shouted to protest out loud before laughing through tears to try and see the bright side.

When her hair had fallen out, Rachel had shaved away the tufts that remained; she had then gone on a shopping spree to buy the most expensive, elaborate and elegant scarves that she could. That was what she wanted to do, that was Rachel's way of coping and fighting. She had told him, time and time again. That she was going to fight, she wasn't going to win, and they still had to be positive.

"Just see the bright side," She had told him. "Remember all of the good things. Remember that Caliope, might seem all independent on the outside, but on the inside she needs your patience. Remember that, when you teach her to drive. Show her, how to change a tyre.. And Koby, don't keep your distance. You need to be a part of his world, let him into yours. For God's sake, learn the rules to Rugby."

Those were just some of his instructions as to what he was to do afterwards.

"If you don't want to do this by yourself, ask someone," Rachel had continued. "Ask your mum, my mum; anyone, just ask and don't do this by yourself."

Once the medics had told them that there was nothing left to do, they had started clock watching. They had now been clock watching for days. With everyone here, the kids and the parents, all that remained was for them to spend time together. His mum was keeping a very close eye on the kids, and already offered her opinion on the proceedings. In her mind, the kids should have been elsewhere and not here with Rachel on her death bed. It had taken a huge amount of self-control to quietly quell her concerns. Raj had gently described to Nandini how Rachel had given the kids a choice and that they had chosen to be here. This was hard for everyone; at a time like this, bickering would only make things feel worse.

This was all now about clock watching. It wasn't a particularly attractive one at that, as it hung between two landscapes on the wall opposite the bed and at something of a tilt. Raj watched the second hand move. There was an audible click over the sound of hushed voices that daren't rise above the sense of fragility that hung forebodingly in the air. Each click was a second that had come and gone, it was a second that they no longer had. A second that was a sigh, half a word and snippets of conversation; life was ebbing away and into the ether.

Everything that he and Rachel had was fading away with each and every second that passed. As he held onto her, there were a hundred and one things that were flashing through his mind. From when he had first seen her, and collided with her in the street; he had been fortunate enough to not end up wearing the black coffee that she was holding. He remembered the moment that they had found that Caliope was on the way, there had been screaming and squealing as they rolled off their bed and onto the floor with an almighty bump. Raj remembered the fight on one New Year's Eve, they had been in the garden and Rachel had launched a terracotta flower pot straight at his head. He had ducked and the plant pot had smashed against the garden shed. It was that point that Raj had learned to never again raise the subject of a red head in red patent shoes and a mink coat.

Raj must have relived so many moments, and over and over again. Time was spent savouring each memory, imagining it all happen and in the here and now. These were moments that would never change, moments that were stitches in the fabric of time and formed the world that he and Rachel had made together. Moments that he would have to hang on to, keep crystal clear and use to get through whatever the world might throw at him and his family. Raj felt that lost, that he didn't realise just how silent Rachel had become as she lay in his arms. He was so focused on keeping her close that he didn't feel the heat start to fade away.

Not a first.

When he could no longer feel her breath upon his neck, Raj opened his eyes. Then he heard it; the sound of a monitor flat lining. He had filed away the sound of the monitor, to concentrate on the ticking of the clock, but now it was loud and unavoidable. The silence had been well and truly broken and the hushed tones of the family pushed away. For those moments, it had been all about him and Rachel; he had filtered out everything and everyone. Just them, him and her.

Rachel had drifted away from his arms and into her eternal slumber. She had gone, and life as he knew it had changed beyond imagination. She stopped fighting and had finally found peace.

17 Saying Goodbye

Journey's End

To wear black was out of the question. Caleb had actually stipulated that in the event of his demise-untimely or not-no one was to wear black or sit around thinking of what might have been. His instructions were fairly simple in the basic sense. There was to be a party, a celebration rather than a morose wake where everyone cried into their coffee. Everyone was invited to say goodbye to him, but they were to do it with a smile on their face and a glass full of champagne. If anyone arrived with less than a spring in the step, they were clearly in the wrong place. Another addendum was that the celebration was to be had with folks dressed to the nines and sparkle if they wanted to.

In the first instance, Daniel was a bit taken aback that his husband had actually thought things out in such detail and outlined what was to happen when he died. He didn't remember having discussed death with Caleb; it had never really come up. Perhaps they were still all new to the idea of being married. The discussion of practicalities had been had been reserved for the future and wasn't exactly in line with the reckless abandon that Caleb filled his days with. Second, Daniel had to plan a funeral that was so far beyond his comfort zone and not in the least bit like funerals as he knew them. The whole process had thrown him for a second time; Caleb was dead, and now this, a funeral.

No black, not in stripes, spots or checks. He had been quite clear, and mostly firm in telling those who had been invited. Yet his sister had turned up in a blackest of black ensemble, with a matching broad brimmed hat and clutching a soggy tissue. Neither he nor Caleb were one for large family gatherings and get togethers; but having his sister there and with her son, did help a little. Caleb's two siblings had made the trip from across the country and had been surprisingly supportive. He had never seen eye to eye with the two women. In their minds, he was a predatory sugar daddy who blinded a naïve and starry eyed Caleb.

Daniel scoffed as he drew in a mouthful of smoky bourbon that was getting warm. He had been nursing it for some time as he thought about the day and all of the different things that had happened leading up to it. He had already removed the claret and blue diamond shaped cuff links from his sleeves and they sat next to a bowl of raspberry ripple ice-cream. Like his bourbon, the ice-cream was warming up; it would not be long before it became a pale pink milk shake. Pushing the pair if cuff links closer together, Daniel half smiled. They been an engagement gift and matched the dark blue shirt and striped tie that he had chosen to wear today. His outfit had been picked out for days, yet he had struggled through the process of choosing Caleb's final outfit. It had taken time and tears, but he had managed to get an outfit together and deliver it to the funeral home.

Caleb had come home and for one last night slept in their four walls. This had been another stipulation that had caused Daniel to scratch his head, but he had no one to argue with about it. He had silently watched as the coffin was carried at waist height through the hall and into the lounge. Positioned on wooden legs, Caleb's coffin had rested in situ until this morning. He had made a coffee, and let it rest on the coffin. Not long after the funeral directors had left the previous evening, the door ball rang and interrupted the stony silence. It was time for him to step back a little, so that others could do the same. The plan was do that by celebrating, remembering and partying the night away. This was no time to be miserable and morose. What was about to happen, was a full scale riot of colour, fun and frivolity.

With the ringing of the bell, a full scale party had arrived. Food, music and festivities burst into the house. Before long the coffin was a make shift bar dotted with mock-tails, cocktails and a selection of nibbles. There was drinking and dancing. He remembered doing a conga around the coffin at three in the morning and wondering what alternate reality had descended upon his house.

At half past three, he had caught sight of clock on the mantle; a cold sobering thought descended upon him. None of this was real and that in a few hours, there would be nothing left of Caleb but a few pounds of ash. He had barked this out aloud and a thudding calm had landed upon all of those who had gathered in the house. One by one, the party goes left; they were all now wearing ashen faced expressions as they too came to grips with reality. There was a final burst of defiant party whistles as he closed the door and skulked off toward his bed. He had to get some sleep, if only a few hours before the day kicked off and with that a whole gamut of emotions that he really didn't want to feel.

This morning Daniel had sat with him for a while, a coaster was carefully positioned below the nameplate and his morning coffee had rested. As he had drunk the coffee, he had noticed that the nameplate was covered with smudges. He had tutted loudly when wiping away the finger prints. Caleb had decided to take his name, albeit with a hyphen and he ran his finger across the copper plate script etched into the metal rectangle. The hyphen had never mattered to Daniel; he had never asked Daniel to adopt it. Seeing his name alongside Caleb's family name was a final reminder of how Caleb had belonged to him, been a part of him. Caleb had been his entirely, his heart, his soul and everything in between.

He must have sat alone and with Caleb for only a couple of hours before the door bell had rung. During those two hours, he had laughed, shouted, screamed, and cried at the coffin. He had spoken out aloud of all the plans that they had made, all of the things that they had wanted to do and now never would. His husband was as dead as a door nail, and had poured proverbial cold water over everything. He had told Caleb that he had been The One; his words had bounced and buffeted against the almost yellow metal of the handles.

He had screamed as to how Caleb's cologne cost the earth, but he would give anything for Caleb to walk passed one more time whilst leaving a cloud of scent in his wake. This was their last few hours together and he had so much more to say.

There was a schedule to keep. By mid-day, there was supposed to be more celebrations and the local community hall had been hired and with a bar, so things could be smoothed over with enough alcohol to sink a small ship. Before that, there the service at the crematorium that he had to go through. To begin, the space in the crematorium had felt too big, and Daniel wondered if enough people would be here to fill it. Soon enough, the seats were filled and the room became less cavernous and intimidating. There was a colour and lots of it. There was a sea of sparkles, sequins, a few feathered head dresses and even a couple of cocktail dresses in the seats. As he stood at the lectern and held onto a deep breath before speaking, he realised just how much Caleb had meant not only to him but also those people who were sat before him. Letting out the trapped breath, Daniel pressed a palm to the piece of crisp blue note paper on the wooden lectern. This was it, this was time to say good bye.

"He tells me not to cry," he said softly, unable to raise his voice to fully annunciate and the back wall. "In this," said Daniel, holding up the blue paper. A note, that alongside Caleb's last will and testament had been stashed safely with a solicitor.

"I am to stay calm, remember what we had and not to cry," his voice broke and he let out a sharp gasp. "I can do calm," he said with a nod. "But I have to cry," continued Daniel, giving a slight shrug of his shoulders. "This was too soon; I was not prepared to say goodbye and not yet. We had so much to do, to see. Now what do I do, and with whom? My best friend, my soul mate and my champion has gone. Caleb was my defender. He kept me safe and built his whole universe around me; he made me a part of his world. And now, now he has gone. Without him, the world is less bright, less warm. The colour is fading, and I do wish it would stay."

He had made it through, eventually and just about. The service had been brief, with his speech and others made by some friends and also Caleb's older sister. There was no mention of Gods, theories or principles; the whole thing was about Caleb. He was the only person that mattered, the only person that they all had in common. It was all very simple. Celebrate Caleb, remember him and all that he had left behind.

Mid-day came and the colours of Caleb's world filled the room on the community centre. One again, Caleb was the centre of attention and yet another shinding kicked off in his honour. Savouring the now warm bourbon, Daniel watched The Birdy Dance start on the dancefloor. He smiled as he saw some of the mourners dance rather awkwardly whilst surrounded by others who were confident and far more flamboyant. The man that he had loved had left, yes; but he would never completely go. Not completely. Not ever.

***

He hated this suit. It was a suit didn't get worn that often and for that he was truly thankful. Putting his empty cup into the kitchen sink, Joel leant against the worktop and passed one hand through the fine follicles of his blonde hair as he tugged his jacket down with the other. There was a horrible stiffness to the fabric that made the suit feel heavy. His mouth turned downwards as he undid the buttons.

Joel felt altogether constrained and cossetted in this, today it was a funeral suit. It was a multi-purpose garment, fit for weddings, funerals, baptisms and other events; the darkness of the fabric combined with square, single breasted tailoring made it suitable for today. He had last worn it to Caleb's funeral, but had accessorised it with a brick red tie that he had borrowed from his father. He had found another today, a special tie and from someone special. The splash of colour had helped to reduce the feelings of suffocation that came from being head to toe in black.

"Joel. There you are," Millie's mum clip clopped across the floor of her kitchen and straight towards him. In her hands was a short stemmed flower with bright pink petals; petals that appeared to be numerous and gave the flower a fluffy appearance. "Did you get some tea?" Maya asked softly as she stood directly in front of him and pinned the gerbera to his lapel. "Oh, that is lovely," she added, momentarily tapping his Fuchsia pink tie. "Goes with the Gerbera, doesn't it. That's the one from Christmas; I knew you'd like it. Millie did too."

"Yes," nodded Joel as he watched the flower be pinned into place, "I did get some tea, thank you," he added, inclining his head towards the sink. "It's bright pink, and it wouldn't be Millie without a bit of pink, now would it. I also hate the suit," he said with a sharp tut. "Pink made it wearable today."

"Hmm, funerals though," said Maya, stepping back a little. "Hopefully things won't go on too long; just this morning to get through. You and the rest; the friends group, are all going out later?" she asked, moving towards the sink and washing up the empty mug.

As Maya stepped away, Joel set about fiddling with the flower. It was more out of curiosity than anything else. He wasn't exactly relishing today. This was yet another funeral, but this time for someone who he had cared about for so deeply, but had never so much as told them. He had never actually told Millie how he had felt about her. He could feel the regret forming in the bottom of his heart and sit with a lead-like heaviness. "We are, yes," replied Joel. "A few are coming today, those that you asked me to call. The rest will come tonight. Hopefully it will be a good night, celebrating and remember."

Maya rinsed out the now clean mug and shook off droplets of water before resting it on a plastic drainer that was populated with a few other pieces crockery. "I hope so," said Maya, a brief smile flickered across her face. "Some of your group called, they even sent flowers," she said it with touch of surprise in her voice. "If you could thank them, Joel; Aldo and I would really appreciate it."

"Course. I will do," Joel looked up from the gerbera that sat against his lapel in contrast to his suit. A couple of the petals had come away and he quickly dropped them into his breast pocket and out the way.

"JOEL!" A third voice sounded across the kitchen.

Both Joel and Maya snapped their heads towards the door as Aldo appeared. In his hands was another mug; this one was full and of tea that sloshed around as he moved towards Joel.

"Did you ask him?" Aldo asked of Maya as he put a hand gently to Joel's shoulder.

Closing her eyes, Maya shook her head. "No, left that to you," she replied, drying her hands on a blue and white checked tea towel.

Aldo took a deep breath and pressed his fingers firmly against the curve of Joel's shoulder. "Joel, will you help-"He paused to look at Maya briefly, and then looked back at Joel. "Maya and I, would like for you to be one of the pall bearers. Plus you are tall enough," he added, a quiet laugh tinged his tones. The last few weeks had given Aldo a lot to think about; everything that had occupied him was etched across his face and gathered at the corners of his eyes.

Caught unawares by Aldo, Joel had nodded his head in agreement as he realised what he was being asked. Even now, Aldo had the power to scare him completely and utterly witless.

Joel carried her. He carried Millie from the hearse and into the church. Joel, her dad, a cousin and another who he didn't know, had borne the coffin upon their shoulders to walk down the aisle of a packed church. He heard Aldo choke and cry from the other side, his sobs just about audible under the soft beat and breathy vocals of a ballad chosen that accompanied Millie's arrival. He exchanged a pained look with Aldo as they positioned the coffin before the altar; they didn't say anything, they didn't need to.

In any other circumstance, they might have had different roles in travelling down that aisle and with Millie. Joel knew, and he knew that Aldo knew; there had been a conversation only days ago, with veiled references that didn't need to be explained. Maya knew too, she had told him. Maya had sobbed her heart out and told him, that Millie had wished for things to be different and had been waiting for him to ask.

All he had to do was ask. Now it was all too late.

More music followed. Notes wafted in the air as a montage of images was projected onto a screen to the right of the altar. Images of Millie as a new born, swaddled in a baby blanket and in her father's arms. He saw Millie on the first day of school and grinning as she wore her uniform. There was a picture of Millie and Joel standing on a shingle beach with Brighton pier in the background.

A rich and vibrant life was documented in the two dozen photographs chosen for the congregation to reflect upon. The last part of the montage was a video, taken only recently. She was sharing her plans to fly away and trek across Peru to raise money for a children's charity. Joel bit his lip, his head sunk and into his hands. To hear her voice, see her smile and smell her perfume; it would never happen again.

He had loved her for so long and with all of his heart. To have never told her or have shown her, that crushed him. If only he had said something, done something; to have loved her and have lost her, was doubly painful. Drawing his palms away from his face, he sat up right to look at Maya and Aldo. Maya wore an expression of resilience, there was a gentle fortitude in the way that she looked at Aldo to reassure him. Aldo himself was less robust and had crumpled into the curve of the pew as he sat beside his wife. Millie had not been his alone. Firstly, she was theirs and always theirs.

***

"Matthew, I want to just sit a while," Albie spoke in hushed tone as he put a hand to his grandson's elbow. Most of the mourners had started to move away from the graveside and into their cars to get to the wake. Sat on a grey framed lawn chair, Albie had watched Lilly's coffin be lowered slowly into the ground. He had been flanked by his son standing to his left and his grandson sat on another seat to his right. They had both protested and loudly, that Albie should not be stood and for over an hour during what was a really quite biting cold day.

Albie had conceded, and decided that he would sit instead. He had sent David packing and to retrieve the chair that in quiet negotiations with his daughter-in-law had been secreted into the boot of Lydia's car. He was not so cabbage as he was green looking, and had hung on Matthew whilst waiting for his son to return.

"In the cold?" asked Matthew, looking sidelong at his grandfather.

"In the cold," replied Albie, sliding aside his thick winter coat and revealing a silver hip flask that was tucked into the pocket of his black blazer. "Just give me and Lilly a little bit longer, eh. Go," he added, tapping at Matthew's elbow.

"But I will be back," sighed Matthew, rising from his seat and placing a hand onto his grandfather's shoulder. "Plan is for you to go with me and Lydia." Pulling his jacket closer, he looked at Albie and then at the open mouth of the grave with the most fleeting of glances. "We'll be back in a bit, Grandad, not staying here too long."

Albie watched his grandson walk away with his hands buried deep in his pockets and his shoulders almost meeting his ears. He and Lilly had watched Matthew grow from a puking, mewling, pink faced babe in arms to a rather sure footed young man with the whole world before him. "Do you think he properly learned to make cake, Lilly?" Albie said out aloud. "You spent enough time teaching him, wonder if all sunk in. No one makes cake quite like you, Lilly. You've given him what David calls a complex. We didn't do too badly with him either, did we? I don't think that I have ever seen David cry and so much as he did today," he said laughing somewhat uneasily; his breath was white as it hit the air and plumed away.

"All those tears, he must have saved them all up. Remember him falling and as a boy? Trying to get him to calm down, saying how big boys don't cry. He'd had enough by now, and just had to let them go. You've left me with them, Lilly. David, his wife, our Matthew." Albie sighed deeply, feeling the freshness of the cold air on his lips as he moved his hand towards his hip flask. Sliding it out from his pocket, he felt the weight and coldness of the metal between his fingers.

Albie flipped open the metal cap of the hip flask and pressed his lips to it to take a sip. "I remember when it was just the two of us and we were starting out together. It was a different time then, Lilly; we were content," he certainly felt it, as he let out a sigh. The warmth of the alcohol settled across his chest and made the breeze feel less fresh.

"Then we had David and things changed. Do you remember how scared we were? You were right, I didn't become my old man," Albie nodded as a quiet chuckle escaped his lips. "I didn't become a monster, and that was because of you. You stopped that happening. I love you, Lilly," Albie's voice broke a little, and he wiped a tear from his eye and on the fabric of his dark trousers.

"You made me who I am, and without that there would be no David or Matthew. I have no clue now though, of what to do next. I am old, Lilly. How long might it be, before I join you down there, do you think? You kept me going and I didn't think we were quite finished yet. I've never been without you and now I am. I don't like this," he said shaking his head. "I don't like this at all."

Albie sat there for a little while longer; he talked out aloud and relived some of the memories that he had made with Lilly. He was so lost walking down memory lane and reminiscing that he didn't see Matthew return and this time with Lydia in tow.

"How much do you think he's had to drink?" whispered Lydia, she had her arm linked around Matthews so that she wouldn't fall over. She was wearing square heeled black ankle boots that had already disagreed with the wet leaves that stuck to the ground and a lot like wet linoleum. Earlier, she had very nearly slipped and gone flying whilst walking to the graveside.

Matthew shrugged at first. "Hopefully not too much," he replied. "We'll soon know. If you take one side, I'll take the other. Grandad?"

Hearing Matthew's voice, Albie started to rise slowly to his feet. He found himself flanked once again, and had a feeling that he was going to baby sat once more. They weren't exactly the sort to frogmarch him, but he knew that they meant well. "I'm not drunk," he stated firmly, tucking his hip flask away.

"Just cold," Lydia offered gently, looping her arm around his. "We should go, Albie."

"Lead on then, Lilly," said Albie, starting to move and dragging the two of them with him.

"Lyd-" Started Matthew, only to receive a glare from his girlfriend. A slip of the tongue was to be expected, things were all very fresh still.

Between the two of them and with a little help from David, Albie was supported through the day. Once all the mourners had gone, Albie wasn't left alone. David and his wife stayed the night, with Matthew bringing left over food and drink back to the house. He couldn't help but look for Lilly as they all pottered around the house. It felt strange that was missing. It would take him time to stop looking for her, calling her name. He hadn't meant to call Lydia by Lilly's name. Saying Lilly's name was almost second nature, and he couldn't have stopped himself had he even tried. Albie watched Lydia and Matthew, watched how they were together. All he could think about was himself and Lilly at the same age. He could also see just how much the young woman meant to his grandson, how he might also be lost without her.

At the back of his mind was a conversation that he had had with Lilly about the young couple. They had talked about whether or not Lydia and Matthew had a future together, whether or not there might be wedding bells. Albie had been unconvinced; they were of a different generation. That for Matthew and Lydia, being together didn't necessarily mean walking down the aisle. Lilly had made him promise; promise to sort out her jewellery and hand over things to be given to Lydia. Lilly had died in hope that one day the two would get married, have children that David might fuss over just as she and Albie had fussed over Matthew.

At the end of the evening, as he watched Matthew and Lydia leave, he was convinced that Lydia had something twinkling in her eyes. There was definitely something preying on her mind, and not just with Lilly passing. Maybe Lilly's hope was valid, may be it wasn't. All he could do now was to hope. Hope that Matthew and Lydia were happy together. Lilly had died in hope but Albie planned to live in it.

***

A cocktail shaker; the urn looked like a retro cocktail shaker. Blue-grey, it was cool to the touch as Christopher picked it up from the shelf. He was stood rather awkwardly in the cupboard beneath the stairs; the ceiling sloped at an angle that if you weren't looking, was likely to smack you straight between the eyes.

He had entered the cupboard through the small door that always made him feel like a giant and flicked on the light. In the far corner a box light about nine inches across threw a harsh light out and onto the contents of the cupboard. Shoes, coats, the rather knackered vacuum cleaner that he had yet to throw away, had all been thrown in or hung up in   rather haphazard way.

The only organized aspect was the shelf. A space had been cleared amongst the cans of air freshener, polish and de-icer for the urn; Adelphi's urn. That had been three weeks ago, when the vet had called and asked him to pick up Adelphi's remains. They had discussed the options beforehand. Options where Adelphi could be cremated with others, disposed of was another phrase that had been uttered.

"Disposed of?!" he had yelled, rather shrilly over the 'phone and the day after Adelphi had gone to sleep. "No, no thank you. Can you go over the cremation bit again, please?" he had asked, his grip tightening around his mobile as he thought twice about throwing the device towards the wall. "You did say something about individual cremations."

Along with the cost of putting Adelphi to sleep, there was the additional cost of an individual cremation. He was prepared to pay for it; there was no part of him that wanted Adelphi 'disposed of' and with other pets. Adelphi was his and his alone, and that was the way it was going to be. Alive, Adelphi had made only smallest of dents in his insurance; he'd been rather robust in that respect. With him now the other side of the rainbow bridge, Christopher was happy to let the insurance take the hit.

For the last three weeks, Adelphi's ashes had been sat

here. Forgotten about, whilst Christopher tried to stoically move on and get on with things. Only today however, he had looked up and away from his laptop; he had looked directly as the spot that Adelphi had used to occupy. He had not done that in a while and at that moment, it had hit him like a bolt of lightning. It was there again, the feeling of having your heart split in two and torn apart.

Using his thumbs, Christopher wiped away dusty residue and lint that had been attracted to the urn in its abandonment. "I'm sorry, Adelphi," he whispered. "I didn't mean to forget you, leave you here. I just couldn't….what am I supposed-" Christopher broke off sharply and groaned. In his reflection, he had moved his head and struck the ceiling. The urn had slipped from his grasp and he fumbled for it awkwardly whilst trying not to fall over the vacuum cleaner. Drawing it close towards him, he held onto the urn as his heart raced.

Taking a deep breath, he turned and pushed the door open to escape into the light of the hallway. Sliding Adelphi's urn to his hip, Christopher slid his other hand into his pocket and dug out his 'phone. His thumb hopped around the touch screen; hearing the dial tone, he pressed it to his ear. "Mum, it's me," he said walking towards the kitchen. "Yes, I know, sorry. I kind of zoned out for a few weeks. No, everything's fine, honest. Thing is," he said letting out a deep breath as he looked at the urn. "I've got Adelphi's ashes. Was just wondering, would you pop 'round and help me send him off. You know, properly."

It was fortunate for Christopher that his Mum was actually free. In the middle of a half term holiday, Joyce braved the rain and made the fifteen minute journey to her son on foot. She was there at his front door half an hour after he had called. Joyce entered the house a little weather beaten and lowering the hood of her rather drenched coat. She was met at the door by Christopher who was still holding the urn and close towards his chest.

Letting Joyce in, he stepped in behind as she walked down the hallway. He was rather intrigued by the white plastic bag that hung from her arm. Christopher's brows knitted together in curiosity. He could see that beyond the rain splattered plastic there was some dark brown black soil and a what appeared to be a couple of twigs sticking out of it.

"Dog rose," Joyce stated, answering the unspoken question that was etched across her son's face. She planted the bag down and carefully removed her coat to drape it across the balustrade at the end of the stairs. "Been looking after it ever since, ever since Adelphi went to sleep," she added, sweeping away locks of hair to look directly at Christopher. "Your dad and I went to a garden centre a couple of days after, and-"She paused as she saw that Christopher's bottom lip had started to tremble and his eyes were welling up. It was an expression that she knew well.

Quickly stepping forward, Joyce put her hands to Christopher's face to cradle his jaw. "It's okay," she whispered as he leant forward and now had his head resting on her shoulder. "This is going to take time," she continued wrapping her arms around his shoulders. He was a lost little boy again, and within her this brought back memories of when he was child. "There's no rush, Chris, do this when you are ready."

Tea and cake were required and in equal measure before Christopher's tears subsided. Everything had been filed away since the blog post and he had used writing that to retreat into his own world. Now it had come out, and had required his mum, madeira cake and mugs of tea help manage dealing with things. Outside, the storm that Christopher's mum had walked through had also squalled itself out. Grimy grey clouds had floated away to leave a blue sky speckled with fluffy white clouds in their wake.

Opening the door to the garden, Christopher leant against it with a foot planted squarely on the threshold. A square lawn edged by fence along three sides was what he called his garden; the south aspect of it was entirely lost on him. The whole thing was deliberately low maintenance. In the far right was the walnut stained shed that he had inherited from the previous owners. If he remembered correctly, there was a fork and spade in there that had borrowed from his father and forgotten to return.

A strip of soil separated the lawn from the fence. In a couple of places, shrubs had been planted but were currently dormant and not in bloom. "He would dig things up," Christopher told his mum. "I would put things in plant them. Nothing would last, he was hell bent on digging it all up," he couldn't help but shake his head. "Nothing was ever Adelphi-proof."

Sat at the kitchen table, Joyce listened and watched over the rim of her mug. Next to her on another chair was the white plastic bag that she had come in with. It was drier now. The rain drops that covered its flimsiness had evaporated in the warmth, and the dog rose-it was labelled as being a pink variety- was still inside. On the table itself, Christopher had left Adelphi's urn. She said nothing as Christopher stepped across the door frame and into the garden. Through the kitchen window, Joyce saw the shed door swing open; she heard it too as the hinges creaked noisily.

Christopher moved around the shed, he was only just visible from the kitchen. Eventually, he hopped out and closed the door behind him. In his one hand, there was an edging spade. In the other a green handed fork that had some rather dirty tines that also happened to be a little bent. Walking across the grass and disturbing the rather lusciously overgrown blades, he felt bottom of his jeans become wet. He made a mental note to ask his dad for his lawnmower and tidy it all up. Raindrops took flight as he moved toward the far left corner of the garden and directly opposite the shed.

Over the next fifteen minutes, Christopher used the spade and fork to dig up clods of brown black, part clay, part loamy soil and make a hole that was a foot and a half wide and about as deep. When he was satisfied that the hole was about right, he flung the edging spade behind him. Landing with a thud on the blades of grass, the impact of the spade caused a burst of raindrops to momentarily fill the air. Standing with his hands on his hips and with his feet shoulder width apart, Christopher could feel his heart beat furiously and shoulders throb from the strain of digging.

"Nearly there, Adelphi," he muttered, "No one is ever going to dig you up, I swear." Cupping his hand across his jaw, Christopher could feel heat radiating from his skin. This was one last thing that he had to and for Adelphi. Taking one last studious look at the hole, he moved off back into the kitchen.

Joyce was watching his every movement. She panned her gaze from the window and towards the door through which Christopher tumbled back into the kitchen.

"Mum, you coming?" he asked, picking up the urn and moving towards the door to exit again. "Bring your tea if you want; the dog rose too. Quick, before the rain comes back again." There was a sense of urgency in his voice as he ran out through the door and across the lawn.

Grasping at the handles of the bag with one hand, and holding her tea in the other, Joyce followed Christopher outside. She could see why her son was in such a hurry. More grey clouds and pregnant with a deluge, were creeping across the horizon towards the house. They didn't have long and it was pointless standing on ceremony.

Christopher could feel that his was heart was still racing and causing waves of nausea to pass over him. His throat was dry and he gulped away the tautness to exhale deeply. He looked at the urn one last time, knowing that contained within it were the early remains of his best friend. Powdery grey material and weighing just less than one and a half pounds, there was not an awful lot left of Adelphi.

He doubted very much if Adelphi had ever weighed less than that as a puppy, and boy, had he grown into a fairly well proportioned dog. Rubbing away the remaining layer of dust and the fine, silky, thread of a long since destroyed spider's web, Christopher moved towards the hole that he had laboured to create and crouched beside it.

Neat mounds of earth surrounded the gap and a little fell back in as he placed the urn onto its side. With his hands, he scooped up some of the dirt from the mounds and threw into the hole to cover the urn. "There are no plans, mate, to ever dig you up. Sleep well," he said, throwing in more dirt by the handful. He turned slightly and looked up towards his mother.

Taking the hint, Joyce walked closer and with the carrier bag that contained a dog rose. Not knowing quite what to say, she held it out towards her son.

Rustling in the breeze, the bag provided a gentle soundtrack as Christopher took a hold of it and with both hands. Reaching inside of the bag, he pulled out a brown plastic pot and letting go of the bag let it flutter its way towards Joyce. Tapping the bottom of the pot, he tugged at the currently rather twiggy shrub to free it. The plant must have been stuck in the pot for some time. The soil within the pot was held together by a complex network of roots with a lace-work like appearance.

He plugged the plant into the hole and on top of the covered urn. Using his hands as shovels, he pulled the dirt heaped around the hole towards the base of the shrub to tuck it in. Rain was falling again, and he raised his shoulders as drops felt to his neck and travelled beneath his t-shirt and down his spine. "I'll see you, Adelphi," he said patting down soil. "Safe journey, bud."

***

It was brilliant white with pale blue embellishments and silver handles that were cold to the touch. What struck Michael was the size. The whole thing was probably no bigger than a foot and a half in length. It was so small, that he might have walked in here with it tucked neatly under his arm. He and Sophie had carried the box-he could bring himself to call it a coffin-between them and the short way down the aisle into the chapel. In between sobs and tears, Sophie had whispered quietly to their son as they had walked. He could see how ashen faced she was, her eyes were bloodshot and her nose was rubbed red with a soggy tissue that pulled repeatedly from the sleeve of her cardigan.

"It's okay, Sam, just sleep tightly," Sophie had whispered. "Mummy loves you, and will miss you. You will always, always my little star."

The three of them had processed down the aisle to the rather muted strains of 'The Dance of the Sugar Plum fairy'. This specific piece of music had been chose as it sounded as though it might have been played in the little boy's nursery and to lull him to sleep. The gentle rise and fall of the piece was a lullaby that would now send him onward to dreams of eternity and beyond.

As they arrived at the altar, Michael caught sight of

the would-be grandparents. Today was a small, intimate family gathering; Michael, Sophie, his parents, Sophie's mum and a sibling a piece. Those gathered here to say goodbye, were those people who would have been Sam's nearest and dearest; family who would have attended his baptism and stood as Godparents.

Religion made today difficult, even more so that it already was. Religion had been a pain and comfort so many times before. When things had gone wrong before, it had given Michael hope; it had given both of them hope. Hope that this might have been part of a plan; that if they remained strong and continued to have faith, then they would have a happy ending. There had been hopes, prayers, offerings and candles. Silent murmurings and pained drawn out, one-sided conversations about how unfair all of this was.

As he sat holding Sophie's hand, Michael remembered coming here late in a Thursday night and ready to rail against the world and the God that was meant to have created it all. Standing not too far away from where he sat right now, he had stood before the altar. He had screamed, shouted at the forlorn figure on the crucifix and demanded that his world be fixed. He had demanded change, that all they wanted was a baby and one to call their own, so that he and Sophie might love the child and create a family. His words had been flung out at the walls, bounced off the wooden rafters and pinged against the contemporary stained glass windows that documented the Stations of the Cross. His raging voice had disturbed the peace of this Holy sanctuary and still that voice was a growl in the pit of his stomach; it was a hissing cur that disturbed his inner most thoughts.

It had taken time for him and Sophie to work out how things would go today. They had discussed with the minister how they might bury their unbaptised baby, if not in sanctified soil. Fortunately, the minister had offered them both comfort and solace. They could bury their son, he and the church saw no bars. Samuel was born of them, of their faith and as such was part of this church. There was no objection to the child being laid to rest in the church grounds and sleep amongst the dozen or so other children who had also been taken too soon. So they had planned today, a final goodbye to hand over their son to the world beyond. He was a child that they had loved so intensely, if only for a short while.

Sat for an hour, Michael heard the minister say his words; there was chapter and verse with relating to peace and comfort. There were words of being thankful; that they may have only been a family of three for a brief time, but they had been a family nonetheless. He heard promises, promises of eternal love and light that would keep Samuel safe; light that would keep his memory alive and keep him a part of their world.

He saw his brother, Andrew, rise from the cushioned but still uncomfortable chair, and stand at the lectern to read a letter. He read out a letter that described his joy at becoming an uncle, of having someone else other than him to terrorise Michael. In this letter, his brother described what he and his nephew might have got up together, had they been in cahoots.

He would have bought the noisiest toys; there would have been football in the park and waiting for Samuel's first day at school. He was saddened, that they wouldn't get do all of these things, but he would not and could not forget what might have been. "You will always be a part of our family," Andrew had said, "There will always be a place for you, a stocking, a memory and a slice of cake. You will always be with us."

Nothing could have quite prepared him for the lowering of the box and into the ground. Michael could not have thought of a more unwelcoming place to send his sleeping son. It was a cold, wet, cocoon of brown and black earth that was teeming with mini-beasts. A place so horrible, that the thought of the creatures disturbing his boy, turned his stomach. This was a hole in the ground, so different to the nursery that had been prepared so lovingly and in such eagerness.

With Sophie in his arms, he pressed his head against hers. Together they cried again, together they trembled with the pain of their loss. His already broken heart felt as though it was fracturing all over again; with each and every breath that he took, it was shattering and into tiny pieces. Their universe was torn up and the fragments thrown to the wind that whistled through the trees and swept through the graves that surrounded them.

Handfuls of earth were dropped into the hole and onto the box; a heaped pile developed on the name plate. His father and Andrew had picked up a shovel each and were starting to fill in the hole to cover the box completely. For the time being there was no headstone. A headstone would come later. Their little boy was gone and he would be sleeping forever. Michael could not think, or focus on what he and Sophie might do next. Everything that they had planned, prayed for, had brought them nothing but unhappiness and pain. He had nothing to say, as Sophie held onto his hand and they walked back to the car.

He had nothing, to offer comfort or even to ask what they were going to do next. It was all probably a little too soon. He looked over his shoulder as Sophie climbed into their car, and for one last glance. A bouquet of blue star gazer lilies had been placed upon Samuel's grave and fluttered in the breeze. His son was somewhere in the heavens and always would be their little star.

***

Straw and honey. That was the colour of Rachel's coffin. Made from willow, it was entirely wicker and felt surprisingly quite robust as it was carried on his shoulders and those of the other pall bearers. Today had been carefully planned in hushed whispers and gentle tones. The word itself-funeral-had never been mentioned; it had been sidestepped as though it was a pot hole to be avoided and at all costs. A word that Rachel had found difficult to say, even though she had told him, once, twice and several times that she was in fact reconciled to what was going to happen. Planning today had been part of her process; that was the phrase that she used and so many times.

"I had no choice about coming into this world, Raj," she had said, "I've done my best to live and do what I needed to. Apparently I have to leave this world, a bit earlier than I would have liked. If I have to leave, then I want to say how and what you need to do for the last goodbye. We already know when, we don't have long left and to argue about it all. Pick up that pen; bring over that bundle of catalogues. Come here and help me plan this thing." Her tone had been firm, laced with calm logic and together they had carefully assembled a plan of what was to happen.

Today was a good bye; this was Rachel's send off and a celebration. The only thing that might have betrayed that a funereal air was the smattering of black jackets here and there, there was the odd black dress and matching pill box hat. Those invited to attend today, had actually been asked to wear the colour purple or something sparkly in Rachel's memory. Most had taken note, he had seen a purple fascinator on someone's crown. It sparkled with crystals as though for good measure.

Rachel's ceremony-she had baulked at the word service-involved all of the family. He had spoken at first, to welcome everyone and remind them that today was now about mourning. "My wife," he said, "Was very specific about how misery was not an option today." When the coffin had come to rest at the front of the gathering, everyone present was invited to up and the weft of the willow was interspersed with fresh flowers and leafy foliage.

Raj had taken a depth breathe and stood with his one hand placed upon Rachel's coffin. "Rachel, we would all like to say goodbye to you today," he said biting his lip and then passing the tip of his tongue of over the dry and flaking skin. "Say goodbye and also thank you, for all the many, varied ways that you have touched our lives. For me, that is twenty years of being my dearest friend, my soul mate and the mother of our two beautiful children. You gave me a world, and whole universe and I am so very glad that I got to share it with you. Without you, I am lost but I will learn; I promise that I will learn to keep things going and how you would have wanted them to happen." He pressed two fingers to his lips and sent a kiss towards the coffin.

Then, he moved towards his seat by his children and let his brother-in-law, Phillip, take the floor. He was a little younger than Rachel, and his bottom lip trembled as he read out a eulogy; his shoulders bobbed up and down and he was visibly distraught. Dabbing his pink eyes, Phillip spoke movingly, in a heartfelt way about being a lost little boy who would ask his older sister for help at school. He had become a gawky adolescent and had been unsure about his place in the world, but Rachel had calmed him and counselled him, to truly mean the world to him.

Phillip paused for a moment, his hand grazing clusters of heather in the willow as he found the fortitude to continue; now he spoke about joy, of sunshine and the brightness that Rachel had given him as his sister. For a few moments, it felt to Raj as though Rachel was there with them and she was being addressed directly.

Raj watched as two children left his side and stood either side of the coffin. Koby kept his gaze pinned to the floor but rested his palms on the willow and absent mindedly fiddled with the petals of vivid orange nasturtiums.

"One day," started Caliope, "Mum and I were listening to an old song. It's a song that I've only a few times, but it's a song that Mum liked and knew really well. One of the lyrics is that there is no sunshine when she is gone. That, that is how everything has felt, for me, for Koby." Caliope briefly looked at her brother, before focusing on the people sat before her.

"It's horrible, that Mum isn't here, and that is why that we are here today. But I can't help but think of sunshine," Caliope paused, drew in breath and looked squarely at Raj. "We still have that sunshine, Dad; we will always have Mum's sunshine. There is sunshine, when Dad says her name; sunshine when Koby talks about how he and Mum would watch Rugby. I see sunshine when I imagine Mum's smile and hear her laughter from all the times that we spent hours watching really soppy chick flicks. Mum might not be here, but she did leave alot happiness, joy and so much sunshine."

Looking as if a load had been lifted from her shoulders, Caliope smiled a little. Taking her brother's hand, she led him back to their seats. As she returned to sit by him, Raj noticed how pink rimmed her eyes were; he had never known his little girl to have cried so much and look so lost.

The ceremony had almost drawn to a close when out of the corner of his eye, Raj saw his mother move from beside his aunt. The two women looked almost alike and were both dressed in traditional salwar kameez; both had a white scarf draped across their shoulders and covering their hair. The white scarf was traditional. White was the colour of mourning in Asian communities. She had also worn a rather sober black cardigan with faux mother of pearl buttons, and he knew that the deep pockets were mostly likely stuffed with wads of damp tissue.

Raj watched as his mother shuffled through the semi-circle of chairs and towards Rachel's coffin with a crumpled up ball of tissue pressed to her nose. Alongside the black cardigan and the white scarf, she had complied with Rachel's wishes and wore her favourite lilac salwar kameez. Whilst it was muted in colour, just happened to be shot through with strands of silver thread.

Nestled in the crook of Nandini's arm was a bouquet of pink and white roses with prickly stems and bronze-green foliage. Rather than being wrapped up in plastic or a sheet of tissue paper, the bouquet was tightly bound together by a scarf. This scarf was pale pink and trimmed along the edge by silver ribbon that glimmered in the light. Raj couldn't quite make out what his mother was saying, she was speaking very quietly and to Rachel as she arranged the flowers on top. These were fresh blooms; flowers that earlier in the day, Nandini had cut from the bushes in her garden. He tried to listen and eventually caught some of the words. He heard the word 'daughter', heard how much she would miss Rachel, that she would teach the children how to roll rotis. There was even a few words of prayer. For that moment, his mother was alone with Rachel for one last time. He could do nothing but watch as his mother's face crumpled with hurt and slowly she shuffled back to her seat.

Raj had been dreading today; as the moment came for the committal, he found that his children were holding his hands. The coffin had been removed from trestles and a curtain drawn around it for the closing of the ceremony. It was at that point that he realised that his chapters with Rachel really were at an end. His daughter had been right, they still had sunshine and they would always have the sunshine.

18 Marcy

Someone to walk with

Death. Even the word and just the word is enough to send shivers down your spine or make you pull a face. It makes us comfortable and we choose not to speak about it. Death-depending upon perception-might become our friend, be greeted with open arms and be a release. Or we might treat Death as foe; draw battle lines and gather an arsenal to shout battle cries that carry on the wind and become barely a whisper. Death is something that we hardly ever talk about, yet it happens to us all.

It was however, good to talk and especially to talk about death. If you were talking, then you ought to have someone there to listen. For Marcy, that was her job. For six hours a day, three days a week, Marcy listened and to those who had been touched by death in one way or another. As she looked at her appointments, she could see how Death left a footprint in its wake. For some, the footprint was still quite fresh, as though left in freshly fallen snow. For others, Death's footprint was only just starting to fade and was like ink blanching away in sunlight. Then there were the furrows. The footprint had grown into field and was ploughed on a daily basis. For most of those who came to her, Marcy could listen and without judgement or direction.

Some, she would have to signpost towards someone who might be better qualified. There were those who didn't want to be there; they would rather walk alone and not have anyone share their footfall or that of Death. Yet she sat and she listened. Sometimes she sat with the silence, at other times Marcy would sit with the sobs, the tears and the sound of pain being held onto with an iron grip. Marcy listened and tried to understand; she tried to feel and to see the world through each client's eyes. She had seen every face of Death, the friend and the foe.

Marcy saw endings, where those sat opposite her in Room six were able to see beyond the here and now; if they wanted to see, that was. It was good to talk and to listen. Each journey was unique; some were sudden, others were drawn out. There was pain and in some cases joy. It was never Marcy's place to judge the direction, take the lead in exploring. Ethically, what she had to do was walk with them; alongside and with every single word, thought, emotion and experience.

Death. It happened to us all. Even to Marcy and so many years ago. The memory was a little blurry around the edges, but she remembered the colourful walls of the Pentecostal church and the singing; full bodied and passionate singing during the whole thing. There was sadness; it was after all her grandmother's funeral. Lots of people attended. Some of the faces, she had known and recognised; others were less familiar and most likely members of the family that were too distant for her to have known. As a seven year old, Marcy had found the whole thing chaotic and confusing.

She remembered visiting Granny Luna in nursing home, where she had lived with lots of other older people. Granny had smiled whilst she had sat in her lap. Marcy could remember quite vividly that she had played with amber beads that Granny wore on her wrists. Granny had looked happy and healthy.

As young as she was, Marcy didn't remember seeing or hearing anything that suggested Granny wasn't as fit as fiddle. She had told Marcy stories of travelling to Britain on a boat and how she had come here to train as a nurse. A boat and travelling all that way from the other side of the world. For seven year old Marcy that sounded like an adventure and her grandmother must have been very brave to do it. Years later, Marcy had spoken with her mum and her sister Celeste, to get a better idea of what had happened. She had been training at the time and the whole concept of family bereavement had touched something of a nerve. Aunt Celeste had filled in the gaps of how Luna had developed Alzheimer's and this had led to all sorts of health concerns. This had confused Marcy and hurt her that no one had told her the truth.

There had been a big part of her that felt Death had been hidden away from her. Granny Luna had been a huge part of her life and she had been stopped from saying goodbye; in her mind, as an adult she felt that she had been stopped from grieving. That left her feeling altogether uncomfortable within and she had worked hard to explore it. This exploration in turn shaped her training, helped Marcy to better understand grief and loss. The process became an integral part of her, and now she helped others to do the same.

Her own journey of working through bereavement had shaped her world, changed it and allowed Marcy to look at the world in a different light. For her, her box of bereavement was sealed and stowed safely away. Those that she worked with came to her with similar boxes. Closing her diary, Marcy made her way to room six. She would be meeting with two new clients today, with each being a very different journey.

It was good to talk and about death.

***

The walk had done him good; the bonus being that this place was not far from work. He could pop out and be back without anyone batting so much as an eyelid. It was work that had arranged all of this, counselling was part of the company employee assistance programme. Counselling, it wasn't exactly something that he had thought about, not really.

Today was his second visit; the first had been for an assessment and to meet a counsellor. Counsellor; the word still made him feel nervous. Aldo took another look at the blue clock face that hung on the egg shell wall. It was ten to the hour and a whole five minutes since had last looked to see what the time was. He had ten minutes, it was too late to cancel and walk out of here. He did want to be here, it was just the fear of the unknown that caused him to look for the door. He needed to do this; he couldn't talk to Maya, he just couldn't. He did need to speak to someone though, someone who was outside of his bubble.

His session started on the hour. For the next fifty minutes, he would be sat in a rather comfortable, well upholstered pale blue arm chair.

"What would you like for to me call you?"

"Aldo," he had said, his hands resting palm down on his thighs.

"You can call me Aldo," he let out a deep breath as he focused on the woman sat opposite him, He wondered how old she was, as well as what she could possibly know about Death. Not to mention what Death did to you, how could she possibly know about how it felt to be left behind?

"It's nice to meet you again, Aldo," Marcy gave a slight nod, and clasped her hands in her lap. Their previous meeting had been a two part experience. First, there was an assessment of the concerns that Aldo had. Secondly, they had discussed how they were going to work together, how their sessions together would go. For now, she and Aldo would meet over the next six weeks; beyond that, it was up to Aldo to decide if he wanted to continue meeting. Marcy watched Aldo carefully. There was a definite sadness that glimmered in his eyes; she could also see that his knuckles had blanched when he curled his hands into fists just above his knees.

"This is a safe place, Aldo," Marcy had said, still watching him closely. "Whenever you are ready, if you can say in your own words, what you would like to talk about today." So it started, and Marcy would listen. She would listen, watch, and pick up the box of pastel coloured two-ply tissues that were sat on the nest of tables close by. Tissues would be taken, as Aldo talked, sobbed and let her in to his world.

Aldo had blinked; his eyelashes batted and fanned a

few times, causing a stripy shadow to fall against the darkened hollows of his eyes. Pursing together, his lips had moved. He would have spoken, but his bottom lip quivered and before long was trembling. He felt overcome; inside, a curtain had torn in two and descended to the floor with an almighty bang. With it, his guard had fallen.

Aldo felt his shoulders sink from being held so high and rigid. Moving his hands from his lap, he wiped away tears. One flew through the air and landed on his trousers where it was quickly absorbed into the taupe threads. He tugged free tissue from the box that was offered to him and pressed it against his eyes to let the tears soak through. Before long, the tissue was wet through and he scrunched up the soft tissue into a ball.

"Millie," whispered Aldo. "It hurts and I can't...." his voice broke again and he lowered his head, he let the tears fall. He didn't want to stop them; they had been trapped inside for such a long time. Surely, it was better to let them out and not hold it all back any more. After all, this was a safe place. That was what she had told him; this was a safe place.

Marcy could see the rawness; she could feel the intensity of his loss and the emotions that were being experienced. It was still very early in this journey. Aldo's loss was very recent. She knew that this could take time. In this room, this was his time and his space to use how he wanted to. If Aldo wanted to cry, then he could; he could let his tears fall and that was his choice. It was not Marcy's place or role, to tell him that crying was right or it was wrong. His grief was palpable. Even then, she would not judge or ask him to stop. She would stay there with him, walk with him and experience what he was experience whilst not directly being involved.

Fifty minutes would pass quickly, albeit be punctuated by sobs, sniffles and silences. Aldo left with a weak smile, confirming that he would be back in a fortnight as agreed. He left the building, and Marcy had ten minutes to write up notes about the session. There was barely a moment to breathe, to nip to the loo before the next client was ushered in. As with Aldo, this was another journey about to start. This journey also involved a child. Only this child had not had the chance to live.

"I just want to talk, and about my baby," said Sophie. Sat in the blue chair, Sophie held onto a small blue bear that she had brought with her. It had been a gift, along with some clothes that her colleagues had given to her when she had started maternity leave. "This is Ollie," she said, holding up the bear and looking at Marcy; Sophie wore something of an uneasy smile as she spoke. "He lives in my handbag; he's been in there for ages. Something of a lucky charm, I guess. We had hope this time, and Ollie. Well, Ollie is cute and he is cuddly. My hope lives and he lives in my handbag." Sophie returned the bear to her lap, and her fingers rubbed the velvet trim around its ears.

"Did he have a name, your baby?" Asked Marcy; she was aware of some details from the initial assessment. "Your son, did you give him a name?"

Sophie pressed her lips together, realising that she had seen the name written down, said the name to Michael. But no one outside of the family had been told the name that she and Michael had chosen for their son.

"Samuel," she replied. Clearing her throat, she took in a deep and measured breath. The coolness steadied her somewhat, allowing her to pause and collect some of the thoughts that were running around in her head. One of the thoughts was her son's full name as she had seen it written on certificates. "Samuel Sachin James. It was ready and waiting for him, just like everything else. We had everything prepared, and now…" Sophie curled her fingers tighter around the bear. "I don't think people get how it feels to get so close. So, so close, Marcy," her voice broke and there were muffled squeaks behind the bear that had moved to her mouth.

"I would like to try," offered Marcy. "Perhaps you could help me get it," she added gently, staying with Sophie's thoughts.

"It's really hard to hear," continued Sophie, returning the bear to her lap. "When people say things like, you were so close, such a shame! You would have made such a good mum, Sophie," she sighed a little, and gulped down air. "Then you get those, those who say that they are sorry, and that's it," Sophie tutted and shook her head. "What they were waiting for, was to say congratulations. To pat Michael and I on the back and say well done. But no, it's a sorry, and not being able to even understand. I mean, how hard can this possibly be?" asked Sophie, shrugging her shoulders. "I'm a woman, female. I should be able to be a mum; that is all that I wanted. I wanted to be a mum, and good one."

"It does sound hard to hear," nodded Marcy. "Especially when you might want to hear people say something supportive. You want to be a good mum; sounds as though that is really very important you, as role."

"Feels like a failure," Sophie whispered. "Complete failure, both physically and mentally. Physically, I have no idea what happened; what I might have done for, for...."she paused as the words she wanted to say, felt bitter on her tongue. These were words that she felt so difficult to say. "I have no idea, what I did for my baby to be born asleep. They, the doctors, said that this happens. They said, that more often than not, they can't say why it happens. But there has to be a reason!" Again, she shook her head, and there was heaviness as her words filled the air.

"What is it that would you like to hear, Sophie?" asked Marcy, tilting her head slightly in anticipation of Sophie's response. "What would you like someone to say?"

Sophie looked directly at Marcy, and wondered if the counsellor had children. She wondered if she had ever experienced that overwhelming desire to have a life growing inside of her. Sophie silently considered whether Marcy had felt the mixture of excitement and fear in willing a pregnancy test to change one way or another.

"Anything," she uttered quietly, "Just something, so I can understand why Sam was born asleep. Anything that explains to me why there have been so many miscarriages, and tells me what is it that I have done. Whatever it is, it has robbed me of having a baby. Robbed me of being able to hold my child, alive and in my arms. I wouldn't wish this," Sophie's mouth turned downwards at the corners, and she moved forward to pluck tissues from a box, "and on anyone," she said, pressing tissue to her face and sitting back into the chair.

There was those who were starting their journey of healing; there was immediacy and there a pained rawness to the experiences. Marcy took a moment, placing an inky tick next to the names of those that she had already seen today. Next were those who had already taken the first steps and were now exploring, trying to reach an understanding of what they felt and processing loss.

Most of those that Marcy worked with experienced the loss of a person, a human being; someone who was very dear. Then there were those who had experienced redundancy, retirement. Loss had different shapes and forms, but it was loss nonetheless. Setting aside her diary, Marcy left the room momentarily to find her next client.

It had taken time for Christopher to get used to this. To be sat in this chair, with his arm on the rests whilst talking with a perfect stranger and about his best friend. A best friend who was no longer part of his life; a best friend who bucked a trend, given that Marcy's clients probably spoke about losing people rather than their pets. Having written the first blog post-in fact he had written several since- he had recognised that something wasn't quite right.

His mum had suggested that he speak with someone. She had ruled herself out as being too close; she was also grieving for Adelphi and that made her the wrong person to speak with. His mum had sat with him, helped him look through the online directory and together they had found Marcy and the agency.

That was over three months ago, there had been half a dozen sessions at first. Only that had felt too short and Christopher had felt the lack of Adelphi so keenly, he had asked for more time. Adelphi and his absence had permeated through so many complex layers of his life and being; he had realised that he just couldn't let go as easily as he had imagined. He still needed to heal, and it wasn't going to be done quickly.

"How are you today, Chris?" asked Marcy as she took her own seat and plumped up the indigo cushion that she liked to have tucked behind her.

"Today is a good day, Marcy," he replied. "Yesterday, well that was awful," added Christopher as he sat back a little.

For the moment, Marcy said nothing. She would let him continue and at his own pace. Yesterday sounded significant, but it was entirely up to the client as to what they wanted to speak about and today. She cast her mind back to their first session, and how she had been confused about Christopher's best friend. Some of the timings, with the mention of years hadn't quite tracked. It had taken measured clarification to establish that his best friend sounded human in discussion. In reality, his best friend was four-legged, furry and with whom there was a strong and enduring bond. It had taken time and a chat with her supervisor to better understand how to work with

Christopher and his loss.

"Yesterday, Marcy," Christopher spoke as he curled his fingers around the end of the chair's arms. "I found myself picking up Adelphi's lead, calling out to him and saying that we were going for a walk. I'd been working and fancied a break, just wanted to get out the house and get some fresh air. It's been three months and I've not so much as looked at the lead by the door. I just couldn't, the pain was starting to dampen down a little. It didn't feel as sharp as before. Then yesterday, it was as though I had forgotten. I'd forgotten that Adelphi had gone. I wanted him to be there, I needed him to be there." He audibly gulped and let his gaze settle upon Marcy. His attention was caught by the orange and white bandana that was tied around her forehead like a hairband.

"Picking up his lead, felt automatic," Christopher continued. "It is really, I must have done it a thousand times and it has become a habit. I did it without thinking. With calling out to him, I heard my own words. I could feel them bounce down the hall and even up the stairs. I stood there and I waited to hear Adelphi come down those stairs. I even turned," He moved a little in the chair, as though poised to move.

"I turned to look up the stairs as I went for my coat. For a moment, I thought I saw his face through the stair rods. I didn't," he said sitting back. "I know that

I imagined it; seeing him, hearing him. It's indelible and won't leave me." Moving his arms from the rests, he let his hands rest in his lap. "I don't think I want that to go away, and I am angry. Angry with myself that I let it slip for a while. I shouldn't have, I really shouldn't have. But picking up his lead, I just had to."

"You kept his lead," said Marcy, smiling a moment and revealing pearly white square teeth behind matte red lipstick.

"I can't get rid of it," closing his eyes, Christopher shook his head. "I've got his lead, his blanket, a few chew toys too. I can't bring myself to get rid of anything."

"Could they be used again?" ventured Marcy, somewhat unsure if she ought to ask the question.

"No!" Christopher replied sharply and his tone rising; he had snapped his gaze from the floor straight at Marcy. He was caught somewhat unaware by his own terseness, and the sound of his voice rang in his hears. "Not yet, no way. I can't replace him."

Marcy had felt that the question might produce something of a response. She could see Christopher move a little uncomfortably in the arm chair. His brow was creased and his face had become a little flushed. Given how he looked to be in some physical discomfort, this was clearly not an easy conversation to be had.

"I can't do that, not yet," letting out a deep breath, Christopher once more balled up his hands into fists. "For now, I want to just get once for and all that Adelphi has gone. Get used to it, when maybe I've just been avoiding it. I can't just replace him," Christopher's expression was pained now, mirroring the tone of his voice. "It's not that easy. You wouldn't ask someone if they could replace their sister, a parent or some other family member. And he was family; Adelphi was family. The thought, the very thought of doing that, replacing him," once again he shook his head. "It's just too much for me to think about. I need time, time to adjust."

Marcy could hear the pain and the anger that Christopher was holding onto; those were the very feelings that she could feel rise up inside of her. Perhaps she had pushed a little too hard and really wasn't ready to let go just yet. She could offer time and space, a place to think so that he could adjust. The pace at which he adjusted would be entirely up to him.

All her clients were given time and a place. A safe place where they could find stability and feel less as though they were being though they were being thrown around; a safe place away from chaos and confusion. Marcy offered something constant; she would be there for as long as they needed her.

Daniel twirled the metal band around his finger. "The house is quiet," he said, moving the ring up and down. "Too quiet at times; it is true what they say about silence being so loud that it is deafening. It is heavy too. The way that it lingers; pregnant and ready to burst." Sat here and lost with his thoughts, Daniel felt as though he had drifted away. He could see Marcy, hear her when she spoke. Her words and presence kept him anchored in the room. She had a holding presence as he tried to focus and he found it comforting.

"Most of the time, I feel as though I am waiting. Just waiting for his key to turn in the front door; for him to come sweeping in whilst talking loudly and quickly about whatever drama that he might have had that day. I miss the movement and the noise," he let go of his wedding band and let his elbow rest on the arms of the chair. Pressing his curled fist to his cheek, Daniel looked directly at Marcy and smiled. He noticed that the blouse that she wore with its voluminous bat wing sleeves was a beautiful imperial purple covered in a frantic swirling pattern.

"I miss this, Marcy," he uttered it softly at first, it was a daunting realisation. He looked at Marcy still, her face was kind and he always found her to be really very attentive. He felt listened to. As though he could speak, and as much as he wanted as Marcy would absorb his words. She would absorb what he had to say, and she never batted an eyelid. "Marcy," Daniel continued, moving his hand and sitting a little forward. "I miss having someone sat with me, and just talking with them. It's", Daniels brows knitted together, he could feel the tension spread across his forehead. "Strange," he said looking at with his head a little inclined to the side.

"How so?" asked Marcy, mirroring the way in which he had moved his head to the side. "Help me understand what that strangeness feels like for you." She wanted to understand what he was processing, she wanted to be able to figuratively walk in his shoes and get a clearer idea of his world view.

"Lonely," Daniel uttered the word and let it sit in the air for a while. Let it hang, so that he could process how it felt to say it out aloud. The thought had escaped first his mind and now his lips. Lonely; it was a horrible, wretched sounding word with no warmth whatsoever. In his head, Daniel was imagining and playing out the memories associated with Caleb coming into the house. The times that he had thrown a scarf across the hall and towards the coat stand, only to miss.

Daniel missed the sound of his husband's voice and the thudding of his feet up and down the stairs. He missed being kissed in his ear. It might have only been a shopping list spoken out aloud with double entendres, but it was a sure fire way of making him blush and smile coquettishly.

"He-Caleb-filled the house," he continued, refocusing as Marcy moved her hand into her lap. It was perfectly innocuous but the movement broke his thoughts a little. "Every inch is covered and with him. Colours, fabrics, cushions and candles," said Daniel. "As though he stamped himself upon the house; he certainly stamped himself across my heart. I let him," he all but whispered, and the words came out in a single drawn out breath. He bit his lip to continue. "I let him into my world, and it was colourful. Was also chaos at times, Marcy, but it was never quiet. He left me with the quiet and it makes me feel alone. It reminds me that he is gone and that is never coming back. It was quiet before him, but it was a different quiet; it was an empty quiet. My life was full of a nothingness, there was no colour; it's unfair to call it a life. This quiet, the one that exists now is too full. It is too full of him, memories, chaos and colour. And there is no one, no one to share it with."

As the last of the words tumbled out, Daniel drew breath. "I can see now, hear, just how much he was a part of my life. The richness that was Caleb, it filled the walls of my home, my whole universe. Now there is a void, a big grey hold where he used to be. It is a Caleb shaped hole and it is vast. I feel it is massive and difficult to grasp." Daniel could hear his words; feel them cascade out one after the other. Every one of them had built up, been stoppered by the silence of his empty home. In this space, during these fifty minutes he could let those words out.

Marcy could feel the emotion in his voice heighten. There was a flicker in his eyes with every mention of Caleb, a sense of realness and of proximity. Daniel still felt Caleb in his world and perhaps wasn't ready to let go and completely. "Your world has changed," she commented. "Caleb was such a big part of it. Now with the Caleb shaped hole, the world is very different and lonely." She carefully repeated Daniel's words. "I could feel the richness that you described; it very much feels a part of you."

Daniel nodded as he sat reflecting on his words being repeated back to him. "My world is different," he said after a moment. "It is completely different to the world that I had before Caleb. That is a world that I very rarely think about these days. Looking back on it, it feels a world unlived in. My world with Caleb, that was good world; I lived in that world and I loved it. I loved Caleb. He was part of the fabric and in each and every thread. It is this third type of world, the post Caleb world that is making all of this so difficult. It is a world where he exists only in memory, a world where I have to adjust to him not being physically there. Even though I can see his keys, occasionally a catch a waft of his scent on a scarf. There are pictures of our wedding; he is no longer here. I have to adjust but I don't know how, how it might get easier." Adjust; he had heard himself say it out aloud. How could he, when his heart wouldn't let him.

Adjust and to loss. Not having your loved one near and knowing that they wouldn't be coming back would certainly mean change. To adjust was by no means easy or likely to happen overnight. Then there was the notion of being in a different world that was littered with shadows of what had been and tinged with memories that could spark at any given moment.

Marcy let time settle and briefly with the gap between clients. Each one was unique, a different journey with different twists and turns. Each client would come with different expectations of what they thought might happen, as well at what they wanted to achieve. Each of the clients that she saw was a different thread in the fabric of the universe; diverse and varied, but the common denominator was Death. She had seen rawness, immediacy, tempered with attempts to manage and trying to understand how the world had changed. Next came those who had journeyed as far as they needed to, and were on the brink of a new chapter.

Bright pink wrapping paper covered the box that sat upon Caliope's lap. It was hot pink to be exact and it was patterned with silver glittery flowers. These were flowers that glistened as they caught the light that flooded in through the window behind her seat. She held onto the box, her fingers splayed across the pink ribbon that was stretched across the lid and was topped off by a bow that sat squarely in the middle.

"Christmas could be hard," said Caliope, not looking up as she held the curve of the pink bow between her thumb and index finger. "Mum would make a real fuss over Christmas. We'd be all together with lots of food, drink, and people visiting. There's always been a lot of hustle and bustle at that time of the year. This year, it will definitely be different. That doesn't mean it's not Christmas," she said looking up at Marcy. "Of course it will be, you can't really avoid it being the end of the year. Dadima thinks we shouldn't celebrate this year. It just wouldn't be right though, not to do anything. There will still be presents," Caliope smiled at the end of her sentence and turned her gaze back down toward the box.

"That box looks a lot like a gift, Caliope," Marcy ventured. "Is that for anyone in particular?" she asked, wondering if it was or whether there was another meaning to it. Their journey together was nearly over, after this there would be one last session to bring their work to a close.

Caliope pressed her hands delicately to the side of the lid to prize it up and away, before planting the lid onto the floor beside her feet. "It's for Koby and I to share," she replied, looking at the contents. "We spoke about memory boxes a few weeks ago and well," Caliope looked up at Marcy, again she smiled delicately. "It stayed with me. I thought that if I found a box, made it look a little pretty. Perhaps Koby and I might find it easier to move on." Both she and Koby had been meeting with Marcy. School had helped arrange it all. Even though Marcy had spoken about confidentiality, Caliope had shared some of what they had spoken about with her brother.

Together, they had discovered that some of what they had shared with Marcy individually had over lapped between them. "I know you see us separately, and can't share what we say, but still. This is for both of us and he did say it was okay for me to share this with you. Is that okay?"

Marcy had been watching carefully from afar, but now shuffled a little forward in her chair. "Of course, go ahead," nodded Marcy, waiting to hear what Caliope had to say and about the box.

"Okay, this is Mum and I at the seaside," Caliope picked up a glossy six by four photograph. "It's a reprint, the proper one was all a bit faded," she wrinkled up her nose a little as she held the image by the corners and between her hands. "Mum and I, before Koby was born. Think it was somewhere in Dorset. We went looking for shells, that's why I am sat like that. Didn't want my bottom getting wet," Caliope laughed and her face was filled with warmth as her cheeks dimpled. Sure enough, she was there in the picture; crouching and her hands were covered in sand. In front of her were a handful of shells and her mum was sat next to her, looking on with a beaming smile. They both looked a little windswept and in the distance, grey clouds hung above the Palaeozoic coast.

"It was just before Koby was born," Caliope continued. "In that picture, he is a bump. Dad is taking the picture. I remember that was the first time that I had ever been near the sea; was absolutely amazing. Hearing the sea, smelling it, was magical." Caliope slide the photograph back into the box, and put her hands to a yellow knitted hat. "Then Koby arrived, and Mum had a family. He wore this. I remember, when he came home. Dadima made it for him. Mum took it with her in her baby bag. Koby put this in; he thinks it is really special. Doesn't really wear hats anymore," she added, shaking her head.

Delicately folding up the hat, it was returned to the box. Her hand moved to two pieces of paper, embossed with an official looking metallic stamp. "Mum loved rugby and so does Koby. These," she had to stop, as she felt a tug at the back of her throat. "These were for Twickenham. England played against Italy. Koby counted down the days, so did mum; they had a calendar stuck to the 'fridge. They talked about it for days after." As with the other objects, the tickets were returned to the box.

Caliope pulled the box a little closer and looked at the variety of items that she and Koby had packed into it. There was a pocket sized copy of 'Much Ado About Nothing', bound in red plastic that was nudged up against a box of French Manicure nail polishes and a tightly rolled up red and white scarf. There was even a folded up ordinance survey map of the Outer Hebrides with a compass sticky taped to its leaves. Each and every object had a memory, feeling and sense of life attached to it. Some of the memories were sad, such as the broken pencils and the pieces of Wedgewood china mug that Koby had decided to keep.

Reaching into the box, Caliope pulled out a deep purple moleskin pouch. Pulling at the cord that was coiled tightly around the neck, she pulled the pouch open. She held out her left palm and inverted the pouch to shake out the contents. Sat on her palm were two narrow hair pins. One was plated in rose gold and set with pink stones. The other was silver and set with blue stones that looked like tiny peridots.

"These, Koby and I are to share," Caliope lowered her tone; her words were quieter and lighter than before. "One is for me to keep-mum was holding on until my eighteenth-that's not too far away," she said looking up slightly. "The other might not suit Koby so much; but she wanted him to have it. If he ever had a girlfriend, got married or whatever." Cupping her palm, she slid the pins back into the pouch. "I've said my goodbyes, Marcy," her gaze was fixed now upon the counsellor. "The hurt has gone and Mum's not here anymore. That doesn't mean that I'll forget though. Not really."

They would talk some more, there was still another half an hour. Caliope shared what it meant to finally say goodbye and they discussed how they might say goodbye to one another. With only one more session, it was simply a matter of course. Saying goodbye was never going to be easy; but all journeys, be they long or short, generally came to an end.

"Bakewell tart," Matthew pronounced and rather proudly. His eyes shimmered as he spoke. "I made one and all by myself," he added, there was a touch of good humour to his voice today. "Followed Lilly's instructions and to the letter. Every single step," said Matthew, waggling an index finger. "God, it tasted good, Marcy. I have never tasted one like it. Lydia thought it was nice too, but she's been eating all of the bakes that I've been making."

Marcy wrapped her palms around her knee as she drew one leg over the other. "You've been baking a lot then?" she asked, the mention of the Bakewell reminded her of how Matthew had spoken about his grandmother's fondness for baking.

Matthew nodded and clapped his hands together. "Every week and there's at least one bake," he said, his lips falling into a broad, beaming grin. "Albie-Grandad-said that I could have Lilly's tin, the one with all of her recipes. Provided that I actually used them, made the bakes and got Lydia to help."

"Is that what he said, that Lydia was to help?" asked Marcy. She had heard a lot about his girlfriend and how she had become quite close to Matthew's grandparents.

"Oh, yes, he was really very clear about that," Matthew's brows had risen in emphasis. "We were to share the recipes, make them together. Get them wrong, right, but together. It's been nice," he said nodding. "Once or twice, we might have had a fight about them."

"A fight, Matthew?" asked Marcy, a little concern entering her voice as she echoed his words back to gain some clarification.

"Nothing major," Matthew replied, waving a hand somewhat dismissively. "I like to stick to the recipes-rigidly, if you like-whereas Lydia is quite happy to experiment, to chop and to change."

Marcy nodded and absorbed what he had said, before asking, "Do you think, Matthew, that you have a fear of the unknown? There is a fear of deviating from the recipes and not having control."

Matthew's smile subsided and his expression became more thoughtful. He let Marcy's words, her question settle a while. "A little," he replied, having taken time to think. "I know most of the recipes and backwards. All of the times that I baked and with Lilly, the recipes never changed. Lilly never once deviated from what she had written on the card. I am a little scared, I guess. That if something changes, if we add chocolate chips, or we change the flour; that everything will be different, the recipe would be different."

"We," stated Marcy, "You said the word we. And you're grandfather asked for you to share the recipes with Lydia. Perhaps that gives you a little wiggle room; gives you the opportunity to develop-not change-your grandmother's recipes."

"Lydia and I do work well together," Matthew conceded. "And I have no plans to change that, to let her go. The recipes do belong to us both, that is also true, Makes sense, I suppose to make changes, develop them and together. Small changes, those are always possible. I don't think Lilly would mind that really. You know, they both told me to stay with Lydia; Albie told me not to let her go. Lilly left me some jewellery for her. Lydia means the world to Albie, me too. This is so much more than just recipes, Marcy."

"How, Matthew how is it more?" asked Marcy, tilting her head to one side a little to listen closely.

"There are only three women that I have ever, truly, loved," said Matthew. "My mum, my grandma, Lydia. These are three women who have shaped my life and in so many ways. Mum, is still there, and will-hopefully-for a long time." His eyebrows rose again. "Lilly gave me her recipes, and being in her kitchen taught me so much, but she is gone. I can make her recipes and I no longer feel angry or sad. Lydia helps and that feels okay. I feels good, it feels as though that is the way it should be. I'm happy, content when Lydia and I are together. Lilly has-in one way or another-helped that happen. I am where I should be, with the woman I want to be with. The one woman, with whom I want to write more recipes. Lydia, is The One."

This was the end of his journey, Marcy had seen his path fork off beyond where he had originally started. She was no longer needed to walk beside him. Matthew had seen the direction that he wanted to go in and he wanted to move forwards. He had also decided who it was that he wanted to walk beside him and it definitely wasn't Marcy. She thought about all of the different journeys. Each one was different and no one journey was the same.

19 Lydia

Ask

Three days has passed since the funeral. For those three days, Lydia had watched Matthew carefully and tried determine how he was coping. They had barely spoken and it felt as though there was still something of a soggy grey cloud between them. Lilly was still on his mind, and she was also on Lydia's mind. Lydia was sat on the couch beneath a heavy, knitted blanket and barely paying attention to the nature documentary on the television.

As she waited for Matthew to return from Albie's, Lydia thought about one of the last conversations that had with Lilly. Depressing a button on the remote to lower the volume and not wanting to hear the sound of squawking gulls swooping for fish, Lydia replayed the conversation in her head.

Lydia had returned to the lounge with a floral

patterned tray. Sat on the tray were two cups of tea and a saucer of chocolate chip shortbread. Lilly had asked for tea and biscuits, she had been very specific and asked china cups and biscuits. She was also charged with keeping an eye on Lilly for a short while; Albie had gone out for a routine doctor's appointment with David. Matthew had been called into work and volunteered her for the job. Were it not for her fondness for Lilly and Albie, she might have felt a little put out. However, she had known them for such a long time and a genuine loving affection had developed to replace a sense of obligation.

As she carried the tray in, Lydia noticed just how small and frail Lilly looked with a stripped blanket pulled up and around her knees. Her hands were resting on her lap, with her fingers curved with arthritis. A few of Lilly's knuckles were swollen with the affliction and looked really quite painful. Such was the pain, that Lilly had tea in a lighter weighted china cup rather than a heavy mug.

Though there were now struggles with the china cups too, Lydia had seen this and Lilly had once complained of the cup being too hot to hold. She had however been chastised and sharply, for having made tea and handed it over in a mug. There was no making that mistake today. Lydia placed the tray onto the faux walnut coffee table that was positioned close to Lilly's knees. Picking up Lilly's cup, Lydia handed it to her as Lilly slowly raised her hands and curled her fingers around it.

Lilly smiled as she felt the heat of the cup in her hands. "Thank you," she said turning to face Lydia who sat next to her. "You remembered. I don't like the mugs; china is so much nicer to drink from," Lilly arched her brows, before taking a sip of well brewed tea that was only just sweet enough with half a teaspoon of sugar added to it.

"Are you still going to ask him, dear?" Lilly asked gently. Her eyes were rheumy now, but still flickered with a glimmer of mischief. "So brave, Lydia," she added, moving her hand slowly from the cup and onto Lydia's. She held her hand for a moment, her fingers transferring warmth from the china cup. "I've not told Albie, but I do hope you ask him. I would never have asked Albie; back in our day, us girls didn't tend to, not really. Times have changed and you are so much braver than I ever was."

"Not yet," whispered Lydia, giving Lilly's fingers a gentle squeeze and registering the warmth before the hand moved back to the tea. "I fully intend to," Lydia said nodding as she smiled. She laughed quietly and looked directly at Lilly. Lilly's hair was now white and in stark contrast to the warm chestnut that the locks had been in the pictures that Matthew had shown her. Fine textured, Lilly's locks sat close to her exposed scalp but still fell with a loose curl at her shoulders. "I don't think I ever want to walk away from him, Lilly," uttered Lydia, biting her lip.

Lilly nodded; there really was a firm bond of understanding between them. "Ask him," she said quietly. "No one has to walk away, but you walk on and together."

They had sat talking for a while, plotting as to how Lydia might propose. Lilly had even shared how Albie had proposed not once but twice. The first time that he had asked, Lilly had feigned ignorance. "I heard him," said Lilly, giggling wickedly and eyes glimmering. "We were dancing; there was music and yes, it was very loud. To be honest, I was a little shocked. I was expecting it all to be a little more romantic. He did ask again though, and thank goodness. He was that nervous, Lydia, I cannot tell you. I said yes, and well, it all turned out for the best."

Lydia had been that lost in reminiscing that she had didn't hear Matthew come into the house. She was still altogether focused on her memories, whilst her eyes were directed towards the television. So much so, that Lydia was entirely oblivious to Matthew being sat next to her. It was only when she felt the remote control move from beneath her finger tips, that Lydia all but jumped out of her skin and nearly threw the device at Matthew.

"Woah, sorry!" exclaimed Matthew, recoiling back and catching the device that was launched at him. "Lydia, it's me," he said, somewhat stunned by her actions.

"If I asked you to marry me, and asked you now, what would you say?" asked Lydia, still very thoughtful as she shuffled around on the sofa. As she moved, her foot landed heavily against Matthew's knee.

Wrapping his hand around her toes before she jabbed her foot further into his knee, Matthew dropped the remote from his other hand into the space between them. "What?" he asked, there was something of an incredulous tone to his voice, and it was tinged with confusion. His facial expression had also altered, it was no longer placid. His brows were arched; his cheeks flushed and mouth agape.

Removing her foot, Lydia drew her limb back towards her. "I don't know if you are going to ask, so I am asking you," said Lydia. "I want to and to ask you; if you will marry me, Matthew. All things considered, life is too short to let the people that you love, care about, walk away and out of your life. Matthew, do you or do you not want to marry me."

Then it registered. Lydia realised that her proposal, her question was her thinking out aloud. Her words had been trapped inside her head for so long and she had not actually thought about how they would exit and through her mouth. As she looked at him, she could see that his face said it all. Matthew's face was a warm shade of pink and he didn't look particularly taken with what she had said. Slowly, she moved her foot back and towards him; this time there was no jabbing motion. All she wanted was a response, so this time her foot gave a gentle nudge.

Moving his knee away, he drew his legs together and got up from the sofa. "Just leave it for now, Lydia," he said quietly. "Shouldn't have made you jump. I'm going to get something to eat," he said glancing over his shoulder briefly and then leaving the room.

Closing her eyes, Lydia exhaled deeply. As she let out her breath, she started to sob and muffled her crying with the blanket that shrouded her. She felt as though she had been winded and could feel a hot ball of hurt form in the pit of her stomach. "Leftovers!" she called out, drying her tears, "Left overs in the fridge!" she added, dabbing away tears and wishing that she had never asked.

***

He had heard something about left overs. Lydia had told him that there were left overs in the fridge; he had also heard her crying. That was how the conversation had ended, and for days after they had skulked around unsure of what to say to each other. It had been obvious, so obvious that Albie had chastised him. That had been three and a half months ago and Matthew had been kicking ever since. Especially as Albie had given him the box that Lilly had bequeathed him. It was a burning a hole in his bed side drawer.

It had taken Matthew over three months to sort himself out and the contents of the box too. Now, he found himself sat on the end of a luxuriously made up bed and turning a small red box over and over in his hands. He was waiting and for Lydia to come out of bathroom. Hearing the toilet flush, Matthew lost his grip on the box as it fell to the floor, he tumbled after it. The box landed with barely a noise onto the thick pile of the carpet. What he did hear was the sound of the bathroom door opening and Lydia's pencil heels clicking against the floor as she came out. Making a hurried grab for the box, Matthew curled his fingers around it and shoved it sharply into inside pocket of his single breasted, navy suit jacket. As Lydia arrived, he was hadn't moved, and was lying prone on the floor.

It was her toes that caught his attention. Peeping out from the strappy sandals, Matthew saw that Lydia had painted her toe nails bright ruby red to match her dress. He followed the length of her instep towards the hemline that billowed out over rustling petticoats that were only just visible.

He was definitely going to ask her and today.

Lydia stood before him, tucking away a stray lock of hair behind her ear and into heavily hair sprayed hair do. As she moved her head, the only just acceptable levels of down lighting in the room caught the crystal drop earring that hung from her lobes and cast a glimmer at her neck. She looked all too confused, and her brow was creased. Her boyfriend was lying across the floor, sprawled out and there was no clear reason why.

By now, Matthew had propped himself up on his elbows. This did nothing to make him dignified as he legs were stretched out before him; he looked a lot like a smartly dressed teddy boy puppet. "I fell off," he said, all very poker faced.

"Fell off?" repeated Lydia, putting her hands to her hips.

Now; whilst he was done here, he might as well ask. That was the thought had been a bud in his mind, and was starting to bloom. "Fell," nodded Matthew, as he drew in his legs and decided to kneel.

"Oh, really?" she couldn't help but give a drawn out response. Then there was the tightness that spread across her stomach as she watched Matthew move, and the feeling had nothing to do with the passion killing underwear that she wore beneath the dress.

She said nothing as Matthew rummaged inside his jacket; he did look rather smart and that bit more attractive than usual in the tailored suit. There was just something about the style that added a little more bulk to his otherwise slight frame. For a moment, she was about drift off into an impromptu fantast. Only to be pulled back by the sound of her name.

"Lydia?" Matthew said her name a little louder for the second time. Here he was trying to propose, and she looked as though she was tuning out. This did nothing to bolster his confidence, and he moved his feet to be on one knee. A dark tan brogue was pressed firmly against the carpet. The shoes that he wore were rather new still, yet to be broken in properly and he could feel the sole slide a little across the carpet. Matthew had to tense his foot to stay still or end up falling again. "If I wait any longer to ask you, I am likely to burst," his voice quivered, as he held out a box and pulled it open with some force.

Red. The box was bright red and had caught her attention rather quickly. A colour so stark compared to the greys and maroons of the boutique hotel bedroom. It was a red box, and in his hands. Again he said her name, and it brought back into the room. All she could see was the white metal band that was set with square cut diamonds and resting on red wadding.

Stepping forwards, Lydia gathered up the skirts of her dress and lowered herself slowly to the carpet. There was a gentle rustling from the layers of the petticoats beneath the stiff, raw silk red vermillion that had been chosen for the black tie gala that was taking place in the hotel. "Go on," said Lydia, having to blink rapidly or have freshly applied mascara and eye line travel down her cheeks. "Say it, Matthew. Ask me, before everything runs."

Pinching the band between his thumb and forefinger, Matthew pulled it free from the wadding. Setting the box down between them on the floor, he balanced the ring flat upon his palm for a moment to take Lydia's left hand into his. "I'm not going to ask," said Matthew, going for the melodrama, "You already asked me," he continued, sliding the ring from the middle of his palm and towards Lydia's hand. "And I was the idiot who failed to give you a straight answer. You deserve a straight answer, Lydia."

Lydia was trying to hold to breath, and her eyes were starting to look glassy. Tears were starting to form and were welling up at her lash line. "Please don't make me ask again," Lydia gasped, "I couldn't take it, if you went all brooding again." Tentatively, Lydia unfurled her left hand as Matthew held it in his.

"No brooding," replied Matthew. He was giggling nervously, so his tone had become a little sing song. "Just a straight answer, Lydia, it was always going to be a yes." Feeling her fingers unfurl, Matthew threaded the ring band on and towards her knuckle.

"Life is too short," he said looking into her eyes and seeing eyeliner starting to move. "So no, you don't let the people you care about leave and walk away."

Struggling to get any words out, Lydia looked down at the band as she tried her best to not keel over and sideways. She silently counted the stones that the band was set with. Now was probably not the best time to ask where they had come from, or how much the band had cost. The one question that she had wanted to ask, she had asked; there was now also an answer. She had got her answer, and that was all that mattered.

***

She found out eventually; the diamonds that the engagement band was set with had come from Lilly. Some part of Lydia knew that Lilly and Albie had been involved in the proposal. There had been a second surprise, another jewelled one that came later still and when the time came for them to tie the knot. It arrived seventy-two hours before the big day and was really quite useful.

There were probably not many brides who wanted the colour red as part of their nuptials. There were red shoes, flowers, red dresses for bridesmaids that were fashioned from silk and satin. Lydia even spent hours trying to decide what shade of red to pain he fingers and toes as she thrust a box of small bottles onto the dining table. The dining table was already groaning beneath the weight of wedding favours, centre pieces and other paraphernalia. All of which was red, glittery, silver or wrapped up in red organza.

"What is it now, nail varnish?" Matthew had walked in behind her and was wiping away hair from the base of his neck. This was hair that the barber's brush had missed and made him feel itchy all over. He had decided to get his dark hair shorn and days before the wedding. He had heeded Lydia's pleas and kept his hair tufty; being scalped was not an option, and Lydia would have been far less forgiving than the barber. Peering into the box, he counted four different shades of red.

"You dare," hissed Lydai. "You dare ask me how many different reds I need, and I swear that I will brain you, Matthew."

There was sharpness to her tone that caused Matthew to raise his arms aloft in a gesture of surrender and step back. In her defence, he had only noticed Lydia becoming more irate and harassed in the last few days. Things had been relatively peaceful, but he was more than prepared for any tantrums and flying tiaras as the big day approached.

"Wouldn't dream of it, dear," he said, unable to suppress laughter. He shuffled further away and around the table so that it was a barrier between them. "Before I go, there was something I wanted to show you," he took a deep breath and put his hand to a rectangular blue box and slid it across the table towards Lydia. "One last thing from Lilly," he said waggling a finger, "Don't open it yet. Wait til I go."

Lydia picked up the box, and it sat neatly within her palm. She could see from the corner of her eye that Matthew was on his way out and with a hold all slung over his shoulder. He was spending the next few days at his parents. All being well, she would see him again on their wedding day and at the other end of an aisle. She waited, waited until the front door clicked closed. Then she opened up the box and looked inside.

Inside and shining brightly were red rubies punctuated with diamonds. Diamonds that were not too dissimilar to the ones in her engagement ring. The stones were set in a shiny hair slide and made for an interesting addition to her wedding outfit. Matthew had asked and repeatedly, if he would have to battle with a veil. This had been why.

Three days. She could wait three days.

***

Albie rubbed his eye with the heel of his palm. He was tired and it had already been a long day. A beautiful day, but a long one; he was also feeling a little under the weather and didn't know how much longer he would last. He had watched Lydia and Matthew all but hop, skip and jump down the aisle and back again. Albie was proud of them both. Lydia had looked radiantly beautiful gliding down the aisle wearing Lilly's rubies in her hair. He had seen Matthew look as though he had found the one person in the world who could make his heart swell to bursting.

He had watched them take their first dance; they had danced to a song that he didn't know. It was some schmaltzy, modern day ballad that was all too sugar for his taste. Albie gently moved the half pint glass that sat next to his elbow. He had missed the first time, so was exasperated at having to try again. It was the then that the trumpets started and Albie snapped his head towards the dance floor. He knew that song, the beat and the rhythm. Slowly, Albie sank backwards into his seat and felt contentment. He was deliriously happy and to have seen today. Closing his eyes, Albie let the music wash over him and allow him to be transporting back into time. Surely no one would mind, if he closed his eyes and for just a moment.

It was the coldness of his hands that gave it away. Having scooped up her skirts around her legs, Lydia had sat on a chair that Matthew had dragged from the next table and placed near Albie. She had seen Albie sitting with his hands clasped in his lap and had suggested to her new husband that they go sit with him a while. Lydia had placed a hand to Albie's, when he had not responded. She had thought that with his chin resting on his chest, she could wake him.

She had almost recoiled back, but kept her hand on his. She caught Matthew's eye and she could see was his smile.

"Trust you to be asleep," Matthew had said, shaking his head before looking directly at his wife.

"He's not asleep, Matthew," Lydia said softly, her face had blanched entirely. "He's…."

Eventually, the music stopped playing. People started to scurry around, and an ambulance was called. Guests were asked to move to another room. Joy and happiness were suspended and the atmosphere became dense with sadness. This was not how either of them had expected their wedding day to end. There were no words, no actions to make it easier.

As Lydia and Matthew fell asleep in each other's arms, they held each other close. There were sobs as their hearts ached from being torn and today. Today, Lydia and Matthew were together and properly. So were Lilly and Albie; together and for eternity.

20 Aldo

Bunting

The past year had been difficult; there had been so much to go through. So many thoughts, processes, memories and emotions; all of these formed his experience of grieving. The first time difficult, celebrating Millie's birthday and so close to when she had died. Died; Aldo could say that word now. He could say it, think it and about it now and it felt different saying it compare to those very early days.

Today, it was Millie's birthday; the second since she had died and it was going to be different compared the first. He was standing on a ladder in the garden; it was positioned precariously between the lawn and the shed. Aldo's arms were stretched out ahead of him towards the eves of the weathered and wearied blue shed, where he was trying to fasten bunting. There was quite a lot of it too. Snaking across the lawn, brightly coloured paper triangles lay on blades of grass that had been mown yesterday in something of a panic. Once he had tied the first length, the bunting would criss-cross over head with the garden staged for a party.

The first birthday had been somewhat different; a greyer and gloomier day than today, and full of tears and tension. Aldo had found the whole day suffocating and painful; so much so, he had told Maya that he never, ever, wanted to feel that way again. Millie's birthday's had been happy for as long as he could remember, and he wanted to keep things that way.

Aldo had woken up in an awful mood that day. Things were somewhat testy still between him and Maya. Even though there had been a funeral with both of them saying their goodbyes, there was a still a fragile tension between them he was struggling with it. He knew that he would be and on his daughter's birthday. He had rolled out of bed, leaving Maya balled up under her side of the duvet; his morning routine happened without change, Aldo was a creature of habit. Habit and routine were safe, secure, there was no flux.

Or so he had thought.

Deep within, Aldo could feel it. There was a flux. There was no Millie and on that day, this caused the flux to bubble, swirl around his gut with flight and fury. He was able to finish his scant breakfast of black tea and white toast, he felt that wrought up. The feeling of being thrown around and by torrents of plain grief and sheer loss were back and with a vengeance.

He had made it to work and from there he would escape for a few hours. Human resource were aware of his recent bereavement; there had been compassionate leave and they had even arranged counselling. At first, Aldo had been hesitant, within himself and about going. He and Maya were barely talking, and he had no idea if she was talking to anyone other than him. The feeling of flux was bubbling up inside and killing him. It felt as though his insides were being eroded away by the bitter taste in his mouth and bile rising as he thought about the driver who had killed Millie.

He had already been to counselling a few times. Initially, there was only meant to be six sessions, but he asked for further appointments that he would finance himself. He had spoken during these sessions about Millie's birthday approaching, so it wasn't a surprise during the appointment that day. It had been difficult going to the appointments, he wasn't exactly found of talking and especially with someone who was a perfect stranger. This was a safe place, the stranger had listened. Yet on that day, for the fifty minutes that he was there, Aldo may have only uttered a handful of words. Beyond those four, five barely audible words, Aldo had cried. He had sobbed, sniffed, snorted and possibly even wailed. He could that during the session; there was no judgement, no direction as to how he had to be strong and for Maya. Aldo could cry and let it all out. That was all he had wanted to on that day.

His time had gone by quickly, he found it difficult to get used to fifty minutes passing. Before he knew it, it was time to go. He left the four storey building and went back to work. There Aldo had immersed himself in a world of numbers. Numbers that weren't human, but could be systematically crunched, contorted and for which he had no feelings. At five thirty, the office block emptied and he left for home. There had been a fight with Maya and over the last of the milk, of all things. They had screamed, shouted things that neither of them probably meant to say. They had gone to bed without speaking; only for Aldo to wake his wife at four o'clock in the morning.

Maya had swung her elbow towards him when he had abruptly interrupted sleep and turned to face him, ready to rip a strip off him. Bleary eyed, she swept dark hair from her face and squinted at him in the dark. "Unless you apologise, I have really don't want to talk," she had said, wincing as he flicked on the bedside lamp on his side.

His head was framed by a halo created by the low

level lighting. "I'm sorry," Aldo had stated, and quickly before she turned away. "I didn't mean it; I didn't mean a single thing that I said. We can't do this again, Maya; next time, Millie's birthday has to different."

Sitting up and pulling their duvet around her, Maya rubbed her eyes.

Aldo needed to talk; Aldo being Aldo, that didn't happen. "On her next birthday," Aldo had said, "I really don't want to fight."

So they had talked and for a while. He could not remember the last that he had talked with his wife and until dawn. It was only when the alarm clock on Maya's side sounded, that they realised what time it was. Then there was another thing; he couldn't remember the last time that they both called in sick and spent the day together.

A year later and the day would most certainly be different. Today, there would be no crying, no fighting. If there were to be tears, he hoped that they would be of peace, perhaps joy and happiness.

"Do you need a hand?" The voice that cut across his thoughts belonged to Joel, and he walking across the lawn and following the trail of bunting. Dressed in floral print shirt and sporting a garland brightly coloured plastic flowers he certainly looked as though he would be celebrating today.

"Joel. Yes, thank you," replied Aldo, making sure that the bunting was secured before carefully stepping down the ladder. "Nice to see you," he said as they shook hands.

"Wouldn't be anywhere else," Joel said with a nod as he picked up bunting. "I'm glad to be here and today of all days, Aldo."

Putting his hand to the ladder, Aldo moved it across the lawn and to the next point to which the bunting would be anchored. Steadily, Aldo clambered up the steps and waited for Joel to hand up the bunting. "Did Maya say anything?" he asked as bunting landed in his palm.

Joel nodded; threading bunting up toward Aldo and watching it rise from the lawn. The brightly coloured triangles fluttered and rustled with the breeze. He noticed a fluffy bumble bee fly passed one of the triangles and have to adjust it flight path or get swatted out of the way. "She did," he replied. "It was a bit hard to hear, to be honest."

Aldo twirled a length of bunting around a blue-grey metal pole that supported the washing line that was suspended down the length of the garden. "It was hard when she heard it, Joel; it was hard for me too," he said exhaling deeply and turning to face the fair haired young man who was level with his knee. "I can hear it now, say it too. Millie is gone, she is not coming back and we all have to move on. There will always be a gap," he said moving down the ladder and standing next to Joel. "There will always be a Millie shaped gap. Some days it is bigger than others. It is not going to go away, but how torn out it looks will change." Aldo bundled up the ladder and move it to the next point.

Joel followed and noted that this was probably the most in depth conversation that he had aver had with Aldo. Another thing that chimed with him was how Aldo was a little less direct than his wife. A year ago, they wouldn't for so long or so personably.

Aldo leant against the ladder and looked again at Joel. "Maya and I, we've dealt with things, with everything so differently and it's been horrible. I couldn't even begin to imagine how you might have gone through it. But we have, all of us," said Aldo, nodding his head slightly. "I see Millie running around this garden, I see her helping me and her mum hang out the washing. I see water fights and dragons being chased by warrior princesses. I won't forget that, Joel, I can't. I will hang on to it, and keep a hold of it all. Life changes, it cannot stay the same. You should keep moving as it does," Aldo shrugged a little, he had said his piece.

He wouldn't admit it, but he wanted to, he needed to say these things. If he had to practice what he was preaching, saying this to Joel-the same had been said to Maya-it was all part of his movement forward. It was all a part of his path to healing and finally being able to let go. He carried on moving the ladder, and together he and Joel hung up the bunting. Today, they would not commiserate. Today, they would celebrate.

21 Michael

Bundle

Sniffles; that was the only way to describe the sounds. These soft sniffles and squeaks were punctuated by cooing. The cooing came from the adults, and Corey sniffled as he slept in his father's arms. He slept soundly for now. Unlike at three in the morning when he had been experiencing the discomfort of an empty stomach and a rather full nappy which meant a rather damp bottom. One thing was uncomfortable; but when combined with the other two, the boy wanted the world to know that he felt as though he was being tortured and loudly.

"Oh, God, you'd think someone was trying to eat him," Michael pronounced. "He's only small, but man, can this kid yell," he said looking into the crook of his arm. His son's mouth puckered gently, accentuating the curve of his cupid's bow shaped lips.

These were almost pouty lips that Corey had inherited from his mother. The boy's nose definitely belonged to Michael, and had the potential to eventually become fleshy and pronounced with age. Michael was rocking gently on his heels; he had already found out that this helped soothe the boy.

Sophie sat close by. A blue and white mug was nestled in her lap and was full of black tea. "It's very hard to think that he's cute, and at three in the morning when he is screaming," Sophie rubbed her eyes and did nothing to stifle a yawn. "He's here, he's ours. We finally have one," she beamed as she spoke and looked at Maya who sat on the other side of the office. She and Maya had shared this office for years. It was in this office that she had met Michael. They had initially disagreed over whether or not a tender hearted year seven should be placed in detention having lost a text book. A lot had happened since then, and Maya had been part of some of it.

Maya smiled back, but sucked at her teeth as she was likely to cry. Shuffling her feet on the floor, she propelled her office chair towards Sophie. Sat closer to her, she held Sophie's hand in hers. "You do, and you deserve to enjoy it; to make the most of it. He's a very happy baby. Are you taking care of yourself? That is just as important." Maya was more than aware of all the times when Sophie and Michael had been heart broken and full of bleak despair.

"I am. He-" Sophie pointed towards Michael, he was still rocking on his heels. "Won't let me so much as move and to get tea. But yes," She continued, "No more now," she said shaking her head. "After Corey was born, they had to take everything out and away," her voice trembled, and after a moment, Sophie broke down. Freeing her hand, she wiped away tears that had welled up. "So we can't, we can't do this again. We'd discussed that anyway, didn't we?"

Michael nodded as he stopped rocking Corey. He stepped closer towards Sophie and lowered their son into her arms. "He was the last shot, so yes," he replied quietly.

Taking Corey into her arms, Sophie pressed her lips and kissed him. More tears were wiped away as she cradled him close. "Take the last year off was the best thing that we could have done, it kept us all happy," Sophie said sighing. As she spoke, Corey decided to open his eyes. He grizzled a little and his mouth puckered at the sides. Sophie was now well aware of what that meant. Things were going to get noisy. Corey did as expected; he opened up his mouth and made his discomfort known quite loudly. It didn't take long for his face to become an interesting shade of pink.

For a small baby, he could certainly raise his volume. Sophie freed her son from the grey and white blanket that he was swaddled in and was handed a bottle by that was offered to Corey. The boy knew what he wanted and the teat was quickly taken up.

Maya watched Sophie and Michael fuss over their new baby. Some part of her was transported back to when she and Aldo had fussed over a very new, very helpless Millie. The young couple before her had experienced a rockier, more turbulent path to get where they were today. What she saw before her, was the same joy, love and sheer bliss that came with holding your own child in your arms.

Pulling up another wheeled chair, Michael sat himself down. "All being well, we'll make it to the garden party," he said, watching Corey guzzle milk. "Will be our first time out and as family," added Michael, looking away from his son and directly towards Maya. There had been a very brief window between Millie's accident and Samuel being born asleep. Between them, having lost a child was shared grief. There was a similar sense of loss, and the comparable experience of having your world shaken to its foundations. A lot had happened in the last year, but he felt that the loss was still there. It was here within the room, lingering between the three of them as though a heavy scent that refused to diffuse away.

Removing Corey's bottle, Sophie held the baby over her forearm to wind him. Corey had dozed off again and was somewhat milk drunk with his eyes closed and head tilted to one side. "It certainly will be, yes," she said, narrowing her eyes in concentration so that she might hear the squeaky pop of contentment she expected Corey to produce.

"And we can thank Aldo properly for the changing table. It was really very sweet of you both, what with the last one meeting with an accident." She arched a brow at her husband, who was looking rather sheepish at the mention of the table that he had destroyed in a drunken rage. Sophie's attention was however diverted; Corey had been winded and had woken himself up with the noise. Cradling him close, Sophie gently patted the boy's well-padded bottom to try and soothe him back to sleep. As scared as she was about caring for him, she would keep that feeling inward. There would be no saying out aloud, as to how she felt. Outwardly, she was glad and would do her best to look as though she knew what she was doing.

"It was Aldo's idea," Maya sat back a little in her seat, her arms sitting languidly on rests. "Not sure where he got the idea from, but it doesn't seem like a bad thing to do. A year ago, having a party and celebrating would have been unthinkable. It would have been just too painful. Hopefully, it will be fun," she said smiling. She could see Corey wriggle in his mother's arms and was suddenly thrown back to when Millie had been small.

Catching the wistful look, Sophie edged herself closer

in her seat. "Here, Corey doesn't mind cuddles," she said, realising that a cuddle probably wouldn't go amiss. Sophie gently lowered a fairly awake Corey into Maya's arms. She stayed close still; not in worry, but to see how Maya might calm him down and get the boy to sleep.

Sat so close, Sophie hoped that she might learn how to sooth Corey and remain calm herself. Some part of her knew that and was able to understand that no one should have to face losing a child. Regardless of whether the child was a babe in arms or an adult, the pain was still real and couldn't be filed away. It could still destroy you and no matter how hard you tried to forget. Corey had helped, but Sophie wondered if she would ever truly heal.

From the comfort of his chair, Michael watched still and remained silent. The last year had been an interesting journey. At the moment that the pregnancy had been discovered, both he and Sophie had decided that enough was enough. This time, they would do all that they could to ensure that they had the happy and healthy ending that they so desperately craved. They had both taken an extended leave of absence from school; the management had really understood why they needed some time out.

Having time off had allowed them to retreat into their own world, to watch their baby grow and nurture themselves having been so wounded and defeated.

The hope that Sophie was carrying once again, was fragile. Michael had driven himself and his pregnant wife almost quite mad in ensuring that nothing happened to her or their unborn son; son. They had found out pretty early on as Sophie was being closely monitored. He had started again with the nursery; there had been some still quite keen feelings about having destroyed it and in a fit of fury. Michael had stripped the room entirely and to plastered walls so that he might have a blank canvas. As Sophie had bloomed and blossomed, the nursery had also changed. The walls changed from being bare and barren to a soft duck egg blue as the room was filled and furnished in readiness.

Michael held onto the sense of peace that had come with Corey's arrival. The little boy had arrived screaming, exercising his lungs and the whole room had heard it. He remembered the distinct image of relief descending across Sophie's face as Corey's cries shattered the heavy, expectant silence of the room. She had cried, as had he as Corey was cleaned up. After a few minutes that felt like an eternity, Corey was returned to them and suffered a maelstrom of kisses and cuddles.

Then the monitors had started to beep. Sophie was exhausted, and her blood pressure had suddenly changed. Michael had felt as though his world was starting to quiver, tremble in fear as he was shepherded away whilst holding his new born baby. He had been barely able to string two sentences together and ask what was happening to his wife.

He was not prepared to lose her.

In the hours that followed, it felt as though it was just him and Corey. Sophie had been rushed away to theatre, and he had been left with their yet to be named baby. Michael had called the parents, all three of them; they had cooed over and cuddled Corey whilst being on edge

Lost in his thoughts, he did not hear or see Sophie. She had shuffled her chair towards him and gently placed her hand onto his arm.

"Hey," said Sophie quietly, trying to get his attention.

Michael could hear Corey gurgling. There were now touches of grizzling and sniffles that indicated his son needed attention. As he held out his arms, he saw his son's eyes open. Corey was lowered into his arms for even more cuddles. Corey and Sophie were his whole world; they were all that he had ever longed for and would fight for until his dying day. So small and entirely defenceless, Corey needed his parents. With Corey being part of his world, he really did feel a sense of peace; there was also happiness and joy that filled is heart and made it feel as though it would burst.

The pain from everything that he and Sophie had experienced would probably never go away. There would always be a reminder of the tears, the pain and anger. Pain and anger were no longer a ball of fiery fury that bounced around inside. Now that ball just sat in a corner whilst humming quietly to itself. All those emotions that had flooded his mind and singed his soul were contained and sealed away. The seal that had formed was important; it was made of love, hope and faith.

22 Christopher

Paw print

Draco. His name was Draco, and this was one very hot tempered puppy. Draco yapped incessantly. As though he was shouting at Christopher and hell bent making point, whatever that point might have been. There was the occasional growl as Christopher tried to scratch him between his ears or tug at the black and white triangles that were Draco's ears. Christopher lay on the floor of the lounge, his limbs were stretched out across the carpet and he was spread-eagled pretty much like a beached star fish. With Draco sat on his chest, he wasn't exactly alone. Draco hated being aloe and had only recently been separated from the rest of his litter. His predecessor had been black and gold, and a little more docile at the same age. In sharp contrast, Draco was noisier and the gold replaced by bright white. The white was in splodges and all over. Each splodge was a distinctly unique shape, but the ones across Draco's stomach looked a lot like crescents and stars if you were to squint hard enough. It was the splodges that had caught his attention when he had first stepped into the kennel at the rescue home. All of the other puppies had looked a bit nondescript compared to the creature that sat staring at him down a furry snout.

Draco's tail wagged. It was not yet as big enough to cause bruises in the same way that Adelphi's would when it whipped sharply against your legs and at full speed. It would surely grow and Christopher was more than prepared for the propeller blade-like movement of a tail. Sniffing at Christopher's t-shirt, Draco's snout hung low as he moved towards his owner's face. Once there, Draco saw nothing wrong in marking his presence with gentle licks from his pink ribbon like tongue. Wrapping his hands around the puppy's small barrel shaped belly, Christopher sat up and drew Draco into his lap. Draco continue to yap, squeak and growl as Christopher traced a finger along a jagged, lightning-bolt shaped flash of white that ran along Draco's snout. There was just something about this dog.

Over the last fortnight, Draco and Christopher had been getting to know each other. It had all started with Christopher being sat in the back of his parent's car. His mum was sat on the front passenger side, with his father at the wheel. He had figured out that something was afoot. Firstly, he had been asked to pop around for brunch. Secondly, he was asked go out with them and across town; so he found himself buckled up in the back seat of the car and able to make eye contact with both of his parents in the rear view mirror. Christopher felt as though he was eight years old again and they were setting off on holiday to the seaside.

"Where are we going exactly?" he had asked, looking directly at his mother's eyes in the mirror.

"Out," his father had responded, his eyes appearing at the right of the mirror and with brows arched.

"I could have driven," said Christopher, his own eyebrows moving and in protest. "or met you, wherever it is that you are taking me," he added, huffing and a lot like had when a child. He even crossed his arms in childish petulance. The ease at which he had done that had unsettled him a little. He grimaced a little, at having also unsettled the contents of his stomach; he had been fed a full cooked breakfast. Being well fed might have helped his brain clock on a little quicker, instead it numbed his wits. Christopher was a sucker for hash browns and fried mushrooms.

His mother leant a little to the side and scowled at him in the mirror. "Please don't kick my seat," she said her expression softening as she spoke.

As a child, he had done just that. He had learned his lesson; as an adult had no intention of being a child again. Christopher had tutted and rolled his eyes, and wished that he wasn't being treated like one. Sat in the back, he had remained sullen but somewhat lost in contemplation as he considered the route that his father was taking as they journeyed. He studied each turn, every sign that he could spot in a desperate attempt to figure out where he was being taken. There was something altogether uncomfortable about being taken on something of a magical mystery tour and by his parents.

The half an hour that it took for his father to drive was only made further unbearable and disorientating by his mum pushing the buttons of the car stereo every five minutes. Christopher couldn't work out whether she was nervous or deliberately trying to wind him up even further. Thirty minutes of torture finally came to an end as his father parked the car smoothly into a bay of a car park. A car park that belonged to a square one storey building that looked rather dog tired and in need of a face lift.

Then he saw, the name. Cransfield Pet Rescue.

Christopher's father caught his expression in the rear view mirror. "This time, you can pick you your own," his father's eyes twinkled with mischief as he spoke. There was also a sense of excitement in his voice as he grinned broadly.

Looking from the sign and towards his father's reflection, Christopher was more than a little confused.

"Go on," his father urged, albeit softly. "Your mum and I will be right behind you. Apparently there are some puppies, which were rescued along with their mum. Mum thought you might want to adopt one. Adelphi has been gone a while now, and well," his father shrugged as he looked at Christopher in the mirror. "Choose your own," he repeated, trying to spur his son on and out of the car.

He sat for a moment, just looking at his father. It was a year exactly since he had said goodbye to Adelphi. He had somewhat been avoiding thinking about it, and adopting another dog. He certainly didn't expect his parents to have thought about it or to mention it. Moving on was putting Adelphi into his past; he wasn't forgetting or filing him. This was however, about starting again.

"Chris?" said his father, interrupting his thoughts, and bringing him figuratively back into the car. "You loved Adelphi, and Adelphi loved you. It took age, infirmity and death to split you up. Nothing else could have stopped you from being best friends and brothers. All that love that Adelphi had for you and you had for him. It doesn't just stop, kiddo. Go on in there, share that love again; find that next fur ball."

Hesitantly, Christopher unbuckled his seatbelt. His mum had opened the door and he clambered out. His heart was beating hard and nervousness made the hairs on the back of his neck stand up. Closing the door behind him, he looked towards the grey, squat, tatty looking building ahead. As well as a fast beating heart, he could feel both excitement and anxiety swirl around his insides. Then there was the cold, sharp, sliver of betrayal that felt as though it was being jabbed into his sides. If he was to go in there, find another puppy; surely that was betraying Adelphi. Adelphi had been his best friend and he was about to be replaced by another. Christopher's fingers gripped hard onto the door handle, his knuckles fading from pink to white with tension.

Adelphi couldn't be replaced, even now and a year on. Adelphi was still a part of him, he always would be. There was only ever going to be one Adelphi.

His dad was right. What he felt for Adelphi, those feelings would never stop or change.

A gentle nudge at his elbow suggested that he ought to get a move on. Standing slightly aside, his mum was waiting for him to let go of the door and get into the building. He felt the full weight of the glare she was wearing. It was the same one that he remembered from being in trouble as a child. It was a look that needed no words and told him to get a move on. The glare reinforced the idea that he might not want to do something, but it wouldn't half make his life easier if he did it. He was no longer a small child, yet as an adult that glare still had the desired effect and had him moving towards the building. His parents followed him in.

Christopher had no idea how he managed to get to the kennel but he did, and he watched the wire framed door open towards him. He peered inside to see the mess of furry puppies being nursed by their mum who was lying on her side. She was docile enough, lying back as her litter jostled to feed. It was a larger litter than he had expected, and noisier too. The puppies barked at each shrilly with their sounds bouncing off the painted walls.

Choose your own.

Those were his dad's exact words. Stood at the door, Christopher scanned across the wriggling array of puppies. They all varied between black, brown and a speckled combination of the two. He watched silently, trying to decide which one he might take home.

Then he saw it, the coat. It was glossy black with bright white splodges. Splodges that if he narrowed his eyes, were shaped like crescents moons and stars. The creature wearing the coat had white socks and having had enough to eat, was headed straight towards him. With ears pinned back and squeaking as he moved, the creature wore a rather inquisitive expression. A expression that queried who this stranger was, and why his dinner was being so rudely interrupted.

About two feet away from the slightly less furry stranger, the puppy stopped. He sat upon his haunches and his tail sat in a hook like curve against the floor. With is head tilted to the side, the puppy eyeballed the interloper standing before him.

He was waiting for an answer, some form of identification.

Christopher was not averse to eyeballing either. He shuffled forward across the concrete and scooped the splodgy coated puppy into his arms. Christopher didn't have to choose a puppy; the puppy had chosen him.

It didn't take long after their initial meeting for the admin to be sorted. He would have to wait a couple of weeks; there would even be a home visit. After which, Christopher went and by himself to pick up his new puppy. The house was alive with noise again; bark and yaps that echoed down the hall way. Once again, there was the gentle pitter patter of pads across wooden floors. Christopher no longer felt alone, and his life was being shared with a four-legged friend. Shuffling his paws, Draco sat flat upon Christopher's chest with his muzzle resting upon his paws.

They both knew that they had chosen each other and for a reason. This was a reason that couldn't be described but only felt. Christopher had Draco, Draco had Chris. Somewhere across the rainbow bridge Adelphi was probably barking in approval.

23 The Anands

Parting Gifts

Nandini had protested at first. She had protested that it was all too soon and that they might not want to put up the Christmas tree this year. She felt that that perhaps decorating the house with tinsel was not exactly in keeping with mourning. In her mind and therefore in her world, you gave time for things to settle, for things to be sombre for a while so that you could be reflective in mourning.

She had fought with Raj. There had been raised voices that were quickly lowered when Koby and Caliope would interrupt and want to know what the fuss was all about. It was rare for them to hear angry adults, hearing their father arguing with their grandmother most likely altogether rather unsettling.

Koby and Caliope who had taken the decision to put up the tree. They worked together to lower the ladder that led in the loft and then bring down to the ground floor all of the boxes containing the tree and decorations. There were quite a few boxes to bring down, give the number and variety of decorations that they as a family had collected over the years. Together, the children worked diligently to put the three together. It had taken them just under half an hour to slot colour coded boughs into plastic and metal column that acted as the trunk.

Nandini watched whilst undoing a box of decorations. She helped by sorting out the baubles, tinsel and garlands that would eventually adorn the tree. Ove the years, the process of setting up the tree and decorating had become something of a family tradition. This had always been her job, the sorting out of decorations. Tree decorating was usually initiated by Rachel; she would be the one to coax Raj to remove the tree from its hibernation. She would then persuade the children to help put the tree together. Nandini observed as Caliope and Koby did their job, occasionally a bough would be slotted into the wrong place and something of a quarrel would happen. The squabble would soon blow over and they would resume their job in earnest.

As she placed metallic green baubles to the floor, she noticed that Raj had disappeared. This difficult, she understood that. Christmas was always about being together and as a family. This year, a major part of the family was no longer with them. She carried on sorting the decorations, arranging them by colour and style on the carpet.

Raj had drifted away. He had argued with his mother, and fought to have the tree put up. What he hadn't foreseen was his own kids taking the matter into their own hands. To take the tree down, had always been his job. Yet here he was, stood in the loft with his head crane awkwardly below the beams as he looked for the lights that would eventually be draped around the tree.

Then there was the topper; a rather weathered, white, plastic angel that was covered in sequins and glitter that he had to locate. The topper had belonged to Rachel's first ever tree. It had been on a small, three foot, fake spruce that had lived with her in university halls. The angel had made it here; when they had decided to invest in a family tree, there was no question as to what might crown it. His mother had cooed over the glitter; glitter that was starting to fall off in places.

It would take him some time to sort through the bits and pieces before he might find it. Hopefully, that would be long enough for the children to decorate the tree. It would also be long enough for him to let loose some of the tears that he had been holding back since the start of Advent. It was since the first of December, that he had been thinking about Rachel and how different this year's tree decorating was going to be. He would take his time, and let the kids do what they wanted to do.

With all the branches slotted into place, Caliope and Koby circled the tree to make sure that the boughs were even fluffed up and the fake needles were standing to attention. Caliope moved clockwise, with her brother going in the opposite direction and stepped out the way if it looked as though they might collide. They would repeat the process once the tree was decorated. It was Koby who took the first handful of decorations; a set of green metallic baubles that were faintly patterned with white snowflakes. These were snowflakes that had once been quite bold and a brilliant white, but were now starting to fade and flake away. These, like the angel that would sit on top, were also from his mum's university tree.

Caliope took the next batch, a series of brown felt gingerbread men with buttons for eyes and sequins sown down their front. She remembered helping Koby make these when they were both younger. Their mum had cut them out using a template and then watched over them both as they carefully embellished the felt and brought the gingerbread men alive.

Next came candy canes; fashioned from red and white pipe cleaners that were attached to golden threads that Caliope pushed over the boughs to attach onto the tree. She took her time, and could feel the back of her throat catch and also hear herself start to sniff. Caliope remembered each and every one of the decorations that she and Koby had made with their mum. Each and every one, and this year those memories were really quite powerful.

Nandini rose slowly from her seat on the sofa and picked up the decorations that she wanted to place upon the tree. There were quite a few and she clutched at them in her arms as she shuffled towards the tree. One of the baubles made an escape from her forearm and was half way to the floor only for Koby to catch it with unexpected cat-like reflexes. She could feel the gaze of the children as she threaded red glass baubles, one by one onto the tree. Each bauble was suspended from the bough by a silver thread and written across each one in knobbly silver paint was the name of each family member. The names included that of her late husband, and these baubles were rather special to her.

Rachel had found these baubles just after Raj's father had passed away; back then, she had been just has hesitant to dress the tree. Rachel had made it a little easier with these baubles. Nandini's mouth turned a little downwards at the corners in sadness. Just like her husband, there was no Rachel; only her name remained.

For Nandini, to the see the name beneath her finger

as the bauble bobbed, this was confirmation that her grandchildren had done the right thing. It was important to put up the tree; it was what Rachel would have wanted.

There were further baubles to be added, followed by brightly coloured tinsel and garlands. Caliope and Koby circled the tree once more and made sure that it passed muster. They had just finished their close inspection of the tinsel when their father arrived holding a box of lights; on top of which, rested the angel to top the tree.

"Haw, her wings!" exclaimed Nandini, pressing her fingers to her lips. She shuffled towards Raj, and picked up the beleaguered looking angel with its torn wings and rather flimsy plastic cone-shaped base. "Do lights, I'll bring her straight back. Go on," urged Nandini, slapping her son's shoulder as she left the room and muttering under her breath. There was no way that she would allow the tree to be topped off and with the angel in her current state.

Koby shook his head as his grandmother walked away and removed the lid of the box that his father had walked in with. Fortunately for his dad, the lights had been properly returned to the box last year; each bulb was placed into a hole in a plastic sheet below which was all the wiring. Koby lifted the lights out, and let his father put the box down. The lights were always his dad's job. For his part, Koby had already helped

Caliope and felt that his duty had been done.

"Fine," said Raj, exhaling deeply. "But you hold the plug," he added. "Your sister can help me thread them around the tree. Look out for the dud ones when we switch it on, Koby; there might be some that need replacing. That happens every year."

Koby dutifully held onto the plug whilst his dad and Caliope wound the lights around the tree. The lights looked rather dated in the plastic, but it didn't matter, not really. It was always his job to hold the plug as the lights went up. The few times that he had tried to help, Koby had become dizzy and nearly fallen over. The one time, he had nearly taken the tree with him; since then he had been relegated to plug holder.

Sticky tape. That was what Nandini had gone off in search of and she had found some in a kitchen drawer with some scissors. The scissors had been used to carefully cut up sticky tape that was then used to repair the gossamer wings of the angel that had become torn in places. Once the wings had been delicately pieced together, she set about fixing the white cone beneath the angel's white polyester dress.

Over the years, the angel had been plonked so aggressively onto the tree, the base had fractured. There had been previous repairs, dried out sticky tape had left a brown gummy residue that she had rubbed away. It didn't take long, but soon Nandini had fixed the plastic. As she held onto it and returned to the lounge, it had a certain renewed sturdiness to it.

"Mum, you done?" Raj had been shouting as his mother crept back into the room and behind him. The lights were done, and they were waiting for the angel.

"Hold on," she yelled back, half glaring at her son. She held out the angel towards him and with both hands. "Put her up," said Nandini. "And be careful, I had to fix her."

Raj shook his head; his brow knitted and took the angel. Raising her aloft, he had to bend the top spike of the tree before setting her down.

"Left a little," said Caliope.

"Right," offered Koby, tilting his head to one side.

Raj tutted, and looked over his shoulder before tugging at the angel's newly patched up wings.

Wonky. That was what Rachel called the angel. An angel that always leant to the side, not matter how much you tried to reposition her. The angel simply wouldn't sit straight. Shaking his head, he tugged her wings a little to make her sit even more askew. Stepping back, he felt Caliope loop her arm around his. Standing before them all, this was not just a tree. There were memories and shining brightly as Koby flicked the switch of the socket on the wall. There were baubles with faded patterns, gingerbread men that looked a little psychotic and cross eyed, as well as couple of doves with a wing missing. Each and every element was filled with good times, with joy and celebration. As he caught sight of the wonky angel, he saw that the black ink used to draw on her face was starting to fade. It didn't matter really. As a family, they had the tree, the angel, all of the different decorations. As a family, they had Rachel and they always would.

24 Daniel

Adventuring

It started with a map and a notebook. Both of which had fallen out of a holdall that was being retrieved from the back of a wardrobe. It had taken Daniel eight months, but he was getting around to sorting out the last of Caleb's wardrobe. Some of it had already been donated to charity, but there were a few things that lingered still. The bag itself was fairly innocuous looking as he stood on his tip toes and tugged at the black leather strap that dangled down from the shelf and towards him. Grasping at the strap, he gave a sharp tug and caught the bag into his arms. It had moved and with some speed towards him, making his chest hurt as it impacted. There was even a surprised 'oof' as he held it close, closed the door and saw to investigating.

This was not a Caleb-esque bag at all. Made from smooth black leather, the bag was rather warm-not to mention, a little dusty-to the touch. It looked rather well made and from soft premium leather that probably cost half a kidney. Engulfed by curiosity, he pressed his noise to the leather to see if he could smell just how real the leather was. Inhaling, Daniel smelt strawberries and cream; a scent that he felt new leather always carried. Thought that could have also been the scent that Caleb would douse everything in, including the pomanders that were tucked into the crevices of the wardrobe. Strawberries and cream, it was a fragrance that reminded him of a happier time and of adventures. Adventures that he and Caleb had enjoyed together when they had traipsed to the four corners of the globe. Then there were the adventures that they had been planning. With his husband's demise, these adventures were unceremoniously cancelled. There had been no thoughts since of going away, planning an adventure and alone.

The bag in his arms was the sort of bag that he might take with him was he to go away on holiday. In Daniel's mind, the bag was much more his taste and nothing like Caleb's. With that thought in his mind, he moved towards the end of his bed and undid the zip. Opening up the mouth, he tipped up bag and shook out the contents. It had felt heavy as he had caught it, and that led him to believe there was something inside waiting to be found. As he shook the bag, three items fell out. The first item to land on the duvet was a scrunched up Panama hat. He put out a hand to the starchy, pale straw coloured hat and unfurled it. The material sprang to life rather quickly and he ran his thumb across the blue band that it was trimmed with. A hat that was all too sedate, far too pedestrian for Caleb. Caleb's might have been a black fedora, trimmed with white silk and have a feather tucked into it. Picking it up by the brim, Daniel placed it firmly onto his head where sat quite snugly and felt really quite comfortable. Jabbing an index finger into the brim, Daniel pushed it back a little on his head to see what else had fallen out.

There were two other items on the duvet. He picked up the first item; it appeared to a document that had been folded up neatly in a rectangle with rather sharp edges. Carefully and rather slowly, Daniel unfolded the sheet of brown paper with his brow knitted in intrigue. Slowly but surely, the brown paper gave way to a multi-coloured street map. A3 in size, the map looked familiar as he placed it on the bed and smoothed it out before him. In the top left were the words Musei Vatican, and just below the domed roof of Saint Peter's Basilica.

To the right of The Vatican, the three curves of the river Tiber snaked down to the bottom of the map. Beyond the curves were all the different landmarks associated with the city of Rome. Palantine hill, The Forum, The Four Fountains; all had been circled with a black ball point pen. There were aslo fluorescent index tab, as though to make sure. The handwriting on the tabs was unmistakable; the blocky capitals written neatly on the tab, belonged to Caleb. Daniel looked over the markers, there were over a dozen attached to the map. There was even a cat sketched in, not too far away from the Garibaldi Bridge. He would have to work out why that was there. The drawing made him smile; they had discussed adopting a cat. Labelled and all set out, what he saw was the makings of a Roman Adventure.

So he had a hat and a map. There was still a third item, and it was beneath the map. Sliding his hand below the page, he put his hand to it and pulled the item towards him. Nestled in his palm was a compact, soft covered note book embossed with his monogram. Loosening the black elastic that held it closed, he delicately opened the notebook to see if anything was inside. Inside, and not in capitals but curly cursive was more of his husband's handwriting.

"The world has always been our oyster," read Daniel. "We have adventured to most places. Can we go here next? All my love and to the man who became my whole world, Caleb."

Letting out a sharp gasp, Daniel closed the notebook and fastened it shut with the elastic band attached to the cover. "To Rome, he said quietly, his gaze returning to the map decorated with fluorescent index tabs. "And for our next adventure; the world really is our oyster."

***

"Call me when you land, or text," Joel had said and with concern in his voice as they said goodbye. "Let me know that you have got there safely."

There had been had handshakes and a hug at check in, with Daniel reminding his nephew that he was a grown man. He had batted him off with his still rather stiff and yet to be broken in hat. Joel had shaken his head, waved and finally left. At just a shade under two hours and twenty minutes, the flight to Ciampino hardly warranted Joel pacing up and down whilst clutching his 'phone to his breast. Boarding was the easy part; it was the adventuring around Rome that concerned Daniel. The black holdall from the wardrobe was stowed away in the overhead locker and the plane glided into the skies. The adventure that his husband was sending him on, was soon underway.

Beyond the note, there was something else in the notebook. There had been a list, and a detailed itinerary that corresponded with the map and detailed how Daniel might spend four days in Rome. All he had to do was follow the list, starting with his accommodation that was a stone's throw from the Santa Maria Maggiore that was at the top of the prescribed list. Landing had been straight forwards, as was picking up his luggage. A pre-booked taxi picked him up and whilst sat in the passenger seat he was able to take in the hustle and bustle of the narrow Roman streets. Then there was the soundtrack of roaring engines, hooting vespas and the rumbling sound of tyres passing over cobbles. Taking it all in as it moved passed his window so quickly made the forty minute journey feel quite intense. The driver had said nothing during that time and concentrated on the road. Daniel was ignored, and the only sound made was by the rapid and staccato speech that came from the talk radio on the car stereo.

His itinerary allowed him a brief window to acclimatise rest and get his bearings. Over the following four days, Caleb's list had paragraphs describing how to get the best, more panoramic experience of Rome. Landing mid-afternoon would give him the time to take in the locale of Urbana and Cavour. The guest house that he was staying in, sat in the middle of a narrow cobbled street and was flanked by restaurants reliant on the passing tourist trade. It was an assuming building with a weather beaten façade; patches of it were a mottled and terracotta coloured plaster had been eroded away. His accommodation was comfortable enough; his only gripe being no lift.

He had turned the air blue in having to drag his suitcase up the stairs and to check in at reception. Five star and luxuriousness it was not, but it would be home for the next four days and would just about do.

A surprisingly restful night's sleep prefaced the first full day of adventuring. Negotiating the Metro from Cavour, getting to Republica and ending up Attaviano took time but was straight forwards enough. Daniel travelled light, Panama hat on his head, a camera and Caleb's notebook tucked into his pockets. Pre-booked tickets meant that he didn't have to swelter and suffer impatience in the intense sun in the queue that wound its way from the entrance to the Musei Vaticani and around the corner. He did have to wait briefly and did so in the Gelateria across the road, whilst nursing a rather potent smelling coffee. He had also savoured a portion of vanilla gelato, and made a mental note to get some at home. Gelato, that was and not some soulless ice-cream that tasted synthetic and soulless.

Less than half an hour later, Daniel found himself within the guarded walls of the museum and headed toward the one chapel that the world and his wife wanted to see. The route there was tantalising, with tapestries and maps that willed you and entranced you as walked down corridors. As the stream of bodies slowed in their movement and had to negotiate the steps going down to the chapel in sobering silence, there was a sense of anticipation that filled the air. A silence made heavier by the watchful gaze of guards looking for exposed shoulders and bare knees. Slowly and steadily, Daniel moved along with all the other sardines and through a set of dark wooden doors. He along with others was shepherded in and ushered into the centre of the room. His eyes scanned the walls, taking in all the imagery. There was no artificial light in there; the only light that filled the room came from the windows that were open and married with the light of burning candles to illuminate the frescos. It took a while, to let it all sink in. Eventually, Daniel remembered. Remembered what he had to do and raised his eye line whilst trying not to fall backwards.

When you are stood there, and in the Sistine chapel with no room to swing a cat, there is only one thing that you must do.

You must look up.

You look up. Regardless of what you might or might not believe, look to the ceiling. What you see is the product of a human being; what you see is the power and product of human ability. What Daniel saw was what Caleb had wanted him to see. He saw what a human being might achieve when they set their mind to doing something, and something that allows the world to see their potential.

There was life in the images painted onto the ceiling, death too. A whole universe in glorious technicolour and created by a man.

There was no way to take it all in and quickly; it was

impossible to capture every colour and creation. The thirteen and a half minutes that Daniel had spent looking was in no way long enough. There were however, more people wanting to come into the chapel. Before long, he along with the others standing really very close to him were shepherded it out and into the brightness of the sun. From there, he continued and towards Saint Peter's square and the world renowned basilica.

Saint Peter's squared rather surprised Daniel. The sheer size of it was something that that television and still images couldn't do justice to. As with the museum, visitors were expected to swarm them and en masse. Security details standing next to scanners were in stark contrast to the fountains casting a fine spray into the air. He stood next a fountain for a while, he pulled the brim of his hat over his eyes to protect against the sun as he tried to scan across the square.

On the far side, the sun caught shiny metal to cause something of a sharp glare; yellow metal at that. Troupes of Bavarian Brass bands were gathered there, standards raised and aloft, fluttering gently on a breeze that didn't do a lot to cool the heat of the afternoon sun. Brass bands were by far the one thing that he had not expected to see and in Rome. He enjoyed the pit stop as some of the bands started to warm up, and snatches of song were carried on the wind to his ears as he made his way across the square.

As Daniel walked up the stone steps and to the entrance of the basilica, the square was pulled up into something of a breath-taking panorama. He just had to take it all in, and was moved to take out his camera and record the view for posterity. That seemed to him, the only way to make the experience feel permanent and to be able to take it away with him. Tucking away his camera, he turned towards the entrance door; a smaller door next the main entrance draped with a red velvet curtain adorned with a golden crucifix.

La Pieta. That was what Caleb had written beneath Saint Peter's and in tightly curled letters. The words had been underlined three times, indicating weighty importance. Taking out his camera once more, he was clutching at it tightly. Daniel saw people-the back of them, most specifically-lots of them, all gathered before Michelangelo's famed sculpture and trying to get a good view through the thick, bullet proof, glass. All that he could see, was a synthetic halo being reflected off a white marble elbow; the bodies before him did rather obstruct his view.

There was only one thing for it.

What followed, was the very polite and very English litany of 'excuse me', 'coming through' and 'may I pass, please?' so that he might make it closer to the window.

Daniel knew that pose, of Mary cradling the forlorn Christ. He had felt that pain and now he could see it. Mary with her son and after His crucifixion; he lay prone in her lap. She had lost her one and only son. The love that she had for him, appeared to shine out from the marble and resonate in the air. Michelangelo had somehow managed to distil within his creation, the very human feelings of love and of loss. Two heart wrenching emotions were juxtaposed and had been carved out of unfeeling stone.

Yet again, Daniel was awestruck by the power of human beings. He was amazed by how far one person could go and whilst being carried along by the power of belief. He looked on Mary's face. She would have to let go of him eventually and say goodbye. Jesus would be interred in his stone walled tomb. Those that had faith would hear about the resurrection; there would be a transfiguration, ascension to Heaven. Even then, Jesus would never truly leave his mother. Beyond that, he would change the world as it was known at the time; what he would leave, would mean a whole new life and to so many people.

That was what Caleb had left behind and with Daniel. A whole new life, but Caleb was not entirely gone. Daniel turned and pushed his way through the crowd and out onto the other side. To his right, he saw a queue forming and headed towards a roped off area;

beyond the ropes was a maroon curtain that parted from time to time to let pilgrims exit and enter. He moved closer to see if he observe what was beyond. As the curtains parted, he could see pews. Pews that were filled with those who wished to pray or have a few moments of quiet contemplation. He looked away and toward the main altar of the basilica that was directly beneath the domed ceiling that was labelled on his map. With a steady crowd streaming in and people milling around, the Basilica hummed and felt alive.

Daniel stepped aside as a couple passed him and joined the queue for the roped off chapel. After a minute or so, he decided that he too would join the queue. The queue wasn't actually that long, and was moving at something of a brisk pace. He, along with others, shuffled closer across the tiled floor and towards the curtain. Just before the curtain, he was met by two guards dressed in very smart, well cut, dark uniforms and with hair that was neatly slicked back across their scalps. With a nod and exchanging a smile with one of them, Daniel headed through the curtain. Finding a seat at the back of the chapel, there he sat. With his eyes closed, he focused on what he felt within, rather than the gleaming gold monstrance that was sat on the altar.

Caleb had led him here and it was here that Caleb would leave him. In the silence of the reflection, this was a last goodbye to Caleb and a hello to a different life beyond.

ABOUT THE AUTHOR

Punam Farmah is a teacher of Psychology and Social Sciences with horticultural tendencies, a trained listener, and lives in Birmingham, England. Her allotment is a short distance away, and forms the field for the natural experiments documented in this book. She is very appreciative of the help from the rest of her family and acknowledges that without them, this book would be devoid of any words, motivation or happy thoughts. When not teaching or experimenting with the plot, she rather likes Star Trek, Shakespeare, the Whedon-verse as well as seeing what can be made with the preserving pan.

www. horticulturalhobbit.com